MIRRORS

BY

LAZETTE GIFFORD

Copyright 2013 Lazette Gifford

An ACOA Publication

www.aconspiracyofauthors.com

ISBN: 978-1-936507-59-7

Mirrors

A Conspiracy of Authors Publication

www.aconspiracyofauthors.com

Copyright 2015, Lazette Gifford

ISBN: 978-1-936507-58-0

Cover Art Copyright 2015, Lazette Gifford

First Print Edition, July, 2016

TABLE OF CONTENTS

Hither and thither spins
The windborne, mirroring soul;
A thousand glimpses wins
And never sees the whole.
Empedocles on Etna, Act 1 (1852)
 --- Mathew Arnold

DAY ONE:

CHAPTER ONE

I tried to block what I felt from the world -- from *both* worlds -- while my fingers brushed across the ancient harp's strings.

Bright music filled the small room as I played *Carolan's Ramble to Cashel*. Plants trailed flowers at my shoulders, half-masking the front window of the upstairs apartment. The semi-opaque curtains formed a veil between me and the troubles in the world beyond my sanctuary.

I'm not a good musician, but playing helps when I'm troubled. Today I sensed subtle changes in the air and tried to ignore the growing apprehension those changes created. I listened only to each bell-like note in the near silence of my home.

Somewhere else a car honked and people argued, but not here in this place. I created a sphere of peace and tranquility and played, content for at least a few minutes more.

No one else sensed the trouble in the air.

The music wove a balm for my battered spirit. My nightmares had been worse this last week, filled with the whisper of words impossible to understand, like the annoying buzz of insects, and hinting at something gone wrong.

A woman shouted in anger somewhere on the street. *Ignore the world. Ignore everything.* Keep playing....

The phone rang with a discordant yowl, and I missed two notes in a row, but my fingers kept moving over the strings. I wanted to escape, and music gave me the only chance, at least for a few precious more seconds.

The phone rang, once, twice, three times, four, five -- and just as I finished the last golden notes, it dropped to voicemail. I put aside the harp with a sigh. I needed the work.

"Skye? Skye, are you there, baby? This is your cousin, Cherry! Pick up if you're there!"

I leapt at the phone, scaring two little mice who had come out to listen as I played. I regretted seeing them dash away. It wasn't often that I played well enough to draw one of the wild out to listen.

"Cherry!" I shouted and grabbed the phone off the counter. "You still there?"

"Thank God I caught you!" Her voice held a note of panic. "Something happened that needs your help."

"What's wrong?" I sat on the edge of the desk, upsetting one of the potted plants. They'd taken over most of the apartment and spread into the office downstairs. Sometimes I imagined moving through a wild place, far away from the city.

"Give me a minute," she said.

She had called me, frantic for help, and then put *me* on hold? Sometimes even the people I know best amaze me. I waited, trying to stay calm. The sun moved towards the edge of the horizon on this Saturday afternoon. I should have enjoyed a walk instead of locking myself in this jungle of wayward plants.

Cherry took a damned long time. The mice came back out. I slipped around the desk and opened the drawer, finding the crackers I kept for them and dropped a few crumbs. I might have to cut back on their treats. They looked fat.

"You still there?"

"Waiting patiently," I lied and dropped into the chair. "What's wrong?"

"I am working out at a lakeside estate," Cherry whispered. Had she stepped out of the hearing range of others to tell the story? "This is a good catering gig. Big, *old* money. It's a wedding, Skye. A few guests came from Europe."

"And something happened.".

"Yeah. Something odd. The wedding should have started an hour ago. Only the bride disappeared, Skye."

I frowned. Maybe nothing to this. "Cold feet?"

"That's what her parents are telling the guests, but I saw the panic in her mother's face. Lacey didn't run away. Something else has happened. The police are already here. I listened to what they said."

"You shouldn't listen. The police get downright annoyed."

"No pays attention if a Chinese woman caterer putters around with the food. And if I mutter in Chinese now and then, they don't even think I understand."

"You are devious."

"Deviousness runs in the family. You inherited that ability from the Chinese side."

I laughed, but my skin still tingled. This wasn't a runaway bride story, and we both knew it.

"When the police showed up, I listened to them talking," Cherry said, continuing the story. "Lacey was in her gown, Skye and no one saw her leaving in it, not even a servant, though the place is crawling with them today. People stood out front, too."

"There's no chance she changed first?" I asked, though Cherry never called for anything easy. She understands the work I do and the unique abilities I bring to the job.

"No time to change," Cherry whispered. I saw her in my mind's eye, shaking her head, her short black hair bouncing from side-to-side. "A bridesmaid left the room but came right back. The bride wasn't there. This was not a dress you can just slip out of and throw on jeans and a tee-shirt instead. The top is a corset, and someone has to undo that part. Her mother showed me the dress because I needed to design the wedding cake to match. There was no way she could walk out wearing it."

"Okay. You have my attention," I admitted.

"There's one more thing. The bridesmaid mentioned an odd scent when she entered the room."

The hair on my arms stood on end. Goosebumps appeared. "A scent?"

"Oh, you know the kind I mean," Cherry replied. "The scent of cinnamon and vanilla."

"I'll be there as soon as I can, Cherry." I had already stood.

"Need the address?"

"No. I'll come straight to you. Be somewhere I won't

draw notice."

"I'll meet you at the gate."

She hung up. I put the harp away. Odd thing to do, given the circumstances and the conflicting emotions raging inside me. Despite wanting to hurry straight to Cherry, I also wanted nothing to do with a problem that might involve *the other side* of my family.

I changed clothing from the comfortable jeans and tee-shirt to black pleated pants, a plain white sweater, and the good leather jacket rather than my comfortable, scruffy one. I didn't want to embarrass Cherry, so I dressed better than usual.

Cherry had brought me a dangerous problem. Vanilla and cinnamon aren't scents most people consider odd or strange, even outside a kitchen. For me, though, they held definite connotations of trouble.

There are many things humans don't want to see. If they can make a myth or a child's tale out of the stranger moments of reality, then they pretend they no longer have to worry. But sometimes the inexplicable still happens, and someone sees odd lights and hears peculiar sounds. Sometimes there might even be strange scents ... and people disappear.

I stood in the darkening bedroom, pulling my jacket tighter across my chest, trying to hide behind the flimsy cover. The night would soon cool with summer slipping into autumn. Sounds surged louder not far away, but my apartment held emptiness, the faint hint of remembered music, and the nibbling of little mice.

The emptiness suited me, along with the green plants and spring flowers. A sudden premonition made me believe I shouldn't abandon my peace of mind, so I closed my eyes and pulled the peace within me where I needed it. I also picked up a small geranium from the nightstand and walked to the full-length mirror in the bedroom. There I put my hand against the smooth glass of the mirror and stepped forward as I went to my cousin.

CHAPTER TWO

I used the link of our shared blood to follow the magical path to Cherry. Since I know her well, I can separate her from the few other relatives in town. The ability to travel through magical paths isn't easy and requires the manifested guardian give permission. Most turn me away.

The path that accepted my presence is as crowded with green as my apartment. There is always a price for passing through such places, and the guardian is content with the plants I offer her. We both embrace the greens of spring, and I assume that's what opened this way for me.

As I stepped forward, I held out the geranium. Something appeared: a shape of green and light as the guardian reached with long green tendrils and took the little plant.

Time to return to reality for a little while. I sensed the tie to Cherry, still concerned and waiting for me, believing my exceptional abilities could help with the disappearance.

Her hope worried me. The aura of cinnamon and

vanilla meant powerful magic had taken place in that room. Little spells produce little scent. Powerful magic likely indicated fae involvement, and this might prove a complication for me if I had to interact with any of them.

The Fae are the other side of the family. There were never many of the half-fae. The match between human and fae is inexact, both genetically and magically. I can work magic, but I find it challenging to call on the power and to manipulate what I produce.

The magic has kept me apart from the humans. People realize I'm not one of them, even without regarding my odd mix of blonde hair, green eyes, Asian features, and fingers that are longer than normal. I don't think the outward signs drive humans away from me, though. They sense magic even when I cannot often use it.

The fae won't accept me either, not with my human blood. A millennium ago they executed any half-breed out of hand. I live in an enlightened age, even among the fae. The fae will leave me alone as I am no threat to them or the humans.

Not only am I neither human nor fae, but I am also neither male nor female, though that's less evident. Like horses and donkeys mating to produce mules, the genes don't entirely match. While most mules are infertile, I am genderless. Cherry, who once treated me when I was ill, said I have a doll's body; smooth, straight, and with nothing to make me either male or female.

I inherited magic from my father's side which allows me to save time and travel this unusual route where twists of green power brush through the air, reminding me of a bright emerald sea breaking against a nonexistent grassy shore. If I went wading into the green, I might lose myself in those eddies and not care. On one occasion, I disappeared into this void for several weeks and thought it only an hour.

The path here is a dangerous place with for me with the illusion of safety I find nowhere else. Holding on to purpose is tricky here. I concentrated on Cherry, who is from the human mother's family. Our grandparents came from Taiwan and the family still holds to traditions. Her real name is Chun, and she has two younger sisters, Mei, and Li. Everyone always called her Cherry, though, and it suits her catering business.

Cherry didn't believe in magic until we met in a chance meeting a couple of years ago. I saved the life of her younger sister. Li blocked out what happened, but Cherry accepted both the magic and me

Cherry waited. Trouble. I kept going.

I reached the end of the path, marked by a shadowy wall through which I sensed the draw of reality. The new plant already sat by the side of the trail, leaves lifting towards an unseen sun. I smiled and stepped into the normal world again.

A moment of disorientation overtook me between the void and the reality. A misstep now and I might become lost forever, so I forced myself onward, holding my breath and reaching for my cousin.

She caught hold of my arm as I appeared. Cherry had seen me come through the void before and knew I needed a few moments to recover. She said nothing while I gasped and focused on the area around us

Using magic to travel makes me ill which is another side effect of being only half-fae. Cherry helped me through the short time I stood gasping. She had been waiting between two parked catering trucks and not far from the gate to an estate. The guards paced by the gate but didn't notice my arrival.

"I figured I better meet you out here," Cherry whispered as I pulled away and leaned against the van. Everything still had a tinge of green. "My part-time people just left. The rest of the group are gathering stuff to take back to the business kitchen. If anyone asks, I called you to help me with the food. We need to go through the gate. Otherwise, I'd have trouble explaining how I got you inside past the gates, the guards and the dogs."

The men paced back and forth by the gate again. "Is there a reason for this security?" I asked.

"I didn't say, did I?" She straightened, which meant a troubling answer. "This is Ted Weaver's home."

I am not the most politically astute person in this world (or the other), but I recognized the name. Many people predicted that he'd be president in four years.

"Is the kidnapping to get to him?" I asked realizing I wanted nothing to do with that trouble.

"A few of the guests think so. This problem is something else, though, right?"

"Magic? Oh yes." An odd residue of power came from the distant house. "There has been magic here, but it feels muddled. Damn. Let's go inside before more of it fades."

Cherry nodded, looking more worried. Her call to bring me in had been a reaction to panic, and now she had to face the reality of dealing with powers she didn't understand.

"I can leave, Cherry. No one has seen me yet.".

She patted me on the arm and smiled. "No. I can't ignore what we both suspect has happened here. Let's go. The guests are off in their hotels. The family is footing the bill, and Mrs. Weaver told me to take the food and distribute it to shelters."

"Damn nice thing to do when they must be worried out of their minds."

"Yeah, it is," she said as we started toward the gate. "That's the problem, Skye. I like these people. The Weavers have treated me with the same politeness they treat their guests. I hate to see this happen, and I want you to find the answer."

The intensity of her emotions made me determined not to fail her. Cherry had asked nothing from me before, so I followed to the gate without pause. The guards, dressed in simple black pants and long sleeved white shirts, shoulder holsters in sight. Both glanced at her and then to me. I was outclassed even by the hired help.

"Skye sometimes works with me. I told Mrs. Weaver that she would be here."

"Didn't see a car."

"I had someone drop me off at the bottom of the hill," I said, waving vaguely at the road. "Too many cars up here."

The man stared down the road. He should have seen me walking from that direction, but given the choice between missing my arrival on foot or assuming I had magically dropped in, I knew what he'd choose.

"Okay. Please hold for a moment."

One ran a scanner over Cherry and me while the other made a call to the house. They let us in with no fuss.

The long driveway curved up the hill towards an immense brick mansion. With a couple of turrets added the place would make a damned nice castle. Maple trees dotted the side of the road, the leaves just turning golden and red. The yard was an open carpet of perfect green grass, sloping downward to the wall at the street level.

When we reached the highest point on the drive, I turned to look across to the lake. Boats sailed past, the people oblivious to the trouble on the hill.

Guests milled around at the front door, whispering and nodding. A few looked askance at Cherry and me as though servants should not be allowed to walk in their presence. Or did I overreact? These people had reason to be upset and worried, and I shouldn't let my feelings towards rich people cloud my judgment. No one appeared to be hostile. Half a dozen police cars stood in a line by the garages and the number of uniformed people scouring the grounds contributed to the worry from others.

The stone-lined path we took on the north side of the Weaver house went through a trellis gate and into a rose garden filled with blooms nurtured even this late in the year. My heart pounded with joy. The plants drew me closer. I wanted to stop and breathe in everything, accepting the life they spilled into the air. I slowed until Cherry glanced back with a frown.

We came around another corner of the house and met more people. I recognized several of these faces. The rich and famous didn't gather out in front of the house, where they might be spotted. The reporters among this crowd looked sedate and no less worried than the others. Were they rich and famous, too? Did only important reporters get in here?

I tried not to gawk and ignored how people stared at me. The two of us crossed to the fancy tables laden with food. Cherry ordered the others who were working for her to carry the larger items to the truck on the street. Someone grumbled, but not for long.

I needed to find the room where the bride had disappeared, but that would require a little subtlety or a lot of magic. Better not to rush with nervous people watching everything.

We put lids on various foods. My mouth began watering, and I longingly remembered the crackers I'd given to the mice, wishing I had eaten something today. As we neared the end of the table, Cherry paused in her work and looked at me. The others had moved off, so we spoke without drawing notice.

"Skye? What now?"

"Continue with this work." I stacked the lovely china plates and real silverware. "We need to keep acting as though we're doing just what people expect."

Cherry nodded and collected more things with the automatic movements of someone who did this for a living. I tried to mimic what she did. Although I'd helped her before, this wasn't the type of work I enjoyed. Cherry loved catering and did an excellent job. One didn't cater the Weaver Wedding without being the best.

"Tell me what you can about the missing woman," I mumbled. "I need information before I test other areas."

"I met Lacey a few years ago," Cherry replied. Her face clouded. "We used to show up at the same food banks to help make meals for the underprivileged. For a while, I never realized who she was, even when I heard her name."

"You like her."

"Yeah, I do." Cherry stopped and looked at me. "She isn't a blonde bimbo like a few of the other rich bitch children I've had the misfortune of dealing with in this business."

"Was she ever in trouble?"

"Nothing outstanding. Lacey once told me about how she avoided getting grabbed at a frat party when things got out of hand. She'd slipped away before the cops showed up and busted people for drugs. Oh, and she adores her parents and would never upset them."

"So she wouldn't walk out on her wedding day, fancy dress or not. What about the guy she's marrying?"

"Kid next door, literally." Cherry gave a wave towards the white walls of a house so far away that I couldn't say next door applied. The next county? "They've known each other all their lives and they're in love. I am sorry for William. He's going crazy."

"What do you think is happening?"

"This has to be something in your area of expertise. She's a good kid, and I want nothing bad to happen to her."

Or to have already happened. I didn't say that aloud, but she stared at me, waiting for the words.

"Let's go to the room where she disappeared. I assume we'll find a mirror there."

"Yes. Big stand-up one, oval," she said. I looked surprised again. "I talked to her there a couple of nights ago, planning out the last few things for the wedding."

Cherry stopped and dabbed at her eyes. Damn. I had never known her to cry, except the night when someone stabbed Li, and she thought her sister had died.

"I'll do what I can. Let's get inside," I whispered and realized I needed to start my work. Everyone had left the yard. I prepared myself for the ordeal of getting to her room.

Cherry signaled her people to gather the last of the chafing dishes and other odds and ends to take out to one of the catering vans. She told them to leave which meant they wouldn't look for us when we went somewhere we shouldn't.

Cherry's workers recognized me as her odd cousin and didn't wonder why she had called me. The others went off, talking among themselves, guessing at what had happened.

With a bowl of fruit in hand, I followed Cherry into the house. We walked down a long hall, and into a kitchen that gleamed with silver and white. A servant left as we came in and she looked upset. I sensed the emotions of those gathered in the huge building, a cloud of fear and sadness.

Once alone, Cherry grew worried again.

"You can stay here," I offered as we placed things on the shiny counters. "I can find the room. The strongest magic will be there."

"I brought you in, and I'm responsible for you whether I'm with you or not. Let's go."

"We can get there quicker if you play guide."

She put aside the bowl and nodded towards a side door. "We can go through the servant's way or we can take the regular stairs."

"Let's take the regular stairs. Not many guests remain, but I imagine the servants are still working. Fewer people out there."

"Good point. How do you do this for a living? I'm half sick, and we haven't started."

"Well, I rarely go wandering around other people's houses." I pulled my jacket closer again as though the thin cloth provided protection. Sneaking through the home of someone as important as Ted Weaver worried me. "We'll be careful, and we'll be damned quick."

"We could just leave --"

"The fae are involved," I said, looking at her. "And knowing that you realize the police will have trouble finding her, right?"

"Oh. Oh. So I was right to call you?"

I put a hand on her shoulder. She was a small woman,

without an ounce of fat despite the excellent food she cooks and 'tests' each day. Although I stood a head taller than Cherry, she had far more presence than her size indicated. I respected and liked Cherry and didn't blame her for worrying.

"You were wise to call me," I said. "Usually, I stay away from anything involving the fae, but this one, includes humans, too. I want to find out what they're doing."

Cherry nodded, lifted her shoulders and straightened her back. "Let's go."

We left the kitchen and headed farther into the house as we slipped along like two mice looking for cover. Cherry stayed at my back, tapping and pointing when we came to the first intersection. To the right stood a door to the basement, or more likely the wine cellar when I considered this place.

At the first turn, the immaculate tile floor gave way to a plush carpet. Good. We made less sound as we passed. Pictures hung on the wall to my left. To the right, an archway framed the entry hall and a larger room. I heard voices from there and felt a wave of worry almost powerful enough to be corporeal and considered using magic to listen, but getting to the room seemed wiser. The pictures on the wall were not what I expected. Nothing political. Instead, I found family shots from parks, zoos, boats and even a trip to Disney World.

I paused at the end of the pictures. The Weavers only had one child, and here I found a picture of the lovely, blond young woman graduating from high school less than three years ago.

Cherry nodded, touching the picture frame and looking somber. The intensity of her sorrow surprised and propelled me onward to the stairs.

Little paintings flanked the stairwell. I sensed age and money from them. If I grabbed one of the little things and shoved it under my jacket, I could have sold it for enough money to live on for a year or more. We kept going upwards on another flight of stairs, and around the curve of a landing and to the upper floor hall.

Four police officers were leaving a room. I should have realized they'd still be here considering how fast I had arrived. Cherry almost yelped at the sight, but I grabbed her arm and pulled us both into the little alcove by the window. And then I spread magic up around us with such speed my head pounded.

Magic is tough for me, and I wanted to gasp, but instead I put a finger to my lips, signaling Cherry to be silent. I feared she might pass out with fear, but she obeyed me.

The police came closer but never saw us. I had instinctively used my most basic, innate magic in a way which has helped me survive in this world. See what you expect. Mirror, mirror your mind. The cops expected a window and wall. So even when the older black cop looked our way, he never noticed us.

The group stopped at the end of the hall, only a few steps away.

"I don't see this being any of the servants we've interviewed so far. They're dedicated to the people they work for," the black cop said. "Hell, I'm not that dedicated."

"We're checking everyone." The middle man, not in uniform, shook his head. "There have been too many people in and out of the house today. Mrs. Weaver doesn't want to admit anyone brought in others to kidnap the girl, but there were many damned powerful people here, and someone might want their political hand on the next president."

"Yeah." A tall white cop nodded and looked at the paper he held. "Damn. I want the bastards who took her."

Everyone mumbled agreement. I wanted to use magic and wish them to get moving, but then I realized they were going over notes, here in private. Hell, it wouldn't hurt to listen.

"Someone had to see her leave in that dress. No one remembers crates going out. We need to check the caterer, but Mrs. Weaver says she's an old friend of the daughter's, and the quick check shows she's legit, although other members of her family have dicey backgrounds. The guards say she's a small woman. The police checked everything her people took out of the house, though."

"We'll start another room-to-room check of the building and search the grounds again. The media will swarm all over this one."

"We need to find the girl," the black cop said. "I'll go call in more help in for the search. Are the servants downstairs?"

"They should be." The group moved towards the stairs. I had hoped to hear more, but I realized with the fae involved, they wouldn't find anything helpful.

They turned the corner, and we heard them going down the stairs. I lowered the mirror spell, and leaned against the wall, catching my breath. Cherry slid to the floor. I took hold of her arm.

"Let's get to the room."

"I want to leave," she whispered. "Oh hell, Skye. That was way too close."

"We're okay. Let's go."

She shook her head in negation but moved with me

anyway. I still sensed the magic from the room the cops had left, still powerful despite how much time had passed. Someone had confined a powerful spell here.

I used a tiny wedge of magic to push the door open.

"Touch nothing," I warned. The police had dusted the door knob and inside, but we didn't need to leave new prints.

With an emphatic nod, Cherry followed as we stepped into a large room with lots of rich, warm colors. Plants hung along the windows and a carved mahogany bed worth more than my car took up most of one side. I sensed nothing pretentious, though. Teddy bears sat in a haphazard arrangement in a couple rocking chairs in the corner. I suspected Lacey liked the bears.

The only child of wealthy parents? The bears might be longtime friends. They had a worn around the ears look.

I wanted to find Lacey. Maybe the sense of a child lost came from the bears, or perhaps I caught the resonance of her here in this room. She seemed more real to me now.

"Skye?" Cherry whispered.

"I need to get grounded." I glanced at the mirror in the corner by a closet door but didn't approach it yet. "If I don't understand what's natural, I can't find anything out of place." Other than the magic that permeated everything, but I didn't say so. Nothing remained of the spell except the ghosts of the power and a lingering scent of vanilla. "Stay there."

Cherry nodded with an erratic movement and remained rooted in a spot to the side of the door. She would touch nothing.

I wanted to sit in the middle of the floor and use magic to examine every corner and crevice. Cherry would go stark raving mad if I into a trance. Besides, I didn't want to risk the chance of someone walking in on us.

So I confined my search to the mundane and searched everywhere I could see. An open door led to a large, private bathroom, all clean and sparkling. I found nothing out of place except various makeup bottles and cases sitting on the counter. They'd brought in a professional to do Lacey's makeup, but the person left no hint of magic residue.

Lacey had custom-made perfume. Even without touching the atomizer, I caught the sweet scent of flowers in spring rain.

I found rows of clothing arranged by color in the walk-in closet, but also with a few gaps which made me suspicious until I spotted the suitcases at the side of the bed. Honeymoon.

By the closet door, I found the tiniest piece of white lace, no bigger than my fingernail, and unnoticed where it had fallen by the mirror's leg. I lifted the cloth and found myself swept up in a sudden link with the woman. I had expected nothing this powerful.

Lacey had been real, alive, elated. Wedding.

"Hey!" Cherry crossed the room and shook my arm to get my attention. She'd been right to do it, too. I had just slipped too far away.

"How odd. I don't often form such a strong connection with anything. I need to watch the mirror."

"Yeah, but can you help?" she demanded, her voice harsh. "Because if not, I want to leave now."

"As long as I'm here, we'd be stupid to go before trying to find out what happened." I touched her arm, but I held to the lace and still connected with Lacey, her presence still drawing my attention. "I am the only one who might track her."

Cherry stopped, took a deep breath. "I shouldn't be this crazy since I called you here. But this is my ass on the line with yours, and my reputation. I like Lacey. I do. But I saw my future if the police walked in now --"

"Don't worry." She frowned, as though the answer was dismissive. "No, just don't worry. I will do all I can to make certain they don't see us this time, either. If someone did, I would make certain no one ever realizes you had been here."

"You are dangerous, Skye," she said with a show of surprise.

"Only when I'm desperate. Let me work at the mirror and then we can leave."

She stepped away, eager for me finish. Still holding the bit of lace in my hand, I moved closer to the mirror and looked into the glass. I have an affinity for mirrors and use them for more than traveling from place-to-place. The power is related to the instinctive spell I bring up to reflect other people's thoughts back to them. I can use mirrors to recall the moments when someone has stared into the glass. With more difficulty I can bring back images of what has happened in the mirror's view, even without someone there staring at the reflection.

My fingers touched the glass. The surface blurred as colors muted, swirling, melting ... and images passed like a movie running too fast in reverse. I watched as an unnatural darkness swept over the scene and disappeared. I didn't catch what happened the first time. So I ran the 'movie' back and played forward from there.

Cherry, who watched the mirror from behind me, made a surprised sound as the images coalesced beneath my trembling fingers. Damn hard work. This magic took finesse and patience.

Lacey had been the last person to stand here and stare into the surface. She had been wearing a flowing white gown and with a shower of lace folded back away from a lovely, heart-shaped face. Golden hair hung in curls at her forehead and beside her bright blue eyes. She stared at me as though she looked into my soul.

I sensed nothing but joy. Anyone looking into her smiling face would have felt the emotion. Lacey loved this man she was marrying today. She wanted to be with him forever.

Though there was no sound, I watched her laugh and thought the world brightened with her joy. This woman had not intended to run away in the next few minutes.

The realization worried me. I wished there had been something to make me believe she had misgivings and had slipped away on her own.

But I still had to explain the magic, didn't I?

And the magic came in the mirror's vision as a sweep of shadows enveloped the room. I spotted something distant as Lacey turned. A view of a building?

"Is that a castle?" Cherry whispered at my shoulder.

I hadn't realized she'd moved closer, but her words helped to clarify my perception. Or was I mirroring what she expected to see?

I didn't think so. The parapets of one tower rose into a cloudy sky. Someone had opened a portal from somewhere very far away, likely across the Veil. I saw little past Lacey and her frilly dress as she turned, startled. I caught only the hint of shapes behind her, and I tried to stop the scene, to bring them into focus. Four people stood there though they seemed nothing more than shadows.

Hands grabbed Lacey, and pulled her away, towards

the castle. She grew smaller in a heartbeat. The darkness spread out and then cleared. The castle and Lacey had disappeared.

"Damn, damn," Cherry whispered. "Your people can reach in and grab someone --"

Her anger shocked me. "Not my people, Cherry, just as the ones who do drive-by shootings are yours."

She glared, still too enraged to see any reason in my words. "Where did they take her?"

"I didn't recognize the place, but I'll search for information. We need leave."

She still stared at me with angry dark eyes. By now my skin was clammy and either too cold or too hot. I don't have the controls that a full fae does, and the more magic I use, the more it takes from me.

"Can you find her?" she asked, her voice softened as the anger changed back to despair.

"I will try. We need out of this room, Cherry. Now, before I'm too ill to go."

She stared for longer than I had expected given how she wanted out of this room.

"Magic makes you ill!"

"I thought you'd figured that out by now," I replied, frustrated that she still hadn't moved. People would come back here soon. Impending disaster hung in the air.

"Damn, Skye. Let's go. We need to talk about this."

"I don't understand," I said with a welling of confusion as she took my arm.

"I'd never suggest this if I knew it hurt you," Cherry said.

"What does that have to do with finding your friend? Someone used magic to take her. Who else could you call?"

"You are more important than a friend. You are

family."

She stunned me with those words. I was the outcast from both worlds; I was neither human nor fae, neither male nor female and nothing anyone would want to claim as a relative.

The shock and my inability to react might have gotten us caught or killed if it had been anyone but Lacey's mother who walked through the door just then.

CHAPTER THREE

I reached for a mirror spell a fraction of a second too late and stopped; a field of magic surrounded this woman and which would negate a spell.

"Well." Mrs. Weaver stepped inside and closed the door. "I didn't expect to find you here, Cherry."

"I -- I --" Cherry looked at me with eyes gone wild as her face paled.

"And you are?" Lacey's mother asked. I recognized her from the pictures below, but something wasn't right. She wasn't fae, and she shouldn't have magic, and yet the power drifted around Mrs. Weaver like an exotic perfume. She wasn't even a half-breed. I was the only one of my kind to have lived (for one reason or another) in the last few centuries.

"I'm Cherry's cousin," I said. She frowned, and her hand lifted to do a test for magic. "Half-fae."

"Oh, my. You're that one? And you are related to Cherry? Small world, isn't it?"

Cherry 's fingers caught my arm and held on tight enough to bruise. I feared she might faint, so I dared a whisper of magic to help steady her. Cherry blinked, took a deeper breath and looked at the woman standing by the door.

"Mrs. Weaver has magic." Cherry's eyes went large. "But you are not fae."

"No, not fae by birth." The woman looked as though she had missed something by not being born to those people. She stepped closer, and the reflection in the mirror caught my attention. The mirror still held a touch of magic and what I saw....

"Oh," Mrs. Weaver said, looking into the reflection.

While the vision had the same face, the clothing had changed. The dress she wore in the mirror had been out of date a hundred years ago: a long dark skirt brushing the floor, and a high-collared white blouse buttoned up the front. The vision in the mirror had dark hair pinned up in a neat bun and a smudge of ash on her cheek. Smoke drifted past the hazy buildings behind her.

"That is how I used to dress." Mrs. Weaver patted her hair which was short now, well cut and used to having the care of a good salon. The clothing she wore today looked comfortable. She must have changed after the canceled wedding. "I worked as a Gibson Girl in downtown Chicago back then and dressed in that uniform every day. A friend picked me up every day in a carriage -- horse carriage, you understand -- and took me to the offices. I took notes, filed things, watched the days pass and wondered about life five years from then. And here I am, a hundred years later."

The picture faded.

"I can hold the magic for a while," I offered.

She caught my hand. "No. Let her go back to the past where she belongs."

"What are you?" Cherry whispered, as though afraid to ask.

"I'm human. Very much human. But over a century ago a handful of fae had fallen into a dangerous situation during the Chicago fire. I found them trapped in a burning building and helped them escape though I came close to dying. They saved my life and granted me a wonderful, long life of my own. Except--" She stopped, and she looked at me, her bright blue eyes narrowing. "Except, I can't bear children because the magic would taint them. But life -- Oh I've had a long and excellent life."

My mouth went dry. New possibilities became apparent in those last words. Cherry waited for one of us to give the answers to questions she might be afraid to ask.

So I asked the question. "Who is Lacey?"

"I don't know," the woman answered, and despair -- a mother's despair for a lost child -- came through the facade. "No one told me. Twenty-two years ago, a year after I married Ted, old friends visited from across the Veil. They brought a baby and made everything appear to be a typical adoption. No one questioned where she came from after the child was in our care."

Such things have happened in the history of the fae when a child might be brought over the Veil to a place of safety. The world of the fae is dangerous.

"Does Lacey know about her background?" I asked, looking around the room.

"She knows she's adopted, but not that she's fae. I used to call her my little fairy princess. Gods of the fae, I should have told her -- at least before the wedding --"

"Lacey is happy here. There will be time to be

something else, later."

"I want to believe she'll be back."

"Fae don't kidnap just to kill. If a fae wants someone dead, they do the work and without remorse."

"Yes, true." Most of the fear left her face. "Thank you. My friends over the Veil made allowances because I'm human. I never learned much of their ways,"

"Who brought her to you?" Cherry asked.

"I can't say." She shook her head in dismay. "I gave my word."

"But knowing who brought her might help," Cherry said, looking surprised and desperate.

"No," I answered before Mrs. Weaver tried to explain. "One does not break faith with a fae. No, she can't tell us. I understand."

Mrs. Weaver nodded and looked less troubled. "Did you see anything in the mirror?"

"Not much." My fingers touched the glassy surface, but Cherry caught my arm. "No, this might help, Cherry. Mrs. Weaver might recognize something."

Mrs. Weaver tilted her head, watching me. "I had heard magic isn't easy for you. I didn't realize the depth of the problem."

Did she know that much about me? I was famous among the fae, but I never expected them to speak of me to others. A slight surge of paranoia tried to take hold, but I pushed the feeling aside. With my fingers on the mirror, I pulled back the images with ease this time because my magic hadn't faded.

"Oh," she whispered at the sight of Lacey, standing there in the gown. We watched Lacey through those moments of joy.

"There." My voice sounded rough, and I trembled.

Cherry helped to steady me. The picture changed with the darkness seeping in the edges. I slowed the view even more. Mrs. Weaver leaned closer and stared into the mirror, a finger tracing the turret.

"I don't recognize the place," she admitted with visible reluctance. "But the others will be here soon. I'm surprised you arrived first. One of them might know."

"Others." Panic set the picture fleeing back to normal. "Fae."

"Yes. Whoever did this set off the alarms around Lacey and me."

"Oh hell. I need to leave."

I turned to the door, but my legs gave way. Cherry and Mrs. Weaver caught me at the same time. I tried to take deep breaths and calm.

"Skye?" Cherry said.

"I shouldn't be here when they arrive." I looked at Mrs. Weaver rather than my cousin. Mrs. Weaver had contact with the fae, and she would understand. "Because of what I am, and with what happened here, they may believe they have reason enough."

"Enough?" Cherry asked.

"To kill me."

"They'd kill you without even learning what happened?" Cherry demanded.

"They might," I said, glancing at her. I tried to submerge the panic again. Calm. "I'm walking a fine line. They've never allowed my type to live long. So far, they don't consider me dangerous. I don't want to give the fae any other ideas. The fae react in haste and repent at leisure, which is often too late for the other side."

"True," Mrs. Weaver agreed. "Take a few more deep breaths. You're safe. I have personal alarms for when any fae comes through, which is what drew me up here. We are careful, so Ted doesn't find out."

"Whoever comes here can pull back the magic," I said, waving towards the mirror. "The fae will recognize who did the work. With your leave, Lady, I will leave before then."

"Can I get in touch with you later?"

I pulled out my billfold and handed her a card. "Or contact Cherry, if you want to be more discreet."

"Thank you, Skye." She stopped and frowned. "They are getting closer, so you had better leave. Thank you for coming to help."

"I came for Cherry. She heard someone say mention the vanilla and cinnamon scent, so she called me. But ... the moment I felt Lacey in this room, I wanted to help bring her back to this place she loves."

"Thank you. I'll walk with you to the kitchen. People won't ask questions if I'm along. With the others on the way it might be best for you not to be delayed."

I agreed, grateful because I couldn't create a spell to hide us without passing out in the hall which wouldn't help Cherry or me. We left the room. Mrs. Weaver remained calm, and I wondered if that control came with age. None of us spoke as we walked through the hall and down the stairs.

"You will receive payment in full for the food, Cherry," Mrs. Weaver said as we reached the main floor. She didn't say those words for show. No one was in the hall with us.

"There's no need to worry about the money," Cherry replied. "We'll decide what to do after Lacey is back."

"You can find places to take the food?"

"There are lots of locations and people who will be happy with an extra meal."

"Thank you so much for taking care of this Cherry. I hate the thought of the food going to waste. I know Lacey would hate it, too."

"Yes," Cherry said. Her head lifted, and determination came to her face. "Please call if I can help in any way."

"I will," Mrs. Weaver said, but she looked distracted and then worried. "The fae are here. You won't be able to leave the house without notice. Go into the kitchen and stay there for a while. We'll be busy upstairs. I'll tell them you were here, Skye. I believe they'll understand and accept your reasons."

"They will realize my presence once you show them the mirror," I said and fought back the urge to run. That was unreasonable on my part; my family had trouble with me, but so far not the others. "Thank you for being so kind at such a trying time."

She smiled with a slight curve of her lips, there and gone. "Thank you, both."

Mrs. Weaver walked away as we reached the hall by the foyer. A group of people stood by the front door, and the police glanced our way, but they saw Mrs. Weaver leave. They continued talking to an older couple, and two young men.

"Who are they?"

"The bridegroom, his parents and best man," Cherry said, and led me to the kitchen. "That's got to be hell, not knowing what happened to his wife-to-be. They are in love, too. And William is a nice enough guy though somewhat on the 'I'm rich' snobbish side. She was breaking him of that attitude, though."

I paused at the edge of the hall and looked back. The best man watched us. I saw more trouble in his stare, but I said nothing. Not here.

CHAPTER FOUR

C herry and I went to the kitchen where bowls, dishes, and food sat everywhere, but no one else was in the room. I only wished there was a cup of tea to be found somewhere in this mess. I let my cousin work and settled in a chair at the middle work island, waiting.

Not for long.

The swinging door eased open, and the tall, blond best man entered. He appeared to be about twenty if you didn't look into his eyes.

"Darion can I get you any...." Cherry stopped and stared. "Oh hell. More fae."

She had startled Darion. He let the door go closed and frowned.

"I am Darion Sapphire Wilding," he said with a formal bow of his head in my direction.

The man didn't realize who I was, and I couldn't ignore his polite introduction.

"I am Skye Emerald McFaelyn," I answered with a bow, though I didn't stand.

"Oh. Hell."

So I had taken him by surprise. Darion reached out and sat in the nearest chair without checking to see if anything had been on the seat.

"You know about the fae," he said, looking at Cherry.

"Skye is my cousin." Her dark eyes narrowed which meant trouble if this fae wasn't careful.

Darion looked back at me again. "Yes, I can see the resemblance, now. No offense intended, Skye Emerald McFaelyn, but what the hell are you doing here?"

"Just Skye," I replied and held up my hands. "No ring, remember?"

"Ah. True. Please call me Darion. No need for formality here, praise the Goddess." He ran his hand back through his surfer-blond hair and still frowned. "But you haven't answered my question."

"I'll answer that question if you answer one for me," Cherry said before I could speak.

"I will if I can, Cherry."

So they knew each other well enough to be on a first name basis. The revelation surprised me because it meant Darion Sapphire Wilding must often be around here. I didn't mind Cherry stepping into the conversation because my head pounded with pain and I leaned back and closed my eyes for a moment --

"Hey, baby." Cherry touched my hand. I hadn't heard her move nearer to me. "Easy, easy. What can I get you?"

Darion watched me and took pity. "A piece of fruit might help. He ... Skye looks as though...."

"He is fine," I offered. "Most people see me as male."

"Do they?" Cherry held out a half peeled flawless

banana. "I've always seen Skye as female."

"That's because you saw me as a child." I nibbled the fruit, fearing I would be ill. Then I realized I was tasting ambrosia and ate more. Darion watched, still assessing my gender the way most people do when they first meet me. "My mother dressed me in disgusting little-girl pink frilly dresses for most of my life. Honest to God, it's a wonder I didn't strangle her with that lace."

Darion laughed when I grinned, which made the encounter easier.

"Skye is here because I called her after hearing about the vanilla and cinnamon scent," Cherry explained as she leaned against a counter. "I didn't realize you were fae. I wouldn't have brought her here if I knew this would put her in danger."

"You did the right thing Cherry," Darion said. I sensed the worry in him. "Since you realized someone had used magic, your actions were wise. Ask your question, Cherry."

"Skye said she wasn't wearing a ring. Tell me about the rings."

Darion gave me another startled glance and a slight frown as though he feared to overstep a line which was odd. That was how I often reacted among the fae.

"I asked you, not Skye. Sometimes she doesn't want to tell me things. And sometimes she doesn't know the answer. Maybe we can both learn something."

"I know about the rings," I protested. I didn't want her involved with the fae because they were dangerous. Darion gave Cherry a polite nod, and I suspected he hid in here with us.

"There are ten clans in the fae lands," Darion said and held up his hands. "Each symbolized by a ring worn on a designated finger, and each with their distinctive gem. The left-hand clans are Diamond, Emerald, Ruby, Sapphire, and Topaz and the right-hand clans are Opal, Jade, Garnet, Lapis, and Amber. The number of the stones on the ring shows the person's rank within the clan. One stone is a regular clan member. Two indicates a warlord, three an ambassador, four is a councilor and keeper of knowledge, and five is the chieftain."

Cherry pulled out her smartphone and took notes. Darion looked amused.

"I might encounter more fae, and I want to understand as much as I can about them," Cherry admitted and looked at his hand. "Sapphire and --" A glance at her notes, "-- an ambassador? What does that mean?"

Darion held the blue-stoned ring up so I could see. I had not expected him to be someone holding a high station within the clan.

"I'm the ambassador-in-training, and share rank with my mother at the moment. I run interference between the clans and sometimes work with the humans though they seldom realize what I am. But I will soon lose the position."

"Why?" Cherry asked.

I nibbled on the banana, wondering if he would answer. Darion seemed open enough, but I sensed desperation. I dared to ask more.

"You knew Lacey was fae, didn't you?" I asked, hoping he remained calm.

Despair came to his face. "Yes, I knew though she never realized."

"Life must be different for full born fae." I ventured farther into the conversation than I ever expected to do with a fae. "Right after I turned thirteen, things happened around me. Stuff moved, mirrors misted over. It became apparent I wasn't human, even without taking into account the physical aspects."

"You are a famous, case." I didn't see any judgment in his stare. "Why are you here?"

"Cherry called me. If I had known this included fae, rather than just something magical, I might not have shown up. And that would have been a mistake. There is an image up in her mirror. A place. When you get a chance, call it up from my touch and see if you recognize the location. I suspect that's where they took her."

"Thank you, I will." I saw hope which I had not expected. "But Lacey ... Goddess, what a mess! Full fae are awakened to their magic, Skye, as part of a ritual, although sometimes something distressing can trigger the power. That might be what happened to you. I imagine you had a traumatic life with all that lace and such."

Cherry went from annoyed to amused when I laughed. She leaned against the counter and nodded to eat more of the banana.

"I've been skirting around this, haven't I?" Darion asked with a glance at his ring and a sigh that held a touch of frustration. "Yes, I knew Lacey's background since I was here to watch over her. I've screwed that up."

Darion must have been on this side of the Veil for far too long. A fae rarely picks up the local vernacular. They are hardwired against slang in a way which has to do with the relationship between the power of magic and words, and an inbred trigger to make certain the words aren't abused, and magic set lose without full consideration.

"I don't understand how this happened with me right here on the grounds," Darion added, and the desperation had come back. "By the time I felt the spell sweeping in, it was far too late to do anything. Then, with guests everywhere, I didn't dare try to get up to the room. This whole wedding was a problem from the start."

"Problem?" Cherry asked, and I saw her getting annoyed. Lacey was her friend.

"A fae marrying a human --" He stopped and stared at me, shaking his head. Did I upset him or the problem at hand? "My clan leader ordered me not to tell her about the fae. Maybe I should have tried to stop the entire relationship, but I never considered they were planning to marry. They were both young. I forgot how fast time passes for humans, and how that affects the decisions in their lives. And -- well, hell. They love each other."

"I can't say the same of my parents. I think they hated each other from the moment they met. No, Cherry, not rape. A normal fae can't force themselves on someone since they experience too much from the life around them."

"So how --" Cherry stopped with a shake of her head. "Never mind. That is not my business."

"I got the impression she bedded him because he was blond."

"Ah," Darion said as his fingers brushed at his long, blond hair. "Odd humans."

I nodded agreement. When it came to sex, we might as well discuss aliens. I didn't bring up that aspect of my life.

"Do you know who took Lacey?" I asked. Sometimes you need to straight out ask a fae for an answer.

"Who? I have no idea." He sounded very annoyed.

"Let's try another question. Why did someone take her?"

That one brought a moment of surprise, so I had stumbled onto the right question this time. I don't interact with fae often, and I'm glad. Twenty questions must be a fae invention, but for them, this isn't a game. They keep secrets extremely well.

"No one has told you?" Darion asked with a hint of disbelief.

"I'm not on a to-be-contacted list."

He looked startled and then an inexplicable anger grew where none had been before, even with the rest of the situation. The change surprised and worried me. I needed to get Cherry out --

"That's irresponsible behavior from Emerald Clan," he snarled. "And I will file a grievance with the King of the Fae."

"Oh, that's a bad idea." An icy touch of fear formed at the base of my spine. "The less they notice me, the better."

Ambassador Darion looked apologetic. "This is something I must do. They were endangering you by not warning you of the trouble. Every fae needed to be given a warning about the problem. Someone has been grabbing us, Skye. It's not safe to be alone or to be unaware, and in this case, you were both. That is unconscionable, putting you in such danger. Take care, Skye. You are unique. Someone might come you."

"Why would anyone collect fae?"

I must have asked a question he didn't want to answer. Darion paused before he answered and his face changed as though he accepted a job he wasn't certain he wanted. "We don't know, but suspect this has something to do with The Choosing."

I stared at him dumbly. He sighed and shook his head.

"Eat your banana. I'll be back as soon as I can and tell you more. The other fae arrived including a Sapphire from across the Veil, who is indignant I am not at the meeting."

"I thought I felt a prod."

"Hard to miss," he said, touching the side of his head. Darion looked at me and then at Cherry. "Please don't leave until I get back."

"Should we stay? Skye isn't safe with these people around," she said.

Darion did something unexpected. He spread his hand out and whispered a few odd words before he spoke in English again. "I gave you both my protection. They will not harm Skye."

My shock told her this was legit; unexpected and frightening, but totally legit. No other fae would harm us while under Ambassador Darion Sapphire Wildling's protection and risk a clan war.

"Thank you," Cherry said. "We'll be here or loading up the truck. I must get this food to the shelters soon."

He nodded understanding the need to hurry in a way that again showed he'd been on this side for a while. Then he gave a very polite bow and left.

"Well hell." I stared at the half-eaten banana and shook my head.

"Finish that. Want a cup of tea?"

"Very much so."

"You should have asked. I've had free run of this kitchen for a couple of weeks."

"Sorry, I hadn't considered your work here." I ate the rest of the fruit to keep from being ordered again. Sometimes I don't do well with people telling me what to do. "This is a mess. A real, honest to all Gods, mess."

"I'm sorry I dragged you in, Skye."

"You were right to call me. I'm uncertain how to word this because it's a very fae sort of thing, but I sense even my help might be needed this time. I didn't realize there was more trouble out there with the fae."

"We can leave if you want to."

I smiled. "He gave us his promise of safety."

"Do you trust him? Will the others allow him to keep us safe?"

"Yes."

"Just like that." Cherry found a cup and tested the water in a teapot and heated it again. She sounded annoyed. "You can't be so trusting, cousin."

"No, not trusting. But the fae are upfront in what they do. It's a hardwired code that goes with the magic. I trust Darion because he could have killed me with a wave of his hand. And he's an ambassador so people will respect him. Not to mention the clan war they'd start if they tried to harm us now."

"Okay, then we wait." Cherry looked at the bowls she'd stacked on the counter. "I'm taking these to the van. It'll take me a couple of minutes to hike there and back. That all right?"

"I'll help you."

"No, baby. You rest." She pushed a cup of tea over in front of me. "You're still pale. Is it safe to leave you here alone? Hell, will I be safe out there alone since people know I'm with you?"

"Yes and yes." I wrapped both hands around the warm cup grateful for the chance to rest. My head pounded as I considered everything, including the other fae who were now in the building and far too near this kitchen. I offered Cherry a worn smile and a lift of my hand. "Go."

She packed the food in a rolling hamper and left, the wheels clicking on the tile in the hall. No other sounds. Darion had made her so safe that if she walked out in rush traffic, a car would have broken before hitting her.

Odd to feel safe and afraid.

I leaned over the counter and sipped the tea, savoring the warmth seeping into my cold hands, and the scent -- I breathed in life from the dried leaves steeped in water. I wanted to stay there for hours, just holding to the cup and accepting the peace of this little room.

Someone pushed the door open.

Ted Weaver.

He stopped just inside the door looking startled. I slipped from the seat in haste and then grabbed the chair because my left leg had gone numb. I moved like a drunk. Great. Wonderful.

"Sir," I said. "I'm Cherry's cousin. Sorry --"

"Sorry? Nothing to be sorry about; Cherry's a nice young woman," Ted Weaver said. He tried to smile at the little joke. "I need coffee. Something. I'm going crazy."

"Yes sir, I can imagine. I'm sorry to hear about your daughter."

He looked at me with his head tilted as though he sensed the sincerity of those rote words. "Thank you. And you are?"

"Skye." His eyes flickered, still trying to figure out my gender. He didn't act bothered when he couldn't guess. "I came by to help Cherry pick up the stuff, but I'm not feeling well."

"It's good of you to come out then," he said. He wandered over to the counter and found the coffee still warm in the brewer and then opened the cabinet and brought out a cup. "Do you mind if I join you?"

"This is your kitchen, sir."

"Ted. Just Ted."

"I can't call the next president just Ted."

He guffawed and poured coffee. Then he sat on the

other side of the work island and put his hands around the cup, so mimicking how I had sat that I experienced a strange affinity with this man. "Sit back down. And there hasn't been an election yet. Nothing is set in stone."

I settled on the warm chair and wrapped my hands back around my cup. Neither of us intended to drink just then.

"Do you work for Cherry?" he asked, filling the silence which bothered him more than it did me.

"No, but I help out now and then."

"What do you do for a living, if I may ask?"

I looked into his face and suspected another reason I found myself here. He wanted a stranger to talk to who wouldn't judge or condescend. The Gods sometimes move us to places we are needed. "I have a one-person detective agency. I find things for people."

"Ah. How nice," he said and even meant those words. "It's sad to lose something you love."

I didn't want to see him despair. This trouble was fae business, but he suffered without knowing the true problem. I lifted my hand and spread magic in his direction, just a touch that blunted the pain, though I erased nothing. "You will get her back."

"Yes," he said. He straightened and looked at me with more resolve, which didn't come from my spell, or from a lack of having seen disasters. This man had traveled south after the hurricane wiped out entire towns on the Florida coast and helped people rebuild with a hammer and a saw. He had journeyed halfway around the world to help earthquake victims. He had experienced the dark sides of disaster, danger, and death.

And yet he still believed his daughter would come home.

We sipped our tea and coffee, sitting in companionable silence, both of us no doubt wanting his daughter to return soon.

And Cherry came through the door. She yipped.

I sputtered at the sound. Ted Weaver laughed with a short, but sincere, emotion. Cherry looked from one to the other of us and shook her head, uncertain what she should say.

"I do live here," Just Ted reminded her.

"Yes, sir. Sorry. I wouldn't have left Skye here --"

"Why not? Your cousin is excellent company. Can I help you with those things?"

"Oh no, sir!"

"Yes, I can." He grabbed a box from the counter.

I gave Cherry a discreet nod. She understood that he needed to keep busy, and she stopped in her headlong rush to grab the boxes away from him. "Thank you. Yes, that will help. Skye --"

"I'll finish my tea, and I should be better by then. We can get this stuff distributed and afterward I'll go home and sleep."

She grabbed a huge container of something greenish and headed out with the likely next president of the United States carrying a box and following behind my little cousin.

He would win the election. I had a premonition like fae sometimes get. If nothing terrible happened between now and the next election, Ted Weaver would win the election.

A president with a wife blessed by the fae and a fae-bred adopted daughter who sure as hell had better turn up soon. Was this political? I wondered if the fae played in human politics, and if so why? What could they hope to gain from such a move? Human power is ephemeral, much like the humans themselves.

I sipped more of the now tepid tea. The two returned and took out another set of things. Only moments later Darion came back looking even more frazzled.

"Ted Weaver is helping Cherry," I warned.

"Is he? I don't want to be talking fae things when he walks in. Should we go somewhere or do you mind if your cousin listens in?"

"Is it safe for her to hear what we have to say?"

"Safer than not knowing what's going on if she spends time with you. She knows about the fae. She was smart to ask questions concerning the rings. It's an important part of our culture and can counter ill will if you meet someone of importance. Did you know about the rings?"

"Some of it," I admitted and drank the last of my tea. "It might be safer if we went elsewhere to talk. Cherry is going to deliver food to different places. Want to ride along?"

"Good plan. We want privacy, so we don't sound like lunatics to the servants."

"How did the others take my presence?"

"Most of them with a shrug. But one was an Emerald, and she -- well, you don't have friends in your clan."

"Yes, I am aware of that situation." The bitterness surprised me. They were strangers, not family.

Cherry came back with Ted before I said more. She nodded to us both. "I'm done."

"I'm heading out now," Darion said. "Someone told me you were here, Mr. Weaver. I wanted to say we hope everything will be fine."

"Thank you, Darion. I hope William is okay." He wanted things to do, to keep busy, to help people, and to not consider what had happened. "Skye, I'll call on you if I need to find something," he said.

I nodded. "I'll be glad to help."

Ted Weaver went off to search out other work. We remained in the kitchen, silent for a few more moments. Then Darion grimaced and shook his head.

"The others are still checking things upstairs. They want me to stick around until they complete their work. We'll talk here for now." Darion cast a spell. No one -- well, no human at least -- would bother us since the kitchen disappeared from their thoughts for a while. That had been an elegant spell and far more than I could manage with a whisper and a wave of my hand.

Darion sat in the chair Ted Weaver had abandoned. Cherry took another, so I slumped back where I had been sitting. "What happened before the kidnapping?" I asked, curious about how he became part of such a mess.

"In order to watch Lacey, I worked to become William's friend in college. Not easy, by the way. These rich people are damned paranoid, and you can't use magic to fake friendship. Once I became his friend, I could keep a close eye on Lacey without being obvious. They were helpful. They never went out on dates alone. Lacey did nothing to compromise herself and nothing to reflect on her father's reputation."

"They're good people," Cherry said. She glanced from Darion and then to me. "Can you two help them?"

Darion frowned. "They will not trust you without a scan, Skye. I told them if you are willing, I'll do the spell."

I considered telling him to go to hell. Others had this done before because the fae didn't trust me, and there was nothing pleasant about having another riffling through my thoughts, looking for whatever secrets they suspected I might be hiding.

"I'm sorry," Darion said seeing my reaction. "But I can't say more unless we can reassure them you are not involved in the disappearance."

"Hell, why not? It's already been a shitty day."

Darion appeared startled by my change in attitude. I had been more than formal before now, and I regretted the lack of tact. He was the first fae who treated me this well.

He wasn't Emerald Clan and not related to me. Did that make a difference? I wasn't an embarrassment to his clan.

"Sorry. I've had this done before. I'd tell you to go to hell, but I'm caught up in this whole mess, and I want answers. So I will cooperate if this will keep me somewhat informed for a change."

"I'll do this as gently as I can," he promised. "Don't fight me."

"I'll try not to." A measure of resistance always happens; the reaction is natural and instinctive. "I should warn you I have a hell of a headache."

"I imagine so."

My shoulders tightened, and my heart thumped as he moved behind me. There are a few things I abhor. One is to have someone standing right behind me, so close I can sense, but cannot see, them.

And I can't bear being trapped, which came next when Darion put his hands on my shoulders and whispered a spell that locked me to the chair. He had to because my body would react on a subconscious level. The spell was a precaution, but my heart pounded at double time, and a chill sweat swept over my body.

"Skye, baby --" Cherry sounded panicked. "Darion, Skye looks bad --"

"Calm," Darion said, worried. He tried to help calm

me with a touch of magic, but that sent another spike of pain through my head. "You must have had some hellacious experiences with the bastards in Emerald Clan."

"Ha," I said. My voice sounded shaky. "I'm the only bastard in Emerald. You know that."

Darion laughed and massaged my shoulders. A shiver of pleasure went through my muscles. "There. Much better. I'll be quick, Skye. I apologize for this."

His hands moved from my shoulders to each side of my head. My breath caught --

I hated the invasion of magic. However, while the intrusion wasn't pleasant, Darion didn't take a dull-edged knife and cut his way through my mind. He nudged and even winced when he hit a big block of a headache. The pain eased with a touch more of his magic. That had never worked for me in the past.

He found the first group of memories I didn't want to drag out, the ones that never faded away. No one keeps secrets from the fae.

"Just get in the car," my mother said, her face a mask of rage. I understood that look too well.

But the car was something different. We never went out together. I slid into the seat and said nothing. If I had been brave, I would have ... but that is a memory. *I would have's* don't work. Please, just move to another memory. This happened a long time ago.

Calm, Skye. I know you cannot change this. But I must be certain nothing is hidden here, amid the other secrets you want to hide from yourself and from others.

No one had ever spoken as they looked at my memories. The sound of his voice brought someone new into the scene. Darion, respecting my feelings, backed away and observed from outside what had happened. I regretted it. His being there had made the entire experience less personal.

I hadn't trusted my mother since she did nothing pleasant.

We drove across town and stopped outside the bus depot where she reached into her purse and held out a stack of bills.

"That's a thousand dollars. Get out of the car and never come home."

I took the money and got out. She drove away.

Darion's rage grew so powerful that the emotion swelled within me. I wanted to escape and run. He calmed, reining himself back as I tried to decide what I should have done that day instead --

But then he offered me words I had not expected: She is evil. She is an evil, heartless bitch.

I frightened her.

"What's wrong?" Cherry asked, worried.

"We're doing okay," Darion said, but his voice sounded rough. "I won't be much longer."

He bounced around, looking at my work as a detective and studying the little things I did now and then with magic. Nothing outstanding. Then he found another dark, rough spot: The night I had run into Cherry and her younger sister, Li. Li had gotten into trouble with a gang. I saved her without realizing who they were. Cherry became my friend. Not so cut off from everyone.

He approved of Cherry, who knew about me and what I was -- and wasn't -- and didn't judge me.

Anything else?

No, no, no.

But the memory came, a dark seething wound in my

soul that I did my best to cover over, to keep this from bleeding into the rest of my life.

They had put me on a frigid metal table, straps across my arms and legs, my neck, my head, trapping me with no hope of escape.

"It's not human," a woman said, a voice beyond the bright white light they always kept in my face, I closed my eyes for fear of going blind.

"Oh, part human," a man answered and jabbed at my side. "There's a match up in the blood work. This one is a mutation."

"Where did they find it?"

"My agent found it living on the streets in downtown. Put up a fight too. Okay, let's start. Put the gag in."

Something shoved over my mouth.

"Monitor the pain levels."

And they cut --

Darion pulled out, his magic disappearing so quickly that I fell forward and hit my head on the counter.

"Ow!"

Darion rushed to the sink where he was ill. He ran water over the back of his head afterward. Cherry looked from me to him, and back again, frightened.

Darion Sapphire Wilding's eyes blazed with anger so strong that I felt the emotion in the air.

"How did you get away from them?"

"A week later, they got careless. They left me unsecured in a room because I was too weak to run. They were right. However, I still had magic, which I had used to keep myself alive while they ... studied me. With the last of the power, I got out of the window and went straight up to the roof. Two days later I was strong enough to leave."

"Emerald Clan never came for you."

"Why should they? They didn't know."

"You are of their blood." His voice had gone hard, but the fury lessened. It is never wise to make a fae angry because sometimes things happen even they can't control. "They should have known. Your father's link --"

"I've never met him."

"Hell. Damnation. Cedric has much to answer for, Skye."

"I am not fae, Darion. Fae told me that their laws don't apply."

"Perhaps not all the fae laws apply to you." His voice remained harsh as he crossed and took a chair again. "But Cedric created you, and by fae law he's responsible, no matter what else may apply. You never should have suffered through torture. And I want to find those damned humans, so they don't do this again to you, to one of us, or to one of their own kind."

He was right, and I couldn't let my fear continue to put others in danger. " I returned later, but they'd gone. I searched through the place and created links so I'd sense if they came near. No one has so far. Later, when we've fixed this problem, I'll give you what information I can."

"What the hell are you talking about?" Cherry demanded.

"Something unpleasant happened six years ago. Am I cleared for the rest?" We didn't need to linger on the incident, and I didn't want to discuss this with Cherry.

"I am uncertain if what I can tell you is worth what I put you through," he said while shaking his head with regret that almost masked the rage. "Hell, I know it's not. And I apologize. Ask whatever you want."

"What is Lacey's fae clan?"

"I can make a good guess, and I think the person who

sent me to protect her knows."

"Who sent you?"

"Lord Wilding himself," Darion answered with a sigh.

I winced as I imagine the reaction from the Lord of the Clan when he learned his ambassador had not kept the woman safe. "I assume he's not happy."

"Not happy is a mild statement. It's a good thing I love this world so well because he decreed that I am not going back over the Veil until I find her."

"Oh." If Lacey died, he would never go home. I hoped this wasn't the case because I liked Darion, which surprised me. I had expected all the fae to be cold and cruel, but for once I felt akin to one. Perhaps it came from having had him in my head, though I'd had Emerald Clan people there before, and not grown closer to them even if we shared blood.

"If this Lord Wilding sent you, then she's part of your clan?" Cherry asked.

"No," Darion said. "It's complicated. Or perhaps not as long as I don't recite the old history and just tell you the result."

"Sounds wise," Cherry agreed.

"In the past there has been animosity between different clans, but that pales compared to the trouble within each clan itself. The real power struggles are not between the clans since the clans will always be equal. But there are positions of prestige within each clan that are fought over, sometimes to the death. When The Rule of Ten -- the leadership over all the clans -- is due to change, assassinations occur everywhere. So, the bottom line is that guards aren't hired from your own clan because you can't always trust those people. In most cases, if you want your back protected from a political enemy, you go to another clan and make a deal."

"Oh. I see." She looked at me.

"I knew none of this. No one tells me anything." My words sounded childish; the headache had tripled.

Someone came to the door and pushed in, stopped and then came through with a surge of magic sweeping past the spell. Darion intercepted the lady as she took a single step inside the room; small, light-haired and dressed in a style showing she had come from the Veil straight to here. They had no technology on the other side, so she wore a handmade dress of lovely blues and greens and a green cape across her shoulders.

She turned my way, frowning.

"I cleared Skye," Darion said and even moved to stand between us.

"We sensed your emotions upstairs," she replied and focused on him. "Something wasn't right."

"True," Darion replied. "But not because of this matter."

He put a hand to her forehead and after a moment the woman gasped and then cursed softly.

"This evil matter needs to be settled, Lady Starlyn Amber Star."

"Yes." She stared at me, the frown changing from one of distrust to distaste. I could live with the new attitude. "Why has no one reported this before?"

I bowed my head, polite in the face of someone of power. Even though I couldn't see the ring on her hand, part of my mirror ability picked up how she expected everyone to bow to her.

"No one looked. Each time the other fae searched, they were only interested in specific incidents."

"And I suspect they never wanted to see more about

Skye than they had to," Darion added.

"Because to know would make them understand. Yes." She bowed her head to Darion and then to me, and left.

The door swung shut again. Darion came back and settled in the chair and didn't hide his surprise.

"She's not usually understanding. That was the head of the Amber Clan. She's held the position since -- well, before the first European settlement on this continent. And yes, I mean the Viking one."

"Hell," Cherry said. She sat back down in her chair, staring at the door.

"She might have made a hellish amount of trouble. None of the clan leaders are in a good mood."

"I don't like having my experiences passed from head-to-head," I admitted.

"Only a taste of what happened, Skye. Only a moment," he said. "And I apologize. I should have asked you first, but Lady Starlyn is never patient."

"It's done." I couldn't call the fae woman back and tell her to forget the problem. Besides, they had other trouble at hand to keep them busy and out of my life.

Darion stood and then fell back into the chair with a sigh of frustration. "The others want us to stay in case there are other questions. They won't be long."

I remained seated, grateful to relax, even at the order of the fae. I still sensed the others up in Lacey's room, a little buzz of activity around the mirror I had used.

"So you are Sapphire Clan, which means Lacey was not from Sapphire," Cherry prompted, going back to the tale.

"Or Emerald. I had a partner from Emerald."

"Two clans eliminated out of ten, then. Any other guards who came from other clans?" I asked.

"I can narrow this in another way." He met my eyes without flinching, which helped settle my nerves. "We're at a crux time over the Veil. A dangerous time. Once a century the rule over all the clans changes from one clan to the next, moving in the same order as the rings. Three days from now the change occurs. The power is automatic and controlled by ancient magic, and we can't interfere. What isn't automatic is who within the particular clan will take the rule. A quarter century before The Choosing, the birthrate of the next clan in line will increase tenfold, which is not a serious number since the fae seldom produce children otherwise. But still, there will be between fifteen to thirty children born in that year. Many won't survive birth, sometimes for very gruesome reasons."

"That's barbaric," Cherry said, appalled.

"It is. The clans are trying to cure themselves of killing children who don't suit them." He looked at me, and I realized I owed my life to this change. "The closer we get to The Choosing, the more dangerous life becomes for those born to the age. Most will go through a ritual and be rejected as unsuitable, and that saves their lives. Matters remain civilized the first couple rounds as everyone within the proper age is brought out, and the ones who are not going to be chosen are set aside and become regular clan members."

"What sorts of things make them ineligible?" I asked.

"What might be called mental defects is the best way to explain, though these are not the same as humans judge such things. The person who becomes the King or Queen of Fae must possess certain attitudes and magical abilities which would make them reasonable rulers and allow them to have fair dealings with the clans."

"Lacey is from the clan next in line for the rule? And

her people grabbed her because she was marrying a human and ruining her chances?" I asked.

"I wish things were that simple," Darion answered and looked just as frustrated as earlier. "My suspicion is that she's Ruby Clan. However, we've had other fae disappear in the last few months, Skye. Fae from every clan have vanished from this side of the Veil, most right on the border and at the Clan Houses. Only one has turned back up, but dead. And another from the same clan disappeared a day later. They disappeared in pairs, before this. Not both together, but always two from the same clan will go missing within a few days of each other."

"So all the clans are accounted for in the disappearances?"

"Yes. A third member of Ruby clan disappeared, but that may be a political killing though no one found the body. No one else has vanished for weeks. Everything appeared safe." He shook his head, and the worry came back to his eyes. "We weren't watching for whoever this is to take another."

"Perhaps someone else kidnapped Lacey?" Cherry suggested.

"The magic appears to be the same person," Darion replied, "including the tightly controlled magic and the scent -- very powerful magic in a cinnamon and vanilla scent, as Skye knows. There are resonances from other sites."

"So what is going on?" Cherry asked.

"She must be Ruby," he said. "One of the top candidates, in fact, from the level of trouble her disappearance has stirred up. The others rushed here, and they're worried. More so than they over the other missing fae. I'm sure if I checked carefully, I would locate a record of a Ruby baby whom others assumed had died."

"So, what happens now?" I wanted an idea of what to do next. We were going to leave this kitchen haven soon, and I would regret heading back out into the trouble.

"The others will search again. Everyone is worried about the upcoming Choosing since no one knows what happened to the other fae. Now someone who might be the next Queen has gone missing, and that makes matters more troubling. We want to find Lacey before The Choosing."

"You can't stop the event?" Cherry asked.

"No. Ancient magic controls The Choosing, a spell set before man built his first cities. The spell is so old it has become sentient and corporeal. When the time comes, the magic will seek the candidates and pull them together, and the magic will then choose the new ruler. The leaders of the clan, who are often still called chieftains, go. So do councilors, ambassadors and two more representatives of each clan, who will witness the rule passed to a new person. Any other fae can come along to watch. This is one of the few times we gather in numbers."

"Have any of those councilors or ambassadors disappeared?" I asked.

"No. They are all regular clan members. One was the partner I worked with, a woman who tried to become Lacey's friend but she never got far. That would be your older half-sister, Aria."

I winced. I had only encountered Aria Emerald McFaelyn once in my life. A group of fae had picked up the magic I had done to stop a car accident when a stupid, drunken fool ran a light. I had protected the family in the car he rammed, including the baby still in the womb.

When I do significant magic of that sort, someone

always comes to check. They tracked me to the bushes by a park three blocks away where I had passed out. That's as far as I got before the backlash of pain and illness made me curl up and hide.

I had awakened to find a hawk-nosed woman had grabbed me by the hair and pulled my head upwards, as though I were a doll she'd found in the mud.

"Yeah, it's still alive," she had said.

I kicked her.

The meeting went downhill from there. She didn't kill me though I had embarrassed her. I survived because the others laughed and dragged her away, leaving me there in the mud with a raging headache and a cracked rib where she had kicked me in return.

"It is blood of your blood, Aria Emerald McFaelyn," someone had said as they walked away.

I wished I had heard the rest of that conversation.

"Skye?" Darion said.

I blinked several times, pulling back from that dark memory. "Just wondering how I should feel about Aria disappearing in this mess," I admitted. "We aren't close."

"I didn't realize you had a sister on that side of the family," Cherry said, surprised since I hadn't confided. I'd talk to her about it -- later.

"Skye has several half-siblings across the Veil. Most never come to this side. Aria crosses now and then, and people thought she would be a good candidate to befriend Lacey."

"It didn't work," I said.

"I've heard you met her once."

"Briefly. The cracked rib still gives me problems sometimes."

He clamped his mouth shut, but when I smiled, he

laughed aloud. "She's not my favorite person, either. And she doesn't like humans, Cherry. Likes their world, but hates them. There was no way she could ever be friends with someone as bright and friendly as Lacey, fae or not. Your father is distraught over his favorite daughter's disappearance. And to be honest, my life doesn't look worth much since he claims the disappearance is my fault."

"You've lost two people in this?" Cherry asked.

"Yes. It's bad for my ego, not to mention my standing in the clan." He joked, but I saw real worry in his eyes.

"The other candidates --"

"All watched, and none of them are directly involved in the disappearances of the others, let alone Lacey's. But...."

"But one might hire others to do the work for him," I said, and Darion nodded. "And he stays out of the picture while still wearing down the number of potential rivals."

"Yes. Lacey's kidnapping has me rethinking several assumptions. Goddess, I hope this isn't the first of a new purge. There are some fae who want a return to the old ways, making Lacey a perfect target, since she came of age in the human world and in their eyes she is not fae enough."

"Any luck on identifying the view I caught in the mirror?"

"No, but they were happy to see what you found and hope they can figure out more."

"Where did the others disappear?" I asked, my detective background reasserting itself, which was why Cherry had called me here.

"Most disappeared right out of the clan homes or close by those buildings. That's on this side of the Veil." He looked at Cherry and smiled again. "The homes of the ten ambassadors are temporal ports. The doors can open to many places like the fae lands or different cities on earth. If your cousin had a clan ring, the link would always help him find the current location of not only Emerald clan's portal, but that of any other clan. There is also a street you can enter with all the clan houses, but in times of danger, you might link to a clan house other than your own. In the last two centuries, with the changes in the human world and the growing technology, life has grown dangerous. Now we offer safe ports in the storm to any fae in danger, no matter what clan, though we try to go to our own people if we need help."

"If they were in buildings and if there were mirrors anywhere around, I might see something."

He looked at me, startled again. "Some of them were weeks ago, though."

"Strong actions, strong emotions -- those will help."

"I must stop seeing you in human terms. You're closer to us than to one of them."

I had never considered myself to be human or fae. I shrugged. "Are you willing to work with me on this?"

"Why not?" he asked, and he lifted a hand before I listed out the plethora of reasons why associating with me might not be what he wanted to do. "I heard you are good at your work; that you are conscientious, and make logical steps when you are working. Oh yes, the ones who did the scans in the past were at least fair in reporting your abilities."

"But I am still not someone you should team with on this problem. Being with me could be bad for --"

"For my reputation?" He snorted and waved a hand through the air as though to brush that statement aside. "Skye, I lost both my partner and the young woman I was sent to guard. My clan leader says I cannot go back over the Veil until I find at least Lacey. I suspect your father may be ready to swear out vengeance on me for losing his daughter, in which case I would need to kill him and any of your immediate relatives who sided with him. I'm good with magic and a sword, but they're more numerous than I care to take on alone. You cannot hurt my reputation, friend."

"Will your family help you?" Cherry asked.

"Well, I don't see them leaping in to help me so far," Darion replied. I heard the edge of anger in those words. Then he shrugged. "But I never expected them to come to my aide. I've spent too many years on this side. There are blood ties, but the obligations are not the same as in human families. Several clan members will help, but I don't want to drag them into this mess."

"Different cultures," Cherry said and shrugged, which seemed the right reaction

"I'm willing to work with you, Skye," he said, looking back at me. "I should have called you when your sister disappeared. Everyone agrees you are good at your work, and you are gifted in ways which aren't normal among the fae. There are fae who are worried you might misuse the powers since you lack the ties to life fae use."

"Okay, explain that one," Cherry said. Then she looked at her watch. "Quickly, because we need to go soon if your people let us leave. The food in my van will not stay fresh for long."

"Your van," Darion said and closed his eyes and lifted a hand, whispering magic words again. "There, the food will stay fresh. You need not worry any longer. And we can leave soon, but I want to wait until a few of the others depart, so we don't run into them."

"As long as we aren't wasting the food, I don't mind waiting," she admitted and leaned back, looking utterly worn. "Tell me about the fae and why Skye isn't like the rest of you."

Darion turned to ask my permission. I nodded. I might learn something more. Cherry asking questions was a boon for me. I didn't have to admit my ignorance.

"Fae powers come in two parts. The more noticeable is the core of magic within each of us, and upon which we can draw to cast spells. There are fae who possess larger cores than others, and the size of the core appears to be random. No breeding program has ever worked to stabilize the power in the core though the fae tried for a few centuries. Magic in the air replenishes the cores. There is magic all around, Cherry, even here over the Veil. Humans have no core to gather it."

"Ah."

"The second part is a link acts as another sense, I guess. We touch the life around us, everywhere and know how the magic we do is affecting the life balance of the world. Magic upsets balances and can be destructive if a fae unleashes too much at once. The link tempers what we do with a natural feedback. Skye lacks such a link. He has a large core of magic to use for whatever he wants, with none of the usual repercussions. Others like him...." Darion stopped, but I waved my hand to continue. "Such people have been dangerous to both here and over the Veil. Catastrophe followed them, disasters which ripped the world apart because they didn't stop. And that's why the fae killed them whenever found."

"But not Skye."

"Not yet," I said and sounded sullen.

"Skye has a different trigger which stops the misuse of

magic," Darion said while ignoring my statement.

"It's damned painful and makes me ill," I said. I stood. "So I'm safe, at least for the moment."

"Yes, for now," he agreed. I appreciated that he didn't lie. "The others are done. We better go. Skye, I want to stay close to you for the time being."

"We plan to deliver food to various places around town," I said.

Cherry shook her head. "You two don't need to go along with me. I'll manage."

"I can help to feed the poor," Darion said to her. "Skye and I need to talk, nothing more. And there are people out on the streets who might come to me, both fae and others from the other side of the Veil, who might have information. Going with you will be helpful if you'll allow me."

Cherry nodded and started out of the room. We followed, Darion dropping the shield as we stepped out.

The house had gone quiet.

I followed the two while considering this case and wondering if I shouldn't back away right now. Despite Darion's willingness to work with me, the rest of the fae world react in a different way. My Emerald Clan relations were about to be embarrassed for not reporting that incident six years ago, and that would cause more tension.

Hell. I needed to get out of this. I might hold up in my apartment for months and stop using magic altogether. Keep a low profile --

And if I saw a child being grabbed off the street again, would I turn my back and pretend I couldn't help?

No. I had to help others, and that meant even using magic which made me ill. The need to come to the aid of others in trouble was a compulsion so strong with me that there were nights I didn't sleep knowing there were problems just outside -- and I could not, even with magic, help settle all of them.

Still, I didn't need to work on this case. I'd pointed them in the right direction.

I had almost walked away when I saw Cherry pause and look at the pictures on that wall again. She stopped when she saw the ones of Lacey and shook her head with despair.

I was not doing this for the fae. I had come at Cherry's call, to help her and family had to count for something in this world.

Lacey Weaver as the Queen of the Fae would be good. Lacey, who loved a human, and who had lived as a human --

I looked at Darion as we headed toward the front door. "I have a question. Why was the possible next Queen of the Fae raised as human?"

"Ruby Clan has always remained close to humans," he said with a quick glance around, reminding me that other humans might still be in the halls. "When Ruby is in charge, there are always better relations between the two groups than at any other time. We have grown very far apart from in the millennium since Ruby last ruled for their one hundred years. I suspect the clan always hoped Lacey would be chosen because of how she lived."

"They want to bring the fae closer to humans?" Cherry asked, slowing as we neared the front door. "Is that safe?"

"Nothing is safe," Darion replied. "We have magic, and you do not. We are few, and you are so damned many there is no way we could be a danger to all of humanity without destroying both our worlds and ourselves. But we are dangerous to individuals, and to small groups."

Somewhere a phone rang, insistent of attention, and someone answered. There would be a lot of calls tonight and very many anxious words.

We had to get past the police at the door, a group who asked why we had not left earlier. It took Mrs. Weaver's intervention to get us past those people, and then she called the men at the gate and had us cleared there. She looked surprised to see Darion leaving with us, and perhaps hopeful when she turned my way. She knew he was fae.

"You talked to Ted and helped him through this," she said to me. "He found it comforting."

"I'm glad I could help," I said. Was Ted's rise to power fae-created? No. I had sat with the man, and he had been as human and non-magical as they come. "I'll do what I can, Mrs. Weaver."

"Thank you."

I had committed myself by saying those last words, and I felt better for having said them as though marking the decision made the rest of the work easier. I feared Lacey might be dead after all because someone didn't want her to be Queen of the Fae. The kidnapper might not like humans -- or was that my personal expectations of fae reactions interfering again?

I suspected I would find out the answers -- I hoped soon enough to help.

CHAPTER FIVE

M ore police wandered around the yard, and they watched us as we walked down the hill to where Cherry's van still waited. Police had taken over for the estate guards and stood by while she opened the doors and they checked inside the vehicle. Then they went back to the estate.

The night had turned dark with frosty with a thin mist covering the rising moon. I spotted a few white sails out on the lake, like clouds racing across the water. I wanted to be out there, looking back at the shore, and not considering what trouble there might be in the world.

The cool breeze rustled through the trees and grass around us. I had no insights into what I should do next except to go with Darion and try to look at a few mirrors.

Those mirrors would be in clan homes. Fae places, which would bring me closer to the fae again. I clamped my mouth shut against a sudden urge to curse as Cherry closed up the back of the van. I spotted a police cordon down at the end of the street, and a huge lineup of vehicles with bright lights. People stood around with cameras --

"Hell," Cherry said. "We'll never get through."

"Oh yes we will," Darion and I chorused.

And we laughed. Darion brushed his hand over the side of the truck, and the words changed, along with the color.

"Nice," I said. "At least they won't track Cherry down that way."

"Plates, too," he added with another brush of magic. He looked at me. "It's easy enough to change things that aren't alive."

"Is it? I wouldn't know. It's all the same to me."

"When I did the scan, I experienced a whisper of what happens to you. For me, magic is like breathing --"

Magic. Behind us.

Darion spun and threw himself between the magic and Cherry. I moved as well, but he was the one who would have saved her if this had been an attack.

A half-dozen people appeared between us and the gate. The world shimmered, and I realized we were in a magic bubble which kept the others from perceiving what was happening. I glanced at the newcomer's hands and suppressed a shiver: Emeralds. These were members of my clan, and their faces showed they were not happy to see me.

"We're here to warn you away from this, Skye Emerald McFaelyn," a woman said. She'd visited my home and scanned to find what I had done with magic once, and she had been no more polite back then. "This is no concern of yours. You do not want to be part of this trouble."

"I have already agreed to help. I gave my word."

Hisses of sound came from the others. They could have been so many angry cats right then, annoyed with an intruder into their pride. I suspected I wouldn't survive because irritated fae just take care of an irritation with ease and the problem would not bother them ever again.

"Skye is working with me, and he is under my protection."

A half dozen heads turned straight towards Darion, shock replacing their annoyance. A Sapphire had just put an Emerald into his care. I realized he had agreed to be my guard. If I understood the implications, this was the same position he'd talked about in the kitchen.

Darion was more than a Sapphire clansman, though. I doubted ambassadors randomly took on guard positions. Darion had surprised the Emeralds who confronted us. He also surprised me but not as much as the others who looked at him with shock and dismay.

"In your care. Do you swear this?" a young man demanded.

Those words won odd reactions from his companions. A hand caught the Emerald's shoulder, as though to stop him from going any farther into a very dangerous situation.

"Yes, child, I do," Darion replied, looking at him. Several Emeralds paled, no doubt realizing they'd insulted someone of real power. "You know who I am. Skye is in my care and working with me. You do not want to make trouble, now do you?"

"No, Sapphire, we do not. Your care, your help, your responsibility."

"Agreed."

Heads bowed. I saw another glare from the rude young man but in the next moment, they all disappeared in a wave of color and flower scents.

"What the hell was that about?" Cherry sounded as though she'd dealt with enough magic for one day.

"That was a very unsubtle move," Darion replied with a snort of mixed disgust and amusement. "I doubt very much their clan leader knew what they intended to do. Those children will be in all kinds of trouble. They didn't expect me to be here."

"And you made yourself responsible for any mistake I make."

"Yes." He lifted a hand before I could speak. "Skye, my young friend, you cannot possibly make any mistakes worse than the ones I have already made. Let's go."

Cherry and I climbed into the van. Darion followed and sat by the door putting me in the middle which I found uncomfortable, caught between human on the left and fae on the right. We drove past the police. The reporters tried to get closer, but they tripped over each other, and we got clear before any of them followed.

So escaped in more peace than anyone else would have managed for most of the night. A few blocks later, Darion reached out the window and tapped the side of the van, dissipating the magic which disguised us. I sat back and nodded, relaxing for the first time since my arrival at the Weaver Estate. The calm wouldn't last long.

The road curved along the lake shore, past other huge mansions set well back on extensive lawns. Guards stood at almost all the gates, and they watched the van go by, sometimes with hands resting on weapons.

"That's not usual," Darion said, waving towards one group as we passed. "Tonight, though, the people in those houses are worried about their children, spouses, spoils, and riches."

"And those guards will never protect them from what happened to Lacey," I said. Distrust filled the air. Even in the heart of the city, amid the slums and derelicts, I had never experienced this much seething suspicion of everyone who passed by them.

I watched the lake instead where it brushed up within a few hundred yards of the road. Cherry said nothing as we drove past the harbor where more sailboats stood like a stand of trees on the water, their masts wrapped in white. The heart of the city glowed off to the southwest, the direction where we headed.

"What now, Darion?" she asked as we neared the poorer part of town. She threaded van through the traffic with ease.

"Now we deliver all this excellent food to people who needed it far more than the guests at that wedding did. Lacey would want us to, not matter what else happens. As we stop at various places, I will try contacting others throughout the night. I have most of my own Sapphire Clan out looking for links and clues. We need more information about what has happened before we can act on anything."

"She's Ruby," I said. And something in my mind clicked. "Hell, the others who disappeared all have families, right? Why can't you follow them? Blood draws blood. That's how I reached Cherry tonight."

"That's how the magic should work. We have all tried to find our missing clansman, but we can't break through whatever is hiding them from us. The only one whom we found was already dead."

"How did he die?"

"She. She died of starvation, shock and mistreatment. We believe she escaped and tried to get to help."

Cherry turned a corner into an area I remembered too well. The lights and the crowds sent shivers through me. I had lived on these streets, sixteen years old and alone. If I had taken the bus when my mother left me on the streets, I would not have found myself in this mess now. And I didn't like being here, with Emerald Clan pissed at me. I feared I would not survive. Darion could not be there to protect me all the time.

That future problem didn't shock me as much as it should have since I'd lived with the possibility of death for far too many years. I wanted it to count for something more than my older half-sister being embarrassed about my existence.

Aria was among the missing and I might not have to deal with her again. Not that the others weren't also capable of killing me on a whim.

As long as I worked with Darion, I could help a young woman in danger. Nothing else mattered: not what she might become, not whose daughter she was, not the presidency or saving the fae. When I stood in her room, I had felt her joy, and I would fight to bring that back to the world.

Tonight we wandered around town, dropping off container here and there for people who needed a meal. Odd food: crab and lobster, steak and chicken. Salads, desserts, rolls, soups. My headache eased as I sensed the pleasure from those who gathered for the meals. I needed to do this with Cherry more often.

Darion slipped away now and then, followed by whispers of magic from alleys. When Cherry was ready to leave, she'd send me off to get him. I watched him talk with people who sometimes were not human no matter what their outward appearance. Right about midnight I found him in a shadowed alley behind an abandoned building and talking with a tall man with long white hair. I bowed and backed away in haste and then stopped at the signal of the ancient one's hand.

Not ancient in years though that was true as well. The silver-haired fae was one of the First Race. I knew they still existed, but I never expected to see one. The Elder turned and took three quick steps in my direction. He almost glowed with power. One of his kind couldn't walk openly down the streets because the humans would know the truth and never question magic again.

I wished for him to go out into the light and make the people of this world see a power beyond themselves and their petty wars and technology. The world had lost something precious when the humans stopped believing in magic.

He tilted his head. "I never expected to cross paths with one of your kind," he said, the words melodious, soft and filled with power. I didn't reply while my heart pounded but I had the inane idea I ought to tell him I had thought the same thing. "You are not just flesh and blood, young Skye. You are also your thoughts and I saw what you wanted for this world when you spotted me. I witnessed your longing to make things better here. Go in peace."

He bowed his head and disappeared. Gone.

"Hells all," Darion whispered. He came closer and leaned against the wall taking several deep breaths. He looked pale. "Do you have any idea?"

"Some. Gods." I took a few staggering steps and leaned back beside him. "That was far more dangerous than facing a little cadre of my cousins."

"I did not expect to find one of his kind waiting here for me," Darion said. "That they are concerned --"

"What the hell is this?" Cherry asked, coming around the corner. "You want to get your butts in gear so we can offload the rest of this and get moving or is that too much real work for you?"

She spun and went back to the van.

I looked at Darion.

He laughed and headed out to help her. I followed a little later. I'd survived two encounters so far where I had expected someone to kill me.

Third time, I thought.

DAY TWO:

CHAPTER SIX

We gave away all the food, dropping the last of it down by the railroad tracks where the people who lived under the bridges would find it. Then Cherry drove clear across town to her business kitchen in Angelwood Heights, nestled into an industrial area. She worked on a few things in the building and then pulled her van out back, and we took her Subaru home.

We reached Cherry's apartment at a little before five in the morning. The parking lot was empty of reporters, so I assumed Darion's ploy worked. She parked in her small garage, and we climbed out with grunts and yawns.

Even Darion looked exhausted as we took the outside steps to her door on the second floor. We'd agreed to spend the night here -- though night was a euphemistic term for nearly five in the morning. I wanted to go home to my plants and mice, but Darion reminded me I was in his protection, and we needed to stay close during this trouble. Since others had seen Cherry with us, he wanted to watch her, too. Her place seemed the best location, so I didn't argue. I wanted to rest. Anywhere.

Cherry fumbled with her keys and unlocked the door. I thought I wouldn't mind sleeping on the floor with the thick carpeting. After years of living on the street, I could sleep wherever I found a spot.

The phone rang as she opened the door, a sharp, knife-like sound cutting into my already battered brain.

"What the hell," Cherry mumbled. The answering machine flashed dozens of recorded calls. My cousin rushed to the kitchen counter and grabbed the phone. "Yeah! What?"

Darion followed me inside, closed the door and whispered a ward across it, the windows and the rest of the building. He used fae words of power and they overlapped and reinforced his magic. I had never stood within magic this strong.

I'd never been here. The apartment was neat, the colors beige and light blue from the living room and into the open kitchen area. A few prints with an oriental style hung on the walls.

"That ward will keep out anything but another fae," he said. "And even some of them will have trouble getting through."

A cat sauntered out of the bedroom, stretching and limping as she wandered towards the kitchen, looking as though she hoped for attention.

"Li, for the love of God, slow down. Yes, yes. I was there. My cell phone went dead hours ago. Calm down." Cherry reached for cat food and poured kibble in a bowl as the little creature brushed up against her hand and purred while still giving us looks of distrust.

"Li is her younger sister," I explained as we headed for the living room.

"The one you brought back from the dead," he said.

I shook my head. "She wasn't dead. But yes, I saved her."

He nodded and crossed to the sofa, sitting down with a soft groan. He looked older than he had when I first saw him earlier that day, which made me wonder about his real age. I suspected he might have been around for a long time.

"Li, I'm dead tired. I'll talk to you tomorrow. I need to get work done so I won't be home. No, I won't wait for your call. You'll get more information out of the news reports than you will from me. I'm just --" She glanced at Darion and me and grinned -- "I'm just the damned caterer."

Darion almost laughed aloud. Cherry shook her head, signing him to silence. No doubt Li would want to know who came home with her sister tonight.

"Night little sister," she said. "I'll talk to you later. I need sleep."

She hung up, dropped her purse on the counter by the phone, and came around to throw herself into a chair across from Darion.

"I take it your sister would not quite understand about you having a strange man in your apartment?" he said, teasing her.

"She might try to get a look, and then she would just accuse me of taking up after Aunt Tay."

"Pardon?"

"My mother." I settled on the sofa beside him. "She

has a soft spot for blonds. She married a nice, blond banker named Ian Fairbanks. But it was the long golden hair that got her into trouble."

"Ah." He pulled out a strand of hair with a critical frown. "Would darker help?"

Cherry laughed. "I like it blond."

"Must be a family thing," I said with a little shrug.

And she laughed again. Then she leaned back, looking as though exhaustion caught up with her from one breath to the next. "What now?"

"Now we sleep," Darion replied. "At least the two of you do. I am fae and don't need sleep as often as you do. I assume you can go for long stretches without sleep, Skye?"

"Yes. Unfortunately, I've already been awake for several days. So rest is a good plan." I leaned back on the cushions. I had slept in worse places.

Cherry headed for her bedroom and returned with blankets and a pillow for me. Darion moved over to the chair. From the way he sometimes bowed his head and frowned, there must be plenty going on that we could not see or hear.

So I stretched out on the sofa and went to sleep.

I dreamt about the fae. Not a surprise.

From the day I learned what I was, I had done my best to learn about my father's people. A group of fae had arrived in an alley a few days after I parted with my mother and explained what I was and the dangers.

I discovered old books on this side of the Veil, some of which hold a few of the answers. A fae can find them since those books glow a little with magic. Maybe Ruby House leaves them here so that humans retain some knowledge of the fae. I had a hard time piecing together anything helpful because so much happens within the clans, and they are secretive about their affairs. But I learned the sweep of changes and the tides of history.

And that's what I dreamt about during my few short hours on the sofa. My subconscious prepared me for the work of dealing with fae on a more intimate level than I had ever planned to experience. The dream pulled up facts about culture, etiquette, laws, and rules, but everything came in a haphazard fashion. I didn't sleep well.

When I woke a few hours later, I found Darion out in the kitchen making breakfast, which seemed so odd I stopped and stared on the way to the bathroom.

"What? You think fae don't eat?" he asked.

I grinned and turned away. I've never been a morning person. Eating even good food that smelled wonderful didn't appeal to me at this hour.

I came back out after a quick shower and after using magic to clean my clothing. I wanted to look presentable.

Darion gave me a friendly enough smile. "Sit down. You need food. Magic can take out of a person, even me. It has to be worse for you."

"I'm not hungry."

"Don't argue with me." Darion put an empty plate in front of me. "I want you doing well because you have abilities which might aid in this case. You realize you can help, don't you?"

"Me? Looking in mirrors?"

"Yes, that is one. It used to be an ability common in the old ones, like the person you met last night. Later fae no longer held that power. And now the gift turns up in you. What else can you do with mirrors?"

"I can travel through them," I said.

He stopped with a pancake on a spatula, ready to drop onto my plate. "Travel," he repeated, as though we were speaking different languages.

"I need to know the rooms at both ends," I explained. "Though I use mirrors to get to Cherry too, and without a mirror on her end since I sense the common blood we share and follow it. But if I visualize a room well enough, I travel from one mirror to the other along a path where the guardian allows me."

"Well, that is interesting," Darion said. He dropped the pancake onto my plate. "The journey has to be damned difficult, though. You use any normal mirror, which means, in essence, you make the mirror magical before you travel through it and then do the same at the other end. You create enchanted objects. Do you have any idea what it takes to make something magical?"

"I never thought about it." I shrugged and relaxed a little more. He would not change his mind about working with me, at least not yet. "I don't understand what is and isn't possible."

"Your family should have trained you," he said. He looked disgusted for a moment, and I thought it odd he would hold this against Emerald for my sake. Or was this because he now worked with me and I knew so little? "Despite your father's rank --"

"Rank?"

He turned startled again and then sat aside the spatula and came around the side of the table to sit beside me. "They've been wrong to ignore you, Skye. You are of the clan, and they hold the responsibility for your life. That means they should never have left you this ignorant. Their attitude is unforgivable."

"What does any of this matter to you?" I asked.

"If I hadn't met you their clan decisions would mean nothing at all. However, having spent a few hours with you, I can tell you one thing for certain: As much as I would have wished nothing bad to happen to Aria, I would be far more upset if you now disappear. Your sister is a hypocrite who loves everything humans created and still wants to see them gone as though the good things would just keep going without humans. I don't like her."

"She's not my favorite person either," I said and shrugged.

"I imagine not. And you have never met Cedric. That's lucky. They're too much alike. He has always intended for Aria to take his place as ambassador."

"Ambassador."

"Yes, and she would be a bad choice after a bad ambassador. Perhaps your clan leader will counter the decision. Your father is old, and he has hoarded power for a long time. He may have power within the Emerald clan to do what he pleases. I don't know the intricacies of their politics. It's hard enough to keep track of Sapphire. Besides, naming her as heir may not matter at all if we don't find Aria."

"True. Tell me about the other fae who disappeared."

Darion noticed how talking about my family made me uncomfortable, and he took the hint to move on to another subject. We talked about the case. I ate the food he gave me and explained how humans solve mysteries, and how even with the ability to do magic, those human abilities sometimes helped more. I suggested we try to find someone who had been near the scenes and ask about anything out of the ordinary in the area. It need not be magical since the people involved would not want to draw attention. I spotted nothing unusual in Lacey's room, but I didn't know the place either. Mrs. Weaver might help.

Darion knew about Lacey's mother, and she had

known he came from fae, but she had never asked too many questions.

Cherry and her cat came out of her bedroom about an hour later. She looked around with sleepy surprise.

"A man who can cook? I am shocked. Smells good, too."

"Thank you, Lady Cherry," he replied with a grin. "I'll prepare food for you when you're ready."

"I am in heaven," she said.

She showered. The cat sat outside the bathroom door, eyeing the two of us with blatant mistrust at intruders in her home, at least until Darion lured her over a piece of bacon. The cat was a pretty little creature: white, with orange and black spots and bright green eyes. Devoted to Cherry, too -- she took her treat back to door and ate there.

Darion continued telling me about the others who had disappeared, and explained a few theories though they were nothing more than speculation, he admitted. My glimpse of the castle was more of a clue than anything they'd found since this trouble started.

"They disappeared from within or near buildings," I said, adding up what he reported. "Places they frequented often, so maybe none of these were chance abductions, and they set off a pre-made trigger, which allowed the kidnapper to find each person in the easiest place to make the grab."

"Yes, good point. We'll check the possibility."

Cherry, dressed in clean brown slacks and blue pullover, settled in the chair beside me and nibbled at her food and then eating with more enthusiasm. She laughed when Darion gave the cat pieces of egg.

"You'll spoil Yo-Yo."

"Just making certain she has her fair share," he said

and seemed to mean those words. Cherry grinned and went back to her breakfast.

She listened as Darion told me more about the fae than I had ever known, including about crossing over the Veil, and how difficult it would be to direct a spell from that side to this, especially for something so powerful and narrowly defined. I wanted to ask questions about life on the other side, but this wasn't the best time. I filed them away for later and hoped we talked when everything settled.

"What do you plan for today?" Cherry asked.

"I have arranged to take Skye to places where other fae disappeared," Darion explained. "This is not, I fear, a place where a human --"

"I do not want to go," she replied. "But come back here afterward, will you? Don't leave me wondering what's going on."

"We won't forget you," Darion promised and with conviction in his voice. "I'll bring Skye here when we're done and fill you in."

"I'm going down to the work kitchen today, clean things up and see if I any other big orders are coming in. How are you going to get around?"

"My car is in the lot. I had it delivered while we rested." Darion glanced towards the window. "Whenever you're ready, Skye."

"Let's go then," I decided. I hoped my worries didn't show. "I'll talk to you later, Cherry."

She watched with worry as we headed out. I tried to smile in parting, but she knew this would be dangerous for me.

Once outside, Darion glanced back at the closed door and frowned.

"I could make this easier for her," he whispered. "I

can lessen anxiety, at least."

"No. She has a right to her own emotions right now, and she wouldn't appreciate having them toyed with."

"You eased Ted Weaver's worries, though," he replied as we headed down the stairs.

Darion had sensed that magic. No surprise. "Weaver knows nothing about the fae and there was nothing would make the situation better. I had limited options, and he didn't need to suffer for something he can in no way change or even comprehend."

"I agree with what you did for Ted. And about Cherry. Human friends have taken a rather dim view of me trying to help them out that way. I'm learning, which is why I asked this time. I don't like to see her worry over this, but I understand that she is dealing with the trouble in her own way. You ready?"

"Should I be? Could I be?"

"Probably not," he agreed. Someone watched from a window on the lower level as we passed. I imagined what they were thinking about Cherry's company and odd hours. "I wish you were part of a clan structure before now. Bringing strangers into the Clan Houses is never good but I Ruby House gave permission to start there. That will help to get the others to agree. They are all desperate."

"I hope I find something," I said. "There's a good chance I won't."

"I have faith in you."

"I don't need more pressure." We reached the parking lot, and I looked around, hoping my head would stop pounding from even that little walk. "Which car is yours?"

He pointed to a small, racy convertible in a lovely shade of green. "A human-made car," he said, unlocking the door and slipping inside the car. "This car doesn't draw attention. That doesn't mean I don't use magic to keep it going or safe during trouble."

He started her up as I settled into the seat. The engine purred. He smiled as he pulled out of the parking lot and into the street. Despite the cool morning, he put the top down, and magic kept us warm. The breeze blew through my hair and tickled the back of my neck. At another time, I would have enjoyed the ride.

We were heading for trouble, and not even from the real enemy.

CHAPTER SEVEN

D arion whistled a bright tune as the car picked up speed, darting through the morning rush traffic as other people made their way to work, a few watching with envious stares at the car and the freedom it no doubt represented to them.

"You're a morning person, aren't you?" I asked. The sunlight pounded down on me like a drum and pulsing through my head.

"Ah." He looked at me and away. "I love the dawn. I love the night too. I assume you prefer not to be out this early?"

"I don't want to know this time of day exists." I rubbed at my forehead, trying to ease the pounding there. Nothing would help. "No matter. I wouldn't sleep anyway, not with everything that's going on. How difficult is this going to be?"

"Well, I managed uncommon cooperation from Ruby Clan, which is a sure sign of how worried they are about their missing child of the clan." He slowed for a light, but it changed, and we breezed through the intersection. "When I sent word about what you can do, they answered within five minutes. The other clans are less forthcoming, but once we get into Ruby House, others will accept us since they don't want to remain out of the loop."

"I better find something at our first stop."

"It would help." He turned towards the expressway. "But if you don't, we move on. You created quite a stir last night with the picture in the mirror. People are searching for the building. They're hoping you can do it again and give us a few more clues."

"Do I need this kind of pressure?"

"Maybe. I have yet to figure out what works with you, so I'll experiment still."

I laughed, leaning back and enjoying the ride. The brisk, fresh air at least brought me awake. "I want the answers for myself, which often motivates me best. I hate unanswered questions."

"That must make life difficult."

"Sometimes. Other times I stop searching for questions in everything I see. You aren't the same way?"

He glanced at me, away, and then back again. I would rather he kept his eyes on the road, though. "Yes, I am. But how did you pick that up?"

"Mirror," I replied. "It's part of the package. I can sense expectations in a person and what people see in me."

"I've known no one like you."

"I imagine not."

"Oh, and a bitter sense of humor, too." We had paused at a red light, and he glanced my way. Then we were off again. We dodged two semis and a bus. His shoulders shifted as though to dismiss what he wanted to say. "We are going to Ruby House. They haven't admitted that Lacey is Ruby Clan yet. I suspect they're trying to save face and not acknowledge that one of their most valuable heirs was without protection."

"You were protecting her, and you are a high ranking fae, right?"

"Not high enough," he said and sighed. "If I were higher placed, I could command cooperation even from other clans. I wouldn't be popular, but I suspect the King would back me. He's having a hard time, this coming so close to the end of his reign. He's been a good man. I hate that his last days are marred by this kind of trouble. I want to find answers."

"If any of them disappeared inside the Clan Houses, we might get lucky."

"I heard that Earis, the Ruby ambassador's daughter, disappeared from her bedroom. So did your sister and someone from Sapphire. The other from Ruby House sat in the dining hall. I sometimes guest at dinner there. We try to be civilized when we're not fighting. I seem to remember a lot of reflective things which I hope will help."

"Me, too."

We rode in silence for a while as he navigated his way towards the middle of the city, an area of immense structures, narrow streets, and rats. We turned down a dark alley where fog obscured the view to the next street, and we drove through to find --

Tall maple trees spread out on both sides of the road, and the buildings which blocked out the sky had disappeared. Large old-fashioned houses sat on a street of green grass, autumn colored leaves littering the ground.

"Well, that's impressive," I admitted. I looked back. A wall of gray cloud stood behind us. "Where are we?"

"We're on the border," he explained and slowed the car to a crawl. "Do you see the rainbow shimmer at the other end of the street? That's the Veil."

Beautiful. Magic. If I went through there, I would be in the realm of the fae. I shivered at the nearness of what I had always considered the forbidden land.

"This is the clan street, Skye. Five houses, lined up like the hands, thumb to little finger, left and right." He turned into the drive of the third house on the left. "It wouldn't matter what side we came in on or from what location; the places would line up the same way. Temporal magic just works out the logic for itself."

We parked in front of a Victorian-styled place, complete with the scallops and bright blues and yellows, though perhaps a touch overdone. I expected such excess from fae, who tended towards extremes. I followed Darion from the car and up the steps to a bright red door. A sapphire blue door adorned the green and blue house to the side. Emerald had to be the building on the other side of Ruby. Bushes blocked the view.

Darion tapped on the door, and a dour, immaculate man opened the door, standing between us and the interior. I saw him glance towards me, hold the stare for a heartbeat too long to be polite, and then turn to Darion. I sensed an aura of age though he looked little older than Darion.

"Be welcome here today," he stated and stepped aside.

I didn't miss the qualifier; I could enter this place until midnight, but after the bewitching hour my welcome would be questionable again. Fine. I wasn't planning on staying.

"This is Ambassador Peren Ruby Day. And this is Skye Emerald McFaelyn. Shall we start?"

"Yes, by all means."

If the ambassador held any ill feelings toward me, he

hid them well. I found myself at ease as I walked behind him and beside Darion and wasn't a magical spell to keep guests calm. I would have sensed any magic from either of them.

"Where do you want to start?" Darion asked, looking at me.

"The dining hall, if that's all right."

Ambassador Peren nodded and turned. We followed him down a hall and entered a room with one wall lined with glass-fronted cabinets, the inside filled with sparkling, shining things: silver goblets and huge platters, small plates and pieces of silverware. The sight of all that shiny silver gave me more hope though I didn't know where to begin.

"Is there a way to find out where this missing person was sitting?" I asked.

"Lena," Ambassador Peren supplied. "She sat in this chair moments before she disappeared."

He leaned against a chair back, and his eyes closed as though he could call her back with just a thought. This man worried about the missing fae. I liked him, no matter what he thought of me.

So far he had shown nothing but politeness, so I stopped worrying about his reaction and went to work. From the place at the table where Lena sat, I spotted a line of silver plates, and even gold glittered just to the right.

Darion opened the cabinet when nodded to what I wanted. I feared touching anything, but having gone this far, I dared not back down now. I closed my eyes, brought up a thread of fiery magic as I brushed my hand across the plate that seemed in best line for any view.

Very old. Ancient. The plate had been part of this house for so long it had absorbed magic. I sensed an odd whisper of interest, almost alive beneath my fingers.

"Oh." I petted the surface with a soft touch of my fingers. The plate liked the interest and wanted to help. Bad things had happened here, and he didn't want sorrow in the Clan House. He missed the feasts and the laughter.

"Gods," Peren whispered. "I didn't realize the plates could experience anything at all. Now I feel evil for keeping them locked away."

I glanced back at the Ambassador, shocked by the words.

"You woke something there, Skye," Darion said, a hand resting on my shoulder. "That's all right. With the plate aware, you should have an easier time with it, right?"

"Yes, I hope so." My voice already sounded shaky. "He wants to help. Let's see if he can bring back the view."

The plate was like a little puppy desperate to please someone. The exuberance almost made the work more difficult at first. It was a joy to see the excitement and witness the first dawning of just being.

I need a pet.

I took control. He calmed, and we looked for the moment when something bad happened. The silver distorted the vision, but he helped me pull backward in time, through the days. Weeks. Months.

"There!"

I drew my trembling hand away and let the vision freeze. The wave of illness took even me by surprise. Ambassador Peren caught hold of me, and half dragged me to a chair.

"Wine! No, it's too early for wine. Bring Skye tea. Lots of honey!"

Darion dropped into the chair beside me and grabbed my hand. I felt a touch of quick magic, hoping to steady me. "Be still. We have what we need."

"Ah. Good." I closed my eyes while trying to control the waves of nausea that took me.

"Is magic always this stressful for you?" Peren asked. Someone placed a cup of tea on the table and left again.

"I can call magic up with little trouble, but the power . . . eats at me as I use it."

Darion pushed the cup towards me. I refused with a shake of my head.

"You don't want to insult your host, now do you?"

Did he joke? Safer to sip the tea although my hand trembled.

Excellent tea; a taste of life itself. My surprise was obvious as I sipped again.

"Ah, you've never tasted this," Darion said. "I wondered. The tea and honey are from across the Veil."

"I never considered that aspect," Peren replied with a touch of a smile. "You like it?"

"Very much, thank you." I sipped again, drinking in sunshine, spring and flowers. I wanted to hold on to the sensation as long as I dared, but I didn't want to waste time, either.

"The plate showed you something?" I asked.

"More view. Nothing clear, which isn't a surprise, given the nature of the surface. However, we watched as Lena disappeared. The darkness came up behind her, just like with Lacey, so now we are now certain this is the same group. And I even caught bit more of the castle and the land, and perhaps an ocean."

"And no one noticed the spell slip in to get her?" I asked, wondering if I should ask such a thing.

"Too much ambient magic in the Clan Houses," Peren Ruby Day replied. "I might have sensed a slight fluctuation, but that's not unusual."

"Let's try the other room," I said.

"You should rest a little longer," Peren protested.

"No. The work won't get easier, and we shouldn't waste time, sir."

I sat the cup aside with regret and followed the other two out of the room. I felt sorry for the plate I had accidentally awakened and wished him feasts and laughter.

We went to an upstairs bedroom, all filled with frills and pieces of art meant to impress people. I sensed their use the way I had with the paintings at the Weaver house. No matter how hard I tried, I got nothing from the large mirror. The woman came to the mirror, moved away, came back -- days passing as we watched. We judged the time by how the room went dark each night, but she didn't disappear within the view of the mirror.

I worked with care this time and did not to put too much of myself into the spell and ask questions that might awaken the mirror, though because of my affinity for mirrors, the link seemed to hold better.

"I'm sorry," I apologized. This was Ambassador Peren's daughter, and I wanted to help because of his kindness.

"They didn't take her right here," Peren offered as we left the room. "No one else was in the Clan House, so we weren't certain. You eliminated that area from the mystery. Now come downstairs for another cup of tea while I arrange for you to go another of the houses. Diamond next. They owe me a favor. In fact, they have owed me a favor for a long time, and I think this the best time to call for payment."

"You may not want to do that, not for me!"

"You do not realize two things, Skye Emerald McFaeland," Peren Ruby Day replied and took my arm when I almost went head first down the stairs. "We spent months looking for any clues at all, and you provided the first views of what happened. There is hope in having this knowledge. And Ruby Clan is the one which will suffer the most if we don't find answers. If I can use favors owed to help settle this trouble before The Choosing, it will be small payment."

From their point of view, I was a godsend. I didn't argue and especially not about the tea.

All too soon I left the lovely, quiet house. In a few hours, I would not be able to return. The realization made me far sadder than I expected. I wanted to ask if I could come back, but I would not overburden Ambassador Peren with my petty needs, but for a while, I had been comfortable among the fae. I had never been so at ease among humans.

Peren walked with us down the street, past the building with a dark green door. Did someone watch from the window? I didn't look. We went to the next house, and I stood behind the ambassador and Darion, glad to be there when the door opened.

I glimpsed the woman inside and bowed my head in haste.

"I am doing this under protest, Ambassador Peren Ruby Day." The woman had a voice as sharp as a steel knife and the words cut when she spoke. "And I will file a protest with the King."

"I never doubted," Peren answered without a hint of anger. "Now, let us get Skye to the room and be done with this."

"Yes. Quickly, and gone again," she replied and stepped aside.

That would be the best invitation into this place I

would get. Peren and Darion went first, and I followed, my head bowed, slinking along like the worst vermin slipping through the door.

The feeling came, I realized, from mirroring her overwhelming emotions towards me. I couldn't help but pick up those feelings. I tried to lock on to Ambassador Peren and Darion and lift my head again.

Darion slowed for my sake but I gave him a subtle tap on the arm, and he seemed to understand. I wanted this done and to leave.

We went straight to someone's long-abandoned room. The scene would be difficult to draw back after so the passage of so much time. I stepped right to the mirror, closed my eyes for a moment, and touched my trembling fingers against the glass.

The image moved with ease for me; another inanimate object almost come alive in this place of magic. I did not want my longing for something nice here to awaken the mirror which would then be left alone in this room, waiting for notice again.

The images moved and moved and moved. Servants -- or at least other fae -- cleaned at regular intervals. The sight amused me, watching them do the menial work by hand and not with magic.

Back another day. And another.

There. The darkness came, and I pulled the image to just before --

"Oh," Ambassador Diamond whispered.

The picture stabilized, and I stepped away, gasping, and afraid I would pass out right then. I swayed and had the terrifying image of falling and taking down the Diamond woman with me. I went to my knees rather than fall and bowed my head. "Forgive me," I whispered and did my best not to be ill.

But something changed as though I came alive in that breath.

I looked up, startled. The woman's feelings towards me had taken a strange, sudden leap in the opposite direction from what she thought when I entered Diamond House. I didn't understand at all.

Lady Diamond stared at the mirror, and another concern rose for someone she had known longer than I wanted to guess. Then she looked at me, worried. Concerned for me.

"You have a true gift." She didn't say the words just to fill the silence. This woman would never speak just for show. Darion worked some magic of his own beside her. He had been capturing the images I brought to light and melding them into a 3D rendering though only part of the whole showed.

"That is water," Darion said, his hand tracing part of the picture, bringing the area into focus. Then he stopped and looked around the room. He found me still on my knees. "Let's get you somewhere to rest."

"In the bed." The Diamond woman waved towards the other side of the room.

She shocked Darion but lifted me back to my feet. I tried to stand on my own, but everything went out of focus. I wanted to protest and say we should leave. Instead, they stretched out on the bed before I got my wits back.

Better here, I realized. The overpowering painful beat in my head slowed to a dull thump rather than the rapid pounding like a countdown to an explosion.

"No, it isn't easy for Skye," Darion said. I had missed the first part of the conversation. "And there is no reason he should do this for us, all things considered."

"He," the woman said.

"Should I say it instead?" Darion asked, his voice harsh. "Would that word make you feel better?"

"Darion," I whispered in shock. I tried to sit up, but a hand pushed me back down -- her hand, strong and insistent.

"Be still," she ordered. I obeyed. Her hand lingered on my shoulder with the warmth of a slight magic in that touch. I dared look up into her narrow face.

"Flesh and blood, magic and soul," she said aloud. "Be welcome here."

Those words startled both Darion and Peren. Darion sat on the edge of the bed by me. The woman drew her hand back and nodded.

"Someone should have spoken those words long ago," she told Darion. "Rest for a while. I'll send tea and cookies."

"Thank you, Ambassador Syna Diamond Sky," Darion said and bowed his head as though she had done him a great honor.

She glanced at me, then turned and looked at the mirror where her friend still stood, though the magic had begun to fade. Ambassador Syna watched for only a heartbeat or two while the image disappeared, but I realized the vision would be forever etched in her mind.

And forever might be an accurate term in this case.

She left the room, closing the door behind her. Peren dropped into a chair by the bed, and Darion shook his head.

"What?" I asked, my mouth dry, my head still pounding. "What happened?"

"It was a small thing," Darion said. "It won't mean much to you. But in Fae, when a child is born, an adult says the first words: Flesh and blood, magic and soul, be welcome here. Those words are a sign that the child is alive and one of us. She admitted that she saw you born and become real in her eyes."

"Oh." I had sensed the change in her attitude, but not realized the full significance. I tried to sit up, but Darion pushed me down again. "We need to keep going. We can't waste time --"

"Lift your arm."

I did so by a true test of will, but the arm trembled, and I looked like I was having a seizure.

"You are resting for now."

"Skye doesn't realize how much he stresses his body," Peren said, still sitting by the window. I suspected the view might not be into the world I knew. The bit of sky appeared to be more green than blue and whatever flittered by was not a bird.

I rested a few minutes rather than argue. Calm. A small plant sat on a table by the bed, well-tended while the room's owner was . . . away. I brushed my finger over a velvety leaf. Life.

Tea helped. The cookies were homemade, still warm from the oven. They smelled of oatmeal, spices, and raisins. I ate three without argument.

Ambassador Syna came to the door to let us out. She nodded with a touch of reserve, but that seemed to be her nature.

"Where will you go next?" Ambassador Syna asked.

"We might as well get Emerald out of the way and then on to Sapphire," he decided with a frown. Emerald Clan would not be easy. "Those are the last two where members disappeared within the clan houses."

"Ah. Skye, will your father be cooperative?" she asked.

"I don't know, Ambassador." I bowed my head to her, maintaining strict politeness. "I've never met him."

Silence. Held breath. A bird chirped outside in a tree, and I wanted to look to see if it was an earth bird or something more exotic.

"You have done well, Skye Emerald McFaelyn. Go in peace."

We stepped outside the building. The door closed behind us. I walked down the steps and still ill, but I still felt better than I had when we entered Diamond House. I didn't know how to sort out my feelings about what had happened.

"Well, that will set all fae abuzz," Peren said with an unexpected laugh. He stopped at the edge of an incongruous sidewalk that could have been anywhere in the city. Nothing here seemed right. "I'll leave you two now. If you need help, call on me."

Ambassador Peren bowed to Darion, and then to me before he headed back towards Ruby House.

I studied the house that stood between Diamond and Ruby. The dark green of the door seemed to draw me closer though I knew better than to expect welcome here. This felt akin to the pull I got when I went to Cherry last night. Blood calls to blood.

A woman answered and ushered us through the door. She worked very hard at not seeing me as we passed the entry hall and headed towards the steps leading upstairs. She wasn't the ambassador. That would be my father. Not having him meet us helped. I didn't need more stress.

Then, as we passed an archway, I sensed my father sitting in the dining hall to the right. To hell with him. I had more important things to deal with right now. I found strength in the thought. Darion even gave me an odd glance but said nothing.

The Emerald woman took us to a lovely room. I tried not to see the wood walls, the velvet curtains, dark green spread over the bed. This could have been my room.

Why did I torture myself? This room wasn't important! I like my home and my life. The lives of other people, even relations didn't matter --

And then I realized this wasn't what I felt. Was I mirroring the woman who brought us here? I suspected a little came from her -- but most of the emotion came from Darion. He took my odd situation in life far too personally.

Working in the Emerald House proved easier. I pulled up the vision with one quick try. We lucked out this time because the young man who stood before the mirror had just leaned down to adjust his boot when the darkness came behind him.

"There!" Darion almost shouted. I hardly trembled at all. "There we have it. That's a much better view."

I stepped back from the work and looked at the image which showed an entire quarter of the castle and the surrounding scenery. The castle sat on a small and barren island.

Darion shook his head. "I've never seen this place." A touch of regret and annoyance showed as he captured the image for his composite picture. "Someone else should recognize the place, though. Excellent work, Skye. There's one more mirror here for you to try. Shall we do it right away?"

"That would be fine." I kept my voice calm. The woman gave me a quick glance as though a stray dog spoke.

We went down the hall past other doors, reminding me, in a sad way, of Lacey's house. I had almost forgotten her in the mass of other disappearances that now haunted my mind. What I did would help Lacey and the others.

A chill passed over me as we entered the bedroom. The place was messy. Dusty. No one had touched anything since the moment the owner disappeared.

Cedric McFaeland sat on the edge of the unmade bed and seeing him brought another chill. The blood ties were stronger with him than with anyone but my mother. Tall, blond, hard-faced and with eyes that stared at me with open hatred. He brushed his hand against the covering on the bed.

"Aria's room," he explained with a wave of his hand. "Can you find her?"

"I have found no one yet," I answered. As the first conversation with my father, this one had rather ominous overtones. No interest in me at all and everything about my half-sister whom I despised.

"They tell me you are talented."

"I didn't know the power was anything special." I met his eyes for the first time. "No one ever taught me about fae powers."

And he flinched. Gods, I hadn't expected that reaction. He looked away, and his embarrassment improved nothing. I glanced at Darion and shook my head in disgust at myself for falling into this petty game and went to work at the mirror. This mirror proved easier to manipulate because the room had remained dark and empty from the time Aria disappeared. I found her without a problem, and we watched. The scene was about the same as most of the others, though for once we glimpsed someone grabbing her, and perhaps a huge, black bag in his hand. A normal arm, at least -- young and well-muscled, but we couldn't see a face.

"That's enough." Darion took hold of my arm and

pulled me away from the work. "At least now it's certain where Aria disappeared."

Darion stared at Cedric. Ah. A disappearance in the Emerald Clan House meant Darion wasn't responsible for losing Aria.

I did not want to rest in this room or even this house. Darion had already captured the image, and he turned me to the door as we started out.

"Wait."

I almost cursed at the single loud word from my father. He stood from the bed and walked towards us, grim-faced and glaring. Did I look anything like him? I had my mother's Chinese features, but I had his eyes and hair. He came too close, and if I hadn't been so damned shaky, I might have run ... or attacked. Flee or fight? Darion moved to my side, and I forced myself to calm, standing so still I couldn't feel beating of my heart.

The man stepped before me, cutting off the exit to the door. "The clan leader says he will replace me as Ambassador after The Choosing," he said. No regret showed in his face. "I'll go back over the Veil, away from this place. I made far too many mistakes here."

He looked at me and away. A mistake -- just another of his many mistakes.

He moved out of the way and let us leave. I didn't understand what he believed he had proved, or if he thought I gave a rat's ass about where he would be after The Choosing. He didn't follow us, at least. The same woman led us out of the building. As we stepped into the same bright sunlight, I stumbled, so ill I almost went to my knees again.

"Hey!" Darion put a hand under my elbow and helped me. Darion gave me a little magical aid. "Hold on. Rest a moment."

"I'd rather not stay anywhere near this place." My right arm swung towards the house, moving like a wild creature attached to my body.

The anger in my voice surprised me. I had dealt with my mother's betrayal years ago. Had I harbored hope for something better from my father? I didn't believe in all the fairy tale sweetness and light stories about the fae, but I had read about the fae's dedication to family and clan. I realized that I had expected something better.

"There is only one more mirror," Darion explained, breaking into my darker thoughts. We were back on the sidewalk, away from Emerald House "And that one is at my Clan house. We'll do the work, and then we'll eat lunch -- I insist. You need to rest, and we can talk about the images."

I wanted to protest and tell him to take me back to the real world, but what good would that do? So I nodded with resignation in every movement of my body before I considered how Darion deserved a better attitude from me.

"Why is he blaming you for Aria's disappearance if it happened in the Emerald Clan House?" I asked.

"Because he won't blame himself and I'm convenient. I had a link to her, but I couldn't follow it."

"I'll be glad when we finish. It's not that I don't want to go to Sapphire House," I added. "But I want away from everything I can't even pretend to be for these people. Out where I grew up -- out in the human world -- I could fake being male or female, whatever suited me. But here I can't affect their judgments."

"I don't appreciate what's happened much myself," Darion admitted. A warm breeze brushed past us, and I wondered if it came from the fae lands, blowing through the Veil. The touch of the wind seemed alive and pleasant.

Someone met us at the door to Sapphire House.

"Your mother has gone back across the Veil, Darion." The man stepped aside as we came into the building. "She says she'll stay there until after The Choosing and to we should tell you to do what you will."

I looked up, startled and fearing the statement meant his mother was unhappy with her son's decisions in the last two days.

"Ah. And so I am the working Ambassador again!" Darion laughed. "Someone might have told me, you know."

A couple of others lingered nearby, and they laughed. Odd. I dared a glance at Darion, but not the others. I didn't want to feel worse about being here. Darion smiled and shook his head. "Don't worry. My mother goes scuttling back over the Veil at every occasion she can find. She says the same thing every time -- Do what you will. She's rather old-fashioned. That happens when you are over a thousand years old, I fear."

"You'll never be that way," a woman replied and slapped Darion on the shoulder.

This meal was my first experience with the true camaraderie between fae, and the shock helped, even though I feared I wouldn't be one of them making this stay in Darion's house even worse.

"We'll get the food ready for when you come back down, Darion. Will this be just the two of you?"

"The rest of you are welcome to join us," Darion offered with an exaggerated sigh. "I'd hate to see you starve after you worked so hard."

Laughter again. No one had laughed in the other places. Because of my presence? Or did everyone worry about the missing people? That might be the problem with

Ruby House, and Emerald House had to deal with my father's distress over his daughter. I felt an edge of worry here because they had lost two of their own. However, I also sensed a touch of hope because Sapphire House had already been trying to solve the mystery. The others, I thought, did nothing more than sit and wait.

Here people were more at ease. Four of them laughed and disappeared around a corner. I wondered how they fixed food here.

"Don't let them worry you," Darion said. We started towards the inevitable stairs at a nice, slow pace while I settled my frayed nerves. "Those in this house are my people, Skye. They trust me, so you can consider yourself accepted."

"Your people. Not your mother's?"

"Not hers. She doesn't stay on this side often enough for her followers to want to be here. Last year we talked with Lord Wilding, and he agreed that after The Choosing I would be the new permanent ambassador so my mother can retire home for a few centuries of quiet."

"Do posts pass within the family from parent to child all the time?"

"No, not always. I imagine Emerald will go with a new branch. No one is pleased with Cedric right now."

"Because of me."

"Because he is a bombastic pain in the ass who has considered no one outside himself and his daughter and has let more trouble slip through his fingers than any other ambassador in Emerald House history. You, my friend, are merely incidental."

He made me laugh. We reached the top of the stairs and headed down another hall. All the houses seemed alike in layout and even colors. What did that mean regarding fae culture? I'd always heard that because of magic, the culture was stagnant, and many innovations came from the human side of the Veil. I hoped I could ask more about it later.

"Here." Darion pushed open a door to a neat room, all in dark blues. "I'm afraid others have been in here since Heron disappeared. The condition of Aria's room was strange. I don't know what the hell that was about with your father and his daughter. The man needs a nice long vacation."

"He needs to get Aria back.".

"That's an odd thing for you to say," Darion answered as we stepped inside the room. "Why? What makes you think he needs her?"

"Because she was one mistake too many for him. He can no longer see his future in her."

"She didn't trust him."

"Because of me." I paused by a mirror set in the wall. I didn't want to talk about my family, but doing this magic would not be easy since I had no reserves left.

"Yes, finding out about you upset her. She never forgave him. If he had killed you, things would have been far better between them."

"Not a surprise," I said. Then I stopped and frowned. My hand rubbed at the point on my chest where she had cracked a rib in our one meeting. "Why didn't she kill me instead?"

"For the same reason, no one else has. Right after the fae learned of your existence, the King of Fae ruled that until you showed sign of being a danger, if you ever did, killing you would be a sin against our own kind. He sent out a lengthy proclamation about living in a new age, and how we must change our views, and how being born was not your fault."

"Ha. That's one I hadn't heard yet. My mother seemed to think being alive was my fault."

He looked at me, frowning again.

"Sorry. That was bitter. Let's do this work."

"I can dig out the proclamation if you want to see it."

"Thank you. I would enjoy reading it -- later. I don't imagine many people get handed things telling them they have the right to live."

"True."

I turned to the mirror and called up the images. The work proved to be harder because many people, including Darion, had come through the room and sometimes paused by the mirror. I saw their reflections of emotion. They were angry and afraid and worried for their friend. Darion spotted Heron, a young man with long golden hair who looked like he might have been a rock star or a fashion model if he tried.

He pulled on his clothes, adjusting the scarf at his neck. Darion gave a slight chuckle at that view, but then Heron walked away, and we never saw what happened. I hated to disappoint Darion, but he told me I had done more than anyone else so far.

"We will find them," Darion said.

We rested and then went downstairs to the dining room. Food sat in platters across the huge table, and silver plates and silverware glittered in the light. Cups and goblets sat at every spot. I looked at Darion, who had stopped at the doorway, startled.

"We wanted your friend's first House meal to be memorable," a woman explained, going past with a vase of flowers. She stood taller than both of us and her short blond hair curled around her face.

"Thank you!" Darion appeared pleased and nudged me forward. "Oh, don't get that panicked look, Skye. We're never formal. My mother doesn't let us eat off the pretty dishes, either. Oh, and be careful. We don't want them all awake before you leave."

"Awake?" the woman asked looking down at the plate before her as she sat with the others.

We took our places, with Darion on my left and another woman to the right. Darion explained about the plate at Ruby House. They appeared amused by the tale, but I saw many of them brush fingers over the plates before them.

"Gods and Goddesses keep us safe," Darion said. I realized this was an invocation and stilled my movements. "Bring peace to both worlds and bring our friends safely home again."

And then the meal began. People talked. They asked me questions and treated me as though I belonged here. However, I realized something as the meal continued. All of them wore rings with bright blue stones that sparkled as their hands moved. All of them belonged here. I did not.

Still, I regretted the end of the meal. I felt stuffed, content, and even relaxed, which I had never expected on this street. I bade farewell to the others -- Blue, Star, Sand, Malen, and Rose. Darion herded me back out of the house into a bright, warm day, and we walked towards the car still parked at Ruby House. I needed the exercise.

Neither of us expected to be attacked.

CHAPTER EIGHT

Something exploded in the back of my head, and the already constant headache became unbearably worse. Then I heard Darion gasp and realized something more must be happening. I tried to grab him as pain struck the back of my head again and we both fell.

Attacked. I twisted, realizing I had to go for the enemy, not help my friend, but the movement made me dizzy and ill. I saw no faces. The figures stood in a black cloud, obscured by magic. The sight scared me at first and then annoyed me.

Someone kicked, hard in my side. I grabbed the leg, and he lost his balance and fell. When the next one kicked, I mirrored the pain right back at him.

He gasped, cursed, and someone else kicked. I couldn't mirror fast enough to keep up with them. Something hit me in the face. And again. I tried --

Cloth slipped over my head. Ties snapped around my arms and secured them behind my back. The people holding me moved silently and efficiently, and they used a little magic, so they didn't draw attention. I tried to speak, but the cloth blocked my mouth. Two people grabbed me by the legs and pulled, dragging me on my back. We moved over sidewalk, grass, street, curb, grass, sidewalk and then grass again.

Somewhere across the street. They kicked as we went, and everything fuzzed in the blackness.

They would kill me.

I hoped Darion survived.

Someone picked me up, swung me over his shoulder and shuffled forward, grunting with the effort. We had gone inside a building which meant a Clan House.

"Wait," a muffled voice said, petulant and annoyed. "I want to see it."

The person put me down on my feet and caught me by the shoulders. He held me up while other hands grabbed at my shirt, pulled upward. Another pulled down my pants. I almost got ill as they held me up, while one of them -- icy cold fingers -- jabbed at my skin, turned me around, jabbed.

"Disgusting," the voice said, still muffled through the cloth. I wanted to scream as cold fingers pinched at my skin though not from the pain, but rather the humiliation as this pervert examined me. "How can even a Sapphire dine with this thing? Take it along. Throw it out."

They grabbed me by the arms and legs and carried me along, silent again. A door opened. We stepped outside the building.

We weren't where we had started. Cold air swept over my bare skin. They had not pulled my clothing back into place, which I realized was on purpose in this cold. We moved. And then we moved by magic, which proved disorientating. We came back to reality after a quick passage, and the chill swept in around me once more.

Someone mumbled words.

And then they dropped me.

I fell a long way.

Cold. Hurt. Very cold.

I grew up in an area with ice and snow, so I knew what the weather could do to a person without proper protection. I was lying face down and unable to move until I used magic to release my arms and damn it hurt when the blood flowed to my hands again! My fingers were numb and swollen, so I had to fight to get the cloth from around my head. Everything still looked black until I realized the bastards had dropped me into a place of night and stars, ice and snow.

Cold, cold, cold.

I rolled over and pulled myself into a ball, trying to find warmth somewhere in my body. Everything felt frozen. I tried to stand and to pull my pants up because I was . . . well, freezing my ass off.

I laughed with a hollow, hysterical sound.

Something howled in return.

I stopped even shivering at the sound as though that little movement might attract the creature's attention. I forced myself to stand and looked around as I pulled my clothing into place. My eyes slowly adjusted to the night, and I looked up at the stars but no moon. The ground had a snow covering in three directions and behind me, a high cliff stretched off to the right and left, white and icy as though the wall had slid up out of the ground. The snow provided enough white to see by and --

Nothing at all. Nothing anywhere. No lights. No sign of humans. Nothing, but white, frozen snow.

Something howled again. Whatever was out there, it

wasn't a wolf, at least not the ones I had seen in the movies.

Nowhere to go.

I sat back down, knowing I would die here in this cold white world.

But I was never good at playing helpless.

A little magic gave me warmth, and I spread the power out over my body, even though I felt as though I glowed. I wouldn't be able to hold the magic for long. The began to grow like something alive inside of me.

I held on, gasping and hoping to survive even against these odds. Darion would search for me. If he had survived the attack --

Too soon the magic died away and left me ill and feverish, but that helped. I didn't feel the cold so much now and knew I should have been walking while I had the warmth. I needed to --

Walk where?

They had dropped me.

If I climbed the wall, I might find their tracks. I didn't want to lie down here and die. I was too angry.

My fingers clawed into the icy surface of the cliff which crumbled away, and I fell backward before I had climbed a yard. I looked around, hoping for an easier way up and found nothing at all. So I called on magic once more and climbed the cliff like I had occasionally climbed buildings when the need arose. When I reached the top, I dropped face first into the snow, too close to unconscious again.

I would have died there except for the magic-made fever burning across my skin. I had used more magic in the last two days than I had in most years, and I had known there would be a backlash. Now I suffered through the fever. The food came back up. My stomach cramped from illness and the beating. My head still felt ready to explode.

I struggled to my feet, swaying as though the slight breeze would push me over again. I would find those bastards. They didn't have a right to --

Darion. They had hurt Darion, too. I panicked at the thought of what might have happened to him, but if they hadn't straight out killed me, I saw even less reason for them to have killed him. The panic had gotten me moving, though.

I followed the footsteps in the snow which seemed to lead towards a distant line of stunted trees. The people who brought me here had walked from that direction. Cold. Difficult to keep thinking. Wanted. . . .

I wanted to go home to my warm apartment, my plants, and my harp. I'd never asked for anything else, so why did these people want to kill me? Anger kept me walking. Then I realized there were no footprints to follow any more, but I saw the line of trees. The group had traveled part of the distance by magic, and we had not been in the spell for long. If I knew how to do such magic, I could have gone somewhere else. I wish I could find a mirror. Ice? Would the frozen surface of a pond work? I wanted a path back to my apartment. It might be my only hope because my feet had gone numb, things ached, and I felt increasingly ill.

Later I realized something had followed me, the steady even crunch of four feet moving effortlessly across the snow where I often stumbled, knee deep in the drifts.

I sat in the snow. Anger abandoned me and pain spread through my body. The rib where Aria had kicked me hurt like hell, and I feared it might be cracked again. Fever made me so hot while the snow and ice kept me cold at the same time. I coughed and found blood on my fingers.

I am going to die here.

Fine.

Sat down, but I hurt. Every movement hurt. And the damn thing howled somewhere far closer as a shadow moved in my direction. The creature would reach me before I died.

Hell. If I couldn't comfortably lie down and die, I might as well keep going.

I stood. My hands and feet felt frozen my eyes watered. I coughed blood again. But I walked.

Something glittered ahead. Mirror! Reflection! Yes, go there, go there.

I remembered the cold days on the street right after I had turned sixteen. It snowed on my birthday. I had taken part of the money my mother gave me and bought different clothes, warm and without a hint of pink or frills. Being able to sense others emotions helped. I knew the used shops to avoid.

I had wanted to take a bus to somewhere southern and warm. I had stayed in the cold city because I met a young girl huddled outside the bus station, crying, desperate and lost. I experienced the emotion when I neared at her. Alice was younger than me and very much alone and afraid. She had come on the bus from New York and didn't have the money to go anywhere else. She'd left a bad situation that showed in her eyes and the bruises on her face and arms. I wanted to send her on, but where? She wouldn't be any safer somewhere else with no one to watch over her. She had already drawn the attention of the vultures.

I could help her find a warm place. Warm would count for a lot on a miserable snowy day, and she trusted me. I might have inadvertently used a little magic without realizing. Someone followed us through the alleys. Dark shadows swept in behind us as evil men hunted young girls alone on the streets.

They didn't get us. I don't know if Alice realized I used magic, but we got away. We spent a few days together, and I convinced her to call her aunt in California. She went to stay with that family afterward, and I knew she was safe.

Not me. Not here. Cold, cold. Shadows following, so close I could hear breathing.

I turned around, angry at the bastards who would come out to prey on children --

The creature stood only a few steps away, and not anything which had ever walked on earth. The animal stood as tall as me at the shoulders, shaggy-furred and blunt faced. I would have called it a bear, perhaps, except the creature had the legs of a wolf, and the tail looked like it belonged to an annoyed cat, buffed out and twitching.

The head bowed low to the ground, the mouth drawn back to show sharp, long teeth, as it growled. I panicked. I mirrored. And that was not the wisest thing I had ever done, because now -- I realized in a moment of terrified clarity -- I had a creature that hunted alone, and suddenly thought he faced another of its kind. Predator. Territorial. Hell! I had just gone from being prey to being a dangerous enemy.

He didn't expect to face a predator when he'd been tracking prey. The creature backed up a couple of steps. My fingers lifted as I called up lights, sound and wind as I created a tiny storm in the night and threw everything at the creature, warping the spell to stick to the animal for as long as the magic lasted.

And then I ran. I wouldn't get another chance.

Run where? Was I closer to the trees and that glitter of light? I didn't think so, but I still ran, knowing the creature would follow. It might be a little slower now, but it would come, wondering if I was prey this time or a dangerous enemy.

Keep going. Keep going. . . .

"You are a tenacious little bastard."

Someone caught my arm. I swung and hit though not with any force. The person threw me down in the snow and kicked.

"Cover up!"

I had blinked, faces almost clear for a moment before I lost the vision behind a black curtain again. Finding them had angered, annoyed and frightened me. I had gotten away, only to run right back into my enemies again.

"Let's just get the little bastard out there again, before that Chub reaches us. We don't want to deal with it, do we?"

"I'd like a nice chub fur coat," someone said with a sound between annoyance and smugness. I would remember that voice.

"Right. You can stay and fight it. Grab the slippery little bastard. Let's strip it this time. Break a couple bones."

I fought. I kicked as my shirt tore --

"Unless you want to lose that hand, you had better let go of Skye."

I knew the voice though I couldn't name the person. The others had beaten me down into the snow. Cold. Bleeding. Hurt like hell.

They stopped pummeling me. Someone took hold of my arm. I tried to pull away, but nothing moved in coordination with my thoughts.

"Easy, Skye. Easy. It's me, Star. Darion sent us since he can't come through to the fae lands."

"Star." The word came garbled between gasps and blood. She knelt in the snow gently moved me, but it still hurt like hell. Someone helped me sit. "Blue."

The ones who had brought me here sat in the snow. Sand had them held by magic and Malen moved from one to the other, pulling out their hands and yanking off rings.

My attackers looked angered. Everyone looked angered.

Blue's fingers traced a warm pattern down my bare chest. I could breathe, but nothing hurt less.

"We're taking you back," Sand said. She'd left the others sitting in the snow. "I'm damn tempted to leave them in much the same shape as you. Sorry, we took so long for us to find you, Skye. We had trouble at first, but you have a powerful aura. Unique. The King of Fae found you and we came running."

"King," I said, gulping at chilled air as we stood.

"No one is happy with what happened." Sand looked back at the others, still sitting in the snow. They looked startled and worried.

The creature -- Chub? -- howled much closer.

"My, that doesn't sound good," Blue said with a touch of amusement. He put an arm around my waist, and someone else draped a cloak over me. Then he looked back at the others, still sitting on the ground. "Sounds like a very annoyed, and likely hungry, chub. Good luck."

And then we left.

I had never traveled with others like this, or at least not conscious enough to appreciate the journey. They pulled the void around us, with magic circling like water in a drain. I sensed how this travel wasn't easy for them and how much they had done to help me. I wondered why.

But the place we traveled glowed in rainbow colors. Blue, white, brown and gold faded in and around us, along with a mist of green running through everything in bright surges.

"We have a new color," Sand said beside me, holding to my arm. We walked as I did from mirror-to-mirror. They had the focus of where to go. I couldn't have gotten us anywhere. "The green must be yours, Skye."

"Yes," I said. The word took almost more breath than I had. "Didn't -- know. Other -- dif --"

"Different colors? Yes. Easy. We're almost there."

"I -- bring . . . her plants."

I sensed more than heard the collective surprise my statement brought. Blue and Star both paused in a moment of shocked silence.

"The guardian of your path comes to you," Star said, though very softly.

"Yes."

"Well, hell," Blue mumbled as we walked. I couldn't breathe. I couldn't move on my own any longer. But I felt this place, and the magic, and the changes --

"She come -- come -- coming now," I managed and waved a hand to where the green rippled and moved, collate and become a human-like shape.

"Oh dear gods," Blue whispered and went still.

"It -- all right."

My head pounded, and I couldn't think though I wanted to explain the kindness the Green Lady showed me. She came from the void towards me, human shaped but in no other way human. A silhouette of green, an arm, a reaching hand.

She brushed fingers against my face. Kindness. Worry

for me, which I had never sensed from her before this. The pain and haziness faded but didn't disappear.

"Thank you," I whispered. My hand reached, brushed a little against her outstretched fingers. Warmth, life, hope. "I -- I promise to bring a plant first chance I get."

A bow of the head, turn, and she left us, not so much by walking away but simply by not being there.

No one said anything the rest of the way out. I suspected knowing a guardian of a void path might make me a little stranger than being a half-breed genderless bastard, though.

Life is full of surprises.

CHAPTER NINE

e came out of the magic and back into Sapphire
House. Darion rushed forward, grabbed me
around the waist and hurried off with me.

"Slow down, for the love of God," I said. My head
pounded, and the world swam around me. "Are you all
right?"

We had gone part way up the stairs. Darion gasped
and cursed while the others babbled behind us, half dozen
voices or more in a cacophony of words and echoes.
Darion slowed as we went up the rest of the stairs, and
even the voices of the others calmed and began to make
sense.

"I have never -- never -- seen anything like it, Darion!"
Sand said as we reached the upper hall. "A full form and
human in shape. She touched him and gave him enough
strength of her own so Skye would survive the journey
through the path. I feared we wouldn't get him this far.
He was bleeding out life at every step."

I looked at Sand, surprised by the intensity of her words. I had been accepting something others found extraordinary. This marked me; I could see it in their eyes.

Darion faltered. The injuries he suffered in the attack must have been serious since magic hadn't healed him. Sand took hold of Darion and me let go without complaint. I noticed Blue moved in to help Darion the rest of the way.

I looked back, shaking my head. "Fool. You didn't have to take hold of me."

"I feared they'd killed you, Skye, and I would have to track them down and repay them, each, in kind."

"No, no, no. Not for me."

Darion wanted to say something, but he clamped his mouth shut. I had to look away since we had turned down the hall back to Heron's room. They put me in the bed and the blankets felt warm and safe and still. I gladly rested under the covers, finding peace and calm.

Darion settled in a chair someone brought close to the bed. He looked pale, his face bruised across his right cheek, and from the way his hand rested at his left side, I suspected an injury there. Malen arrived with tea, and the scent took my mind away from everything else. They helped me sit up with pillows at my back, and Malen held the cup while I sipped and sipped again, accepting the special magic imbued into my soul. I felt alive even though I ached.

Darion, always a gentleman, waited until Malen put the cup aside before he spoke again.

"Tell me everything," he said.

I told him, in excruciating detail, what had happened from the moment I mistook the pain in the back of my head. He nodded but said nothing. Neither did the others though Malen kept handing me the tea to sip whenever my mouth went dry. When I got to the part about the creature, Sand supplied the name --Chub -- and I kept going.

"And then these fine people arrived and rescued me." I waved a trembling hand to the group. "And I am very grateful."

"Our honor to do so," Sand said, and the fire of rage came to her eyes.

"No idea who the attackers were?" Darion asked and sounded very annoyed.

Malen came over and held out his hand. Four rings, the stones glittering with a golden light, sat in his palm. Darion lifted his hand, and Malen dropped the rings there while he recounted tracking me with the help of the King (that still stunned me), of finding the people, doing battle, taking their rings, and leaving them there.

"They'll have gotten free by now," Darion said at my look of worry. "And they're likely home. Blue, please send word to Ambassador Sun that I would like to see him here. Immediately."

Even I winced at the order, and I didn't envy Blue having to deliver the message, though he looked content to do the work. I glanced at Darion wondering if I dared ask him not to pursue this with so much vigor -- but then I saw the bruise on his face and realized the people who wore those rings had been quite stupid to cross him.

"This sort of thing doesn't -- happen often here?" I shivered, as though the cold had caught up with me.

"No, not often. Not in this day and age."

I nodded, sipped more tea, holding the cup myself and wishing the pain in my chest would ease enough for me to take a good, solid breath. "Well, at least we both survived."

He looked at me, his eyes narrowed. "You forgive too readily."

"Forgive? Not at all. It's a damned good thing I'll never know if I come face-to-face with those four because I have a long memory. However, right now there are far more important things to worry about than what almost happened."

"This wasn't a case of almost," Darion said. "They did, in fact, take you."

"Yes, but they failed in their foremost task. I'm back."

He nodded, though he still had a predatory stare when Ambassador Sun -- a tall man with close-cropped hair -- came into the room. The man looked at Darion, at me, and sighed.

"Who was it?" he asked, neither annoyed, worried, nor particularly angry. He sounded like someone who'd had his patience tried a few too many times and recognized the signs of yet another such incident.

Darion held out the rings. Sun came and took them, one at a time, nodding over the first three, and wincing at the last. "My son," he said in explanation. "Where are they? "

"In fae and perhaps a bit cold and bruised," Darion replied. "If any of them are dead, it was not at the hands of any Sapphire, or even Skye Emerald McFaelyn, though the gods and goddesses know he had every reason to demand blood-for-blood at this point."

"Yes," Ambassador Sun agreed with a glance at me. Then he frowned looking down at the rings in his hand. With another sigh and a shake of his head, he held them back out to Darion. "You should keep these until the four have redeemed themselves to your satisfaction."

Darion hadn't expected the action. He sat up straighter and his hand moved away from his side. He looked into the ambassador's face, as though they could exchange information without words.

Darion held out his hand. The rings fell back into his palm.

"I shall not question the honor of Topaz again," Darion said. "Every house has its wild children."

"Yes, we all do. And some have even worse. I learned a few minutes ago that the good Lord Iron came from fae to the house for a brief and unannounced visit this afternoon. He did not stay to see me, for which I am grateful." Ambassador Sun looked over at me this time and gave a gracious nod of his head. "Lord Iron is a tedious old man who has outlived his role and his world. He wants the humans returned to pre-technology so he and his friends can be gods again."

I remembered the cold hand as I stood naked before something evil and disgusting. I nodded, swallowing back the bile. He had told me the one thing I wondered and didn't dare ask. And I realized he had, by giving Darion back the rings, put himself at odds with his own Lord. Darion had studied the rings, but now he held them out to Ambassador Sun.

"Take them," Darion said. "I have more than enough young fools of my own to worry over."

"No, Darion. It won't help my situation. I cannot abide by Lord Iron's ways any longer. He is worse than the children the clan sent me to shepherd, the ones he turns loose on this side of the Veil. After The Choosing . . . well, we'll see who goes home to fae in triumph or shame. Keep the rings. I won't send the boys to you until after the rest of this is settled. We'll let them sit out the most important moments of the century, powerless, shall we?"

"Yes," Darion replied. He leaned back and his hand went to his side again. "Your son is far too fond of knives."

Sun winced once more. "He will have more than you to answer to for his actions. This behavior is inexcusable. I will name a new heir."

Despite my intention to stay out of this, I shook my head at that last statement, and the movement didn't go unnoticed by the Topaz Ambassador.

"You can't feel any sympathy for my son," the man said.

"None. I hope he--" I stopped myself. No need to be rude or crude with this man. The fever, illness, and growing pains played on my mind, and I fought not to lose my control. "I have no sympathy for anything that happens to him. However, I also don't need to make enemies, and anything that happens to him now will be linked to what happened to me. He's in favor with your Clan Lord. Should I want to see more trouble there?"

"Skye Emerald McFaelyn, I will tell you a truth. Use it as you may. There is nothing I can do to my son that will make you any more popular with my current clan lord. Knowing so, what would you have me do?"

I hated the kinds of questions that pitted my anger against my reason and wanted to tell him to strip all four of them naked and drop them in the middle of Antarctica. I wanted his son to have a go at a chub with that knife of his. Or better yet, let me kick the shit out of him for a while as others held him down like he, or one of his friends, had done.

But none of those ideas would help.

"I would like you to do that which will keep from creating more trouble for you with your clan Lord," I said. I shrugged. "You've been more than reasonable. Should I throw your help away for vengeance?"

"Very logical. That must be quite tedious to live by in someone your age. I didn't understand logic until well past my hundredth birthday."

"I grew up fast on the streets," I said, daring to be a little braver in my words. "There either you made logical, and wise decisions or something came along and ran you over and didn't even notice."

He nodded. Then he reached towards me. I flinched so much that if there had been any tea left in the cup, I would have splattered both of us.

"My apologies, and with your leave." He held his hand out this time intending to touch me. I looked to Darion, uncertain, but he nodded, so I did.

Ambassador Sun brushed a hand over my head and whispered something. Warmth spread down through my body, and I felt -- felt -- bones knitting together, bruises fading, and my lungs clearing enough so I could almost breathe without an ache. When he drew his hand back, he still frowned, though.

"My people are healers," he said. "You need rest, Skye."

"I will rest as best I can." I felt tired and warm, safe and comfortable. I fought to keep my eyes open. "Thank you."

The man bowed his head and left again. Darion waved the others away. They'd been privy to a lot of information, and I saw more shock and amazement on their faces. And worry, but that might just be because they found themselves part of something larger than they had expected.

After they had left, Darion dropped the rings on the stand by the bed.

"If you asked, the ambassador's son would have been

your slave and for as long as you wanted. The clan would have given him and his friends over to you, and they would have lived by your rules and never dared complain."

"I had that feeling. And what would it have won me, except the indignation of more people who are already unhappy with my new connection to the fae?"

"Oh, that's true enough," Darion said. He shrugged a little and shifted showing a touch of discomfort. "But I suspect you can't wait to get away from this connection."

"If that were true, I wouldn't want to drag that group along with me. No thanks."

"You're smart. Your sister took offense at something a Diamond did, and not even to her. She demanded retribution."

"I am not my sister. Or my father. Or my mother. I'd like to be more like Cherry. She cares about people, and she does things--" I stopped, and worry surged through me again. "I need to get back to her place. She's got to be going crazy."

"I contacted her earlier, not long after you disappeared, and told her we had a link and I'd have you back to her tonight." He shifted in the chair again and nodded. "Yes, you're right. We need to get back to her soon. I thought you would spend the night at Sapphire House, and I'd talk to her, but Ambassador Sun has helped in that respect."

"Very much so. I feel well."

"And you lie well, too, when it suits you. Rest for an hour. I have a few matters to settle, and then we'll both go back to your cousin's for the night."

"Sounds good. Comfortable bed," I admitted.

"Yes, it is. I've slept there often myself." He stood, went to the door and stopped again. "Any other questions?"

I glanced at the rings still sitting on the table beside the bed. "Are there often cases where people lose their rings?"

"No. Clan rings are sacred. It takes a work of extreme cowardice or depravity for a clan to demand the return of a ring from one of their own. In the old days, someone might collect rings in battle, though. Now they do so in tournament and ransom the rings back to the owners."

"You do tournaments? Like horses and jousting and that kind of . . . stuff?"

He grinned and leaned against the door jamb. "Yes, all that kind of crap. It can be fun, too, since we live in a more civilized age, and now people rarely die, except by accident."

"Huh." I shifted on the mattress, trying to ease one last ache in my leg. Nothing active sounded enjoyable. "Everyone a ring?"

"There are rare occasions where someone provides invaluable help to a clan other than his own, and the clan offers him a second ring which is like an adoption, though he doesn't leave his own clan. Oh, and there is one case where someone wears no rings at all. That's if the person is the King or Queen of Fae. During the one hundred years of rule, the person gives back their clan ring and renounces allegiance to the clan in order to serve all clans equally ."

"And after they stop being the ruler? What do they do then?"

"Take a place of honor in the clan. Sometimes they become councilors and advise the new ruler. If the clan isn't held by someone who just doesn't want to give over the rule -- like Topaz with the good Lord Iron -- they become the chieftain for the next round. Nine hundred years is a long time to lead a clan. Most of them tire of the work by then and withdraw to their family estates to enjoy life for a while."

"But not the Lord of Topaz."

"The great Lord of Topaz was a friend to Roman Emperors when he first took the clan. Back in those days, a fae could claim to be a king of a far land no one had ever heard of and live like Kings in the land of humans. They also interfered far too much,"

"The clan is stuck with him?"

"Someone would need considerable backing to remove him from his position. Lord Iron has cultivated the younger fae of his tribe, the wild boys. They'll keep him in power for a while still."

"Ah."

"Tell me what you want, Skye."

I considered the question for a moment. Did I want revenge on Lord Iron? Did I want the four Topaz boys to freeze in hell? And what would that get me?

"I want to find Lacey and the others. I want this to end well."

"But what do you want for you?" he asked and sounded confused this time.

"Why can't that be for me? I want everything to end well, so when I look back, I have no regrets about my part in what happened. Isn't that selfish enough for you?"

"You know that isn't selfish, don't you?" He went to the door and then paused and looked back. "I didn't realize a path guardian had befriended you. How did you manage that one?"

"By being so naïve, I didn't understand it was anything special. I knew there was something beyond the mirrors and one day I was in danger, and I slipped through to the path. She helped me reach another mirror. I came back later and left a plant. I like plants, and since I'd seen so much green there, I thought she would like plants too."

He nodded. "She wouldn't have let you in if she didn't believe you were worthy. Path Guardians are part of ancient magic, and they are extremely choosy about whom they allow to travel through their realms. Not all fae can go through those paths. Most have to make full portals, which takes considerably more magic."

"I've been lucky."

"Or blessed," he said. Darion tilted his head this time as though he appeared far too earnest. "Rest a little, Skye. I'll be back soon."

I relaxed against the soft pillows as he left and succumbed to sleep, either feeling safe or just too exhausted to care.

CHAPTER TEN

S ometime later Blue came back with clothes that he placed on the chair by the bed. Blue jeans, shirt: they looked as though someone had just gone out and bought them.

"Darion says you can take a shower before you change if you like. He'll be ready in about fifteen minutes, but there is no hurry."

"Sounds good," I agreed and fought to move my legs off the bed. "Or maybe just lying down and dying would be better."

"Those people from Topaz Clan should pay for what they did to you." Blue appeared adamant in his decision. "They're getting away with trying to murder you."

"No, they're not getting away with it." I waved towards the rings, still sitting there on the table. "Everyone knows and everyone who doesn't approve of their actions will show their anger. That's good enough for now. We have far more important things to worry about, Blue. Really."

"I suppose so," he admitted, though he still didn't look happy. "Take care, Skye. If you need help, try to get word to us. We'll come for you again."

"Did I say thank you?"

"Dozens of times while we brought you back, even though we feared you would not survive the journey."

"It wouldn't have mattered if I hadn't survived. You didn't leave me there to die in the cold or at the claws and teeth of that creature." I had, until now, been able to suppress most of what had happened. I didn't need the fear or the anger which tried to surge through me. "Even if I had died in your hands, it would have been better."

He looked at me for a long moment before he left. I ached when I stood, and regretted leaving the warm bed, but I forced myself to limp over to the bathroom. I didn't look in any of the mirrors; not then, and not when I dressed again. I didn't want to know how I looked.

Darion waited for me at the bottom of the stairs. I moved slowly down the steps. It had been a hell of a day when I considered everything.

"Ready? Or would you like to sit down for a minute -- or a day or two?"

I laughed. My throat hurt from my trek through the fae equivalent of Dante's ninth hell. And if I ever saw a Chub fur coat, I'd be tempted to take a little frustration out on it. I needed to get back to reality. Not that my world was any safer, but I knew what to expect out there in the world of humans.

We headed back out of the huge house and into the bright, warm light of a late afternoon. Darion's car sat in Sapphire House's driveway, and several Sapphire people stood outside watching over us until we drove away. They waved. I waved in return. The leave-taking seemed benign and mundane and unreal.

I didn't regret when we drove back towards the gray fog wall separating this exceptional street from the dirt and grit of downtown. I glanced back at the last moment. The houses looked as quiet and sedate as any upper-class neighborhood somewhere in the Midwest -- a place created by people with old, comfortable money.

Or just power.

And then the fog spread around us for a moment, and we emerged, Darion breaking at the end of the alley. Three taxies swept by, honking at each other. A drunk sat with his back against the wall by my car door, blinking several times, with a vague 'where the hell did that come from' look on his face.

A glance behind us showed crates and boxes, and cars passing at the other end of the alley and only the faintest hint of mist between us.

"You won't be able to find your way there, Skye. Not without a ring. A ring would tie you to your clan and always lead you to your clan house."

"They took the rings from those four. Did that trap them?"

"No. They were -- as you were -- already across the Veil. They had magic enough to get loose from the bonds and head back to the Topaz lands. I've heard they are safe. Even Lord Iron dare not make too much of standing up for them for fear someone will mention his involvement in the matter. They will ridicule them for having lost their rings, and that's the least they deserve."

"We were in fae? I wish I had seen more. I had always imagined that it was, well, less cold."

Darion laughed but with a hint of longing. We needed to fix this mess so he could go home. He said nothing more as he maneuvered the car out into the street and picked up speed.

A sullen, autumn sunset swept out across the western sky. Twenty-four hours ago I had learned about Lacey Weaver. I had gotten no closer to finding out what might have happened to her, despite the very long day.

"Did you learn anything about the castle and where it might be?" I asked.

"None of us recognized the area which is odd. The king and council are looking now."

"Can they help?"

"Oh yes. There isn't a place in fae -- or in this world -- which isn't known by someone. That happens when you live so long. We can only hope they figure this out in time to save the others."

I nodded and relaxed as he drove the rest of the way across town. We were running out of time.

The sun had disappeared by the time we reached Cherry's apartment building. I climbed out of the car, startled by trash blowing by in the lot and as skittish as a stray cat. A voice half a block away made me jump.

Darion ignored my reactions, and we moved carefully up the stairs. Too damn many stairs today, I thought, as though they had been the problem.

Cherry had opened the door before we got there. She looked at me, shook her head, and stepped aside.

"You look like hell, Skye. Don't these people have magic? Can't they help you?"

"They have," I said, going past her.

She looked at Darion and then back at me. "You must have had a hell of a day."

I dropped onto the sofa and nodded. I didn't want to relive everything that had happened. Cherry, in an act of benevolent kindness, didn't ask. She'd ask Darion instead. I didn't care.

"Tonight we need rest," Darion said. He had stayed by the door. "I need to check with a few people, and I will come back here later if that's all right Cherry."

"No problem," she said, though I heard a hint of uncertainty in her voice. "Will Skye be safe here?"

"Yes, I believe so. I'll return as soon as I can. Skye, rest well for a while. I hope we will have at least the night to recover, but I cannot guarantee anything."

I nodded and waved him away so he would leave and I could sleep, which was all I wanted.

Cherry went with him out the door, and I heard them mumble a few things out on the landing. I had already closed my eyes and leaned back, wanting to sleep, right here sitting on the wonderful, soft sofa.

Cherry closed the door as she came back inside the apartment. I barely lifted my head and dropped back again, trying not to moan.

"Let me get you a blanket and a pillow."

"I'm all right." I wanted to be left alone with my misery. The ride from fae to here had taken all my energy.

"Don't argue, baby. You'll sleep better for being comfortable."

I wanted to argue anyway. I wanted to have control, even over something stupid. Instead, I let her get the blankets and pillow and make a little nest for me while I fought just to remove my shoes. The cat wandered in and out, looking rather annoyed at intruders in her home again. I wondered about having such a creature waiting at home, but I wasn't certain of the upkeep. As I settled into the blankets, I remembered what had happened at Ruby House.

"I need to get a plate," I said, looking up at Cherry.

That was the last even remotely coherent thought or statement I had --

Until someone pounded on the door.

I sat straight up and cried out at the moment between sleep and waking. I heard howling.

"Cherry -- Cherry -- you ho-ome?"

"Son of a bitch!"

Cherry came charging out of the kitchen, a washrag in hand and dripping water. She startled me so much I stood, but my legs wouldn't hold me, and I fell back down amid the blankets. The cat had been sleeping at my feet, and took off at a run, staring daggers back at the door.

Cherry glanced my way, her face set in anger as she kept going to the door.

"Cher-ry, Oh, Cher-ry ba-by --"

She undid the locks and threw the door open so quickly that the tall man standing on the other side took a staggering step backward in surprise. He would have fallen right down the railing if she hadn't grabbed his arm.

Drunk. This wasn't an attack. The man who stood on the other side of the door blinked through watery, bloodshot gray eyes at Cherry, and offered the most inane smile I had ever seen.

"Hey, Baby. I knew you were home."

"What the hell are you doing? What did I tell you would happen if you ever showed up here, dead ass drunk again?"

"You are so cute when you're feisty," he said and grabbed her.

I wanted to cover my eyes, so I didn't see the carnage. She pushed him back out as he tried to step past her, and he made a sound of disappointment and disbelief.

"You are not coming into my apartment, Paul. Get your ass back out of here. It's too cold to be standing here."

"Ah, come on, Cherry baby. I --" He saw me on the sofa. He blinked and blinked again. "Hey, who the hell is he? Are you two-timing me --?"

"Son of a bitch!" she said and with far more anger this time. If she had been fae, I wouldn't have wanted her to get so angry and curse, not with the emotion she put into those words. Paul would have been running away with his tail between his legs -- and I mean that quite literally. "You stupid, bastard -- out. Just out. I will call the cops in about half a minute and have them haul your sorry ass out of here if you don't leave on your own."

"Hey," he said and sounded confused. "Who is he? What's going on? I can't drive . . . can't drive home -- like this."

That stayed her hand. I wondered if I should give up the sofa for the floor, or if she would take him into her bedroom. She didn't look inclined to have anything to do with him, though. I wondered if Paul, when sober, had ever seen that glare of righteous anger. Did he expect to be forgiven because he was drunk?

She turned with the anger blazing in her eyes. "If I take this stupid bastard home, will you be all right?"

"I'll be fine," I said. "But I'm not sure you should be out there alone, Cherry."

"Shit." She looked at me as though she had only just recalled everything else that had happened. Then she turned back to the guy still swaying at the door. A cool breeze blew in around him, and I wished he would just go away so I could rest again. "I'll call a taxi to take you home, Paul. You can pick up your car tomorrow. Don't come to my door when you get it. I never want to see you again."

"Oh, come on baby," he said and draped an arm across her shoulder.

She shoved him away. He laughed and grabbed at her again.

And that was when Darion arrived. He caught Paul's arm before the man even noticed the newcomer. I wasn't certain Darion had come up the stairs. He might have just appeared on the landing.

"What the hell --" Paul began.

"Didn't Cherry say you were leaving?" Darion asked, calm and steady.

"Another blond bimbo? You collecting blonds this season?" Paul said, his voice growing angry and annoyed, though he wasn't half as angry as Cherry. She started to say something. Stopped. Looked at Darion and nodded.

"Can you remove this asshole? He woke Skye. He's drawing attention from the neighbors. And I told him if he ever showed up here drunk like this again, I'd shove his --" She stopped, and I wondered she intended to shove up his ass.

Paul, for reasons I couldn't begin to understand, smirked, and tried to pull away from Darion. Darion took him by the arm and escorted the man down the stairs. Paul protested and got louder. Darion shut him up with a touch of magic, and I had to wonder what went through Paul's fuzzed brain right then.

I settled on the sofa. My head pounded, my mouth tasted like cotton and vinegar. I feared my eyes might fall out of my head. I grabbed at the blankets, shivering.

Cherry remained at the open door and stepped back ahead of Darion. "Should he be driving?"

"Oh yeah. He's stone cold sober now." Darion

grinned. "A shame about the backlash to that spell and the blinding headache. Oh, and all liquor will taste like shit for the next few months."

"Oh my," she said and closed the door and smiled. "Thank you, for me and for him. When he's sober, he's not a bad guy. Not the kind I want to spend my life with, mind you, but we've had fun. But he drinks, and he gets stupid."

"He'll have a long time to consider staying sober," Darion said. He crossed the room and settled into the chair across from me. "You can sleep for a while longer, Skye. Everything is fine."

"Is?" I said, almost coherently.

He nodded.

So I slept again. Just fell back among the blankets and pillow and slipped into a deep, dark sleep. Darion remained nearby, a reassuring hint of magic in the air. The cat came back and nestled into the blankets. Cherry and Darion spoke in the kitchen, and I felt oddly content.

So the police showed up about an hour later.

"I'll avoid this one," Darion said. "They won't notice me here. I can tell they've come about Lacey. Me, the best man, here with the caterer? We don't want that kind of questioning started."

"Good point," Cherry said, fervently nodding. She looked worn and worried.

"I won't be far if there's trouble."

He faded out of view though I sensed he had remained in the room. Cherry looked startled and then resigned when someone knocked. She went to the door while I sat up and tried to make myself at least a little presentable.

Cherry must have said all the right things at the door before she let the two uniformed police officers and one plainclothes detective into the apartment. They looked friendly enough and said this wasn't anything more than a routine check.

"Are you alone --?" the detective said, and then stopped, seeing me still sitting on the sofa.

"This is my cousin Skye. She's ill. I have her staying with me for a few days until she's better."

Perceptions changed as the three looked at me, all of them reconsidering their first view as male, which made my head pound a little worse, though the level of mistrust lowered. I don't know why. It's a cultural fallacy that women are passive and males aggressive, and I would have thought this group wouldn't fall for such easy answers.

"I'm here to discuss the Lacey Weaver situation," the plainclothes detective said. "You were the caterer at the wedding, right?"

"Yes. Come in. Is there any word on her? I've known Lacey for years. We've worked the same soup kitchens together."

"No word, I'm afraid," the detective admitted and made a note on a pad he pulled from his pocket. He came into the living room. I gathered my blankets up around me and tried not to look too pathetic.

"I'm Detective Alan Barber," the man said as he sat in the chair. Cherry settled beside me, patting my hand. The two other cops remained standing and didn't introduce themselves. "This is a routine set of questions. We're talking to everyone who had been at the wedding. I would also like a list and address of all the people who work for you, both on this job and in general."

"No problem. I have everything on a computer in the bedroom. I'll give a print out to you before you leave."

"Thank you."

"I was there, after she disappeared," I said. People had

seen me, and it wouldn't do to gloss over that now. "Cherry called me when she needed help to distribute the food."

"So Skye dragged herself out of bed and helped. I asked her to stay here. I didn't want to be alone," Cherry admitted. The words sounded sincere, even with Darion sometimes staying here. "It's frightening, seeing a woman disappear, right in the middle of her home, with so many people around. I wouldn't have slept at all if Skye hadn't been here."

"You work for her?"

"No. I have a small detective business. Nothing like this stuff. I find things for people. I have a card --"

"There is one on the fridge," Cherry said. "Remind me to give it to you before you leave, Detective Barber."

They asked us questions, all of them routine stuff. Darion stayed hovering nearby, but nothing much would come of this meeting except for another break in my much-needed sleep.

"Do you often help your cousin?" Barber asked.

"Not often enough," I said, and meant those words, too. "But I have the time. It's not like I have a booming business."

Nods again. Cherry went to get my card and her computer list. One of the uniformed officers went with her. I frowned, but I suppose it was only routine. I half expected Barber to ask me something while she was gone. Instead, he only took notes. They left a few minutes later.

After they had gone, I limped off into the bathroom. By the time I came back, Darion had appeared again and frowned a little.

"What's wrong?"

"We may have made a mistake. We should have told

them I went with you two last night to help deliver the food," Darion said. "People saw us all over town."

"Hell." Panic almost me. I didn't want the police to doubt us which wouldn't help now or with my business later.

"I have Barber's number. His cell phone," Cherry said, waving a business card. "I'll call him and tell him that part skipped my mind. And Skye, being so ill, just didn't think of it either."

Darion nodded. He still didn't look happy. The fae made a habit of not drawing the attention of officials.

The police hadn't gone far. She spoke quickly, apologetic, explaining how upset everything had made her, saying Darion had gone with them to help and then got a ride back home from downtown.

The call might have made us look questionable -- but at least she gave them a truth they would have wondered over later. I didn't want to be caught up in anything trying to hide Darion's part in that night's activities.

"You look a little better," Cherry said, handing me a cup of coffee.

"Do I? That's scary because I just saw myself in the mirror."

"At least the police didn't doubt you were ill," Darion offered. "Would you like a little food?"

"Not even remotely interested in eating," I said, shaking my head. I feared something exploded in my brain. I dropped back with a moan.

"Lie down on your stomach," Darion said. I lifted a hand in a gesture meant to stop him, but he came to the edge of the sofa. "Just do so. I'll help you relax."

I kicked the blankets around and settled on my stomach. Darion sat on the coffee table and leaned forward, his fingers plying the muscles in my shoulders and upper back. No magic, just a gentle massage of muscles that had begun to mimic steel.

I understood how a cat felt just then. I would have purred. Honest to God, I would have purred and stayed there all night.

I slept. Darion had left again, but I didn't care. I remained curled up in the blankets, relaxed and content.

Safe.

It wouldn't last.

CHAPTER ELEVEN

At least two hours passed before the next set of uninvited guests arrived.

They at least had the courtesy to appear outside the door and knock. I had sensed their magical arrival, though. I stood before Cherry, pulling a robe around her, came out of the bedroom.

"Magic," I said. "Fae. You better let me take care of this one. Go back --"

"No. They came to my place. There's no use hiding."

I nodded and brushed a hand through my snarled hair before crossing to the door, limping worse again and feeling like shit. With a gentle wave of magic, I cleaned up a little, though, so I didn't make a bad impression. Darion wasn't here, and I wondered if I should let them come into the apartment.

I opened the door and gave a quick bow of my head, mostly, so I see their rings. Was that how bowing started?

The rings held blue stones. Not sapphire blue, though.

These were far darker. Lapis. These were the first four I had met. The man in the lead had two stones in his ring, which made him a warlord. That boded ill.

"Welcome," I offered and stepped aside. I could have left them standing out there, but hell, they had my curiosity. Darion's magic wouldn't have stopped them anyway. They were being polite, so I did the same.

The warlord nodded as they came in through the door, glancing at Cherry before turning back. I wasn't going to like having his attention. The group didn't go far into the apartment, and they didn't look inclined to stay long, which seemed just fine.

I closed the door and waited.

"I am Brand Lapis Landfair," the man said.

"Skye Emerald McFaelyn," I replied, as though they didn't know. "Do you have business with me?"

"Somewhat," Brand answered. He had the look of an older fae -- not in the face, but the eyes, and even the clothing. Conservative. So did his three companions, two more men, and a woman. "We are the ones who brought Lacey Weaver from Fae to this realm after the unfortunate deaths of her parents and brother."

I tried desperately to get my brain working and ask the right questions. "She is Ruby Clan, right?"

"Yes. Lacey Ruby Day. Her mother was of Topaz. Her father was the brother of the Ruby Clan's leader."

"So how did you get her out of fae without anyone in Ruby knowing it? And why?"

He stood for a moment and considered not answering, which told me my position in this meeting. They had only wanted to impart information to someone who wouldn't demand more answers. I could still ask, though.

"Many fae died that year," Brand Lapis Landfair said. I

heard subdued emotions in his voice; loss and pain, longing and worry. "Magic which must have gone wrong and waited to strike had gotten loose. The magic killed dozens before being quelled. Lacey and her brother had been born less than an hour before the attack came. I had been part of the team hunting down the Unnatural, and I managed to save the child."

"But you didn't turn her over to Ruby clan -- ah, no. Because of The Choosing, and that put her at risk, being so helpless. She might be the next Queen if she survives."

"Yes." He seemed pleased I understood so much. "I followed my duty to make certain she went to some place of safety since she wouldn't find such anywhere in Fae, not a child without a family."

"So you brought her to an old human friend."

He nodded once more and then shook his head as though he had already said far more than he intended. At least this filled in a lot of the blanks, and even made sense, in an odd fae sort of way.

"We are concerned, Skye Emerald McFaelyn, about your involvement in this matter," Brand said, eyes narrowing. "There have been questions after your encounter with Topaz House today."

"Was the encounter with Topaz Clan at all related to Lacey's disappearance?" I asked. "Granted, her mother was Topaz, but I suspect what happened to me was personal."

The group had the grace to look embarrassed by the Topaz House behavior. They had confirmed relevant information about Lacey, though.

"We wish to be less barbaric in our request that you step away from the business of fae," Brand said.

Cherry stepped forward, and I feared what she said wouldn't be polite or politic. I lifted a hand to signal her to silence. Brand's hand moved as well, expecting me to cast a spell.

"Calm, everyone. Calm." I spread both arms and saw Brand watching the way they trembled. They wouldn't take me seriously as a threat. I wanted to sit down dared not in their presence. I was damned tired of rude fae.

The door opened, startling us all. Darion walked in, giving a polite enough nod to the Lapis people, a smile to Cherry and a look of rebuke to me.

"Sit before you fall, Skye. And don't worry. Brand Lapis Landfair if you go back to your clan house you will find an edict waiting there by the time you arrive."

"Edict," Brand said. He looked from Darion his eyes narrowed. "The King has issued a statement?"

"Skye is to be left alone in this work. Another incident like Topaz will bring an entire clan into censure."

I shook my head, panic rising once again. "Hell. That won't make me any friends, Darion."

"No, it will not," Darion agreed. "But this will remind your enemies that you do have friends already. The King wants this case solved, Brand. So far we have been trying to find our missing brethren for months and with no clues at all until Skye stepped in."

"How do we know he's not created the castle out of his own mind? No one knows this place, Ambassador --"

"Three Old Ones came at the King's bidding. They recognize the castle."

Silence, except for the intake of breath. Then Brand turned and bowed to me.

"My apologies, Skye Emerald McFaelyn. Good luck with your work."

They all gave quick bows, turned and walked past Darion and back outside again. Darion closed the door behind them. I stood there, trying to figure out if this was good, bad, or worse than I could imagine.

"Sit down, Skye," Cherry said. She grabbed my arm. I must have been swaying as though a wind swept through the room because suddenly things settled a little better. I went back to the sofa and looked at Darion.

"Yes, the King has issued the edict, at my advice. He came as far as Sapphire Clan House to discuss the matter. He wasn't certain until the Old Ones showed up and confirmed that the castle does, in fact, exist."

"Hell. His edict won't make me any more popular."

"Of course not. Nothing will. But this will keep you safe from fools like the rest of the Topaz Clan, who had made noises that they would look for revenge."

"Thank you," I said. "I should have said that from the start, right?"

He shrugged, taking the chair. "I haven't heard what the Old Ones told the King," he said, frowning. "I was waiting for word when Sand said that a group of Lapis, including Brand, arrived here. Brand is --"

"A warlord. I saw the ring. And dangerous, I assume."

"Yes. Very much so. Without an ounce of compassion --"

"Then why did he bring Lacey over and give her to the Weavers?"

Darion's mouth opened. Closed. He looked as though something in his world had just drastically changed and he had not even noticed.

"Hell. That even makes sense. He had been hunting the Unnatural. He must have saved her from one of . . . Hoyle's daughter. God's all! I should have realized."

He considered all kinds of things I barely glimpsed. I

wished I understood more about the fae and their relationships, and the cultural ties that seemed to bring everything into focus for Darion. I would have asked Darion to teach me if I hadn't feared my head would explode if I so much as talked too much.

"Either of you hungry?" Cherry asked. "I'm in the mood for a little late night cafe food. Does that sound at all possible, Darion?"

"Dinner would be nice," Darion said.

"No, no, no." I started to shake my head and changed my mind with a soft moan.

"You need food." Darion came over to the sofa and pulled me up, ignoring my almost coherent protests. "You need to help your body replenish lost minerals from today. Magic takes away from the body's resources. So does healing. Come on, friend."

"Can you get her down to the car? I'll dress and be right down," Cherry said. She looked happy. Another insomniac, I suppose. I stopped arguing since this made both Cherry and Darion happy. They'd done a lot for me the last few days.

We went down the damned stairs. The night was chilly, the sky cloudy with the promise of a wet day to come. A fine mist made cloud-like-luminescence under the parking lot's lights.

"What time is it?" I asked. I limped over to the car.

"About three in the morning," Darion said. "The police are watching us."

"Oh hell." I laid my head on the car. "How do we explain you this time? Or the people who came visiting?"

"I won't appear to be me. I'll be a friend of Cherry's who just got into town. There will be no problem there. The others were just shadows and were careful not to be seen."

"You explain everything to Cherry," I said. "I'm going to sleep in the back seat. I should have stayed there from the start. There wouldn't have been as many visitors to your car."

"Good point."

I climbed in and settled back in the narrow seat. He had the top up since driving around with it down would have looked odd on such a cold night. Although not as comfortable as the sofa, I closed my eyes and drifted away. I didn't look when Cherry arrived though I listened to the conversation the two had. Cherry didn't sound in the least bit upset about the police and magic if they didn't see Darion as himself. My cousin took magic way too much for granted.

CHAPTER TWELVE

We drove through the empty streets and then took the freeway most of the way across town to Cherry's favorite little cafe. I didn't have to worry about the quality of the food and someone even greeted her by name. I saw the waitress eyeing Darion and me as though we had just come up on the auction block. When she stepped away from our table, Cherry grinned. I slid in on one side of the booth, and they took the other.

"Sorry. I hadn't considered how others would react," she said. "Do you want to be my cousin, like Skye?"

"No," he said and quite emphatically. Then he smiled. "I really don't want to be your cousin."

I looked from one to the other. Hell. For obvious reasons, sexual attraction just doesn't register with me. Cherry didn't look displeased. Darion smiled. The waitress came back and put down the coffee we had ordered and stood there, waiting.

"Hey," I said, tapping the table in front of them.

"Food. Remember?"

They both looked at me in shock and then embarrassment. We ordered. The waitress laughed as she walked away. I wanted to laugh as well, but I still had to go back home with these two, and I'd made far enough enemies today.

The food tasted excellent. I felt better after we ate. Despite their initial moment of attraction, the two didn't fawn over each other the rest of the meal. We had dessert, too. From the way Cherry attacked her piece of apple pie, I suspected the first part of the meal had just been a pretense. After the first bite of mine, I agreed.

Something buzzed in my ear, and I swatted. Then I saw Darion frown and put aside his fork. He looked at me and nodded.

"You felt that, did you? That was Blue. He wants to see me. With everything going on --"

"We'll be here," Cherry said. She leaned back, holding her coffee cup in two hands. "Unless you want to take us home first?"

"No. I'll drive around the block and find a dark place and talk to him. I'll be back soon." He slid out of the booth and hurried away, but I sensed that he rushed because he wanted to get back to Cherry as soon as possible.

Cherry watched him with a little predatory look I had not expected, but when she turned back at me again, she sighed.

"I have to ask if you have a problem with this."

"Pardon?" I asked, putting the fork aside. She sounded serious, and I still wasn't capable of thinking and eating at the same time.

"With Darion and me. I don't want to upset you."

"Well, if you mean sex, no it will not bother me at all. I'd be worried if you were talking marriage and babies."

"No!" She said and so loudly the couple two booths over frowned. She shook her head in vehement denial of the words, her short black hair bouncing from side-to-side. I got the impression words like marriage and babies would always win the same reaction from her.

"That's fine," I said. "I'm just . . . I would hate to see another kid to go through what I have, always wondering if the next person who walked into your home would kill you for reasons you never understood."

"Damn," she said. "No. I won't do that to anyone, Skye. In fact --"

"You and Darion like each other." I picked up my cup and sipped -- and then frowned as someone came into the cafe. He looked familiar. "Cherry, is that the guy who showed up at your apartment?"

She turned in her seat and looked. "Hell! The bastard is following me!" Cherry stood up from the table to confront him. I grabbed hold of her, but the guy -- Paul, I remembered -- came past the waitress and straight towards us.

I hoped Darion came back soon. I could handle this -- but Darion would manage it with more style.

"Paul, get your ass back out of here and never cross my path again."

Paul looked annoyed, embarrassed and angry. But not drunk. Darion had made certain that wouldn't happen soon. How could this fool believe we'd think it a coincidence that he showed up here, twenty miles from her apartment and at this ungodly hour of the morning? Was he that stupid? I feared so. And stupid, self-centered people can be dangerous.

"I have a right to be here." He threw himself into the booth across from us and glared. "You and your blond boy toy there can sit back down, Cherry. And where's your other new friend? I saw him come in here with --" He stopped, catching himself. "I assume it takes two to replace me, right?"

I pulled her back to our booth and slid in beside her, putting myself between him and Cherry, which annoyed him. He must have been sitting out in the car at her apartment and here. He'd waited for Darion to leave. I didn't like it.

He ordered coffee and a piece of pie. And not politely, but I didn't care. I turned back to Cherry and gave her a look of warning.

"Let Darion have a go at him again. He doesn't get much of a chance to deal with his type," I mumbled.

"What are you muttering about over there?" Paul demanded. "You talking about me?"

"You were far more likable as a slobbering, shit-faced drunk," I said looking back at Paul. Cherry, made an annoyed sound, probably because I had stopped her from dealing with him.

"Watch what you say, boy --"

"Boy? Are you really that stupid, Paul? This is my cousin Skye. We've talked about her, right?" Cherry said.

Paul went bright red. "You're lying."

He could not change his mind about me, the power of his conviction unwavering. Stubborn, wasn't surprising, given how he had followed Cherry and made an ass of himself because he wouldn't let go.

I decided to have a little more fun at his expense. I pulled out my ID and held it up for him. This time, at least, it said female.

"You sure look like a guy to me, sweetie."

"I am not your sweetie. And neither is Cherry. What do you say you go home, Paul before you make an even bigger idiot of yourself?"

"Where the other one go? What kind of perversions have you three got going on?"

"Cherry, would you like us to call the police and have this person taken away?" the waitress asked from the register. She already had a hand on the phone.

"Yes --"

"I have right to be here," Paul said, standing and glaring at everyone. "I'll have my lawyers down on this place so fast --"

And that's when Darion walked back into the building. Paul looked worried, perhaps with just the faintest hint of fear, knowing Darion had done something odd in their last meeting. Or maybe he hadn't realized how tall Darion was until he stopped right in front of the man.

"This isn't a safe place for you," Darion said looking Paul in the face. "Not safe at all."

I caught a hint of magic and a soft scent of lilacs. Paul backed up a step.

"You want to get out of here now, don't you?"

"I didn't realize -- I thought she was a guy," he said, waving a hand at me, as though that answered for all his bad manners. He inched his way around Darion and headed for the door, past the waitress who had just come out with coffee and a piece of pie.

"I'll have that," Darion said with a bright smile.

Before she had set the pie down, Paul's car screeched out of the parking lot.

"He's going to be a problem," Cherry said shaking her head. "You know, how sometimes you meet someone, but they turn out to be something else?"

"Happens a lot in my life," I offered. Cherry laughed and elbowed me as Darion slid back into the booth across from us. He nodded his thanks for the coffee and pie and waited until the woman had moved well out of range before he spoke again.

"Blue says there's news about the castle," he said. "They haven't found the place, but there is something odd, even for fae, from what I gathered. I need to go to Sapphire House. Can you drive my car back to your place? I'll be there as soon as I can, Cherry."

"How are you going to get back to Sapphire House?" I asked.

"Blue has a portal ready." He ate another bite of pie, and then apparently decided the next bite would kill him. He shoved the plate clear across the table in front of me. "Finish that."

I looked up at him, ready to take offense at being ordered but he and Cherry smiled at each other and hell, at least this gave them a couple more minutes together. I nibbled at the pie and drank a little more coffee. He settled the bill and left a very nice tip.

When we left, Cherry had the keys to his car. I had rather hoped to drive, but maybe this was one of those rites of a relationship where you trust your chosen mate with something of great value to yourself. I gave up trying to figure it all out and climbed into the car.

By the time we pulled away, Darion had gone somewhere else. I looked back at the cafe. I saw no one in the parking lot at all, but I saw a car in the next block started up as we pulled out. Paul couldn't be that stupid -- but he hadn't shown good sense yet.

"What kind of car does Paul drive?" I asked.

She looked in the rear-view mirror, startled. "Hell, is he back there? His father owns a big car dealership, and he has a different car every time I see him."

"I'll watch just to be careful," I said and turned a little sideways.

"Put on the seat belt. If that is Paul -- well he's been kind of crazy. I can't believe the stupid bastard showed up at the cafe!" Cherry still drove at a nice sedate pace, despite her worry. I would have wanted to race home, so Darion had made the better choice when he handed over the keys. "That was horribly embarrassing."

"You did well," I offered.

As we stopped at a light, she looked at me, glaring a little. "Never think I can't take care of my own battles."

"I never did," I protested. The light turned green, and she eased back out before the other car caught up with us. I had a serious suspicion I was right since it had followed us through three turns already. "But that doesn't mean I can't help. What would you have done if you'd gone there alone and he'd shown up?"

"Told the waitress to call the cops," she said. "And then I would have knocked the stupid bastard down and sat on him until they got there. Skye, he's not backing down."

"You'll be fine. Darion and I can make sure of he won't get dangerous. We won't hurt Paul, but you saw what happened when Darion told him he should be afraid. He needs a little fear. I'll talk to Darion, later. There are subtle things that might help him to lose interest in bothering you anymore."

"That would be helpful," she said with an emphatic nod of her head.

The car followed us onto the freeway ramp. Cherry looked in the rear-view mirror and made a sound of worry this time.

"Cherry, I need to ward the car," I said. "Tired as I am already, I might be groggy afterward, but this is a good idea, just in case."

She nodded. "I told him months ago to take a hike and not come back. But there he is, bothering me again. I never thought he would be this kind of person."

"You don't know sometimes," I said. I tried to keep the conversation calm. I didn't have to work very hard to ward Darion's car after all because he had a spell ready to be triggered. "There, done."

"Warded?"

"Yeah. Darion had the spell ready. Very nice."

"Just in time," Cherry said, glancing into the rear-view mirror. "He's making his move."

Her fingers held white-knuckled to the steering wheel and her face looked pale, even by the dashboard light. The car roared up beside us; a big SUV, dark and foreboding. The passenger side window rolled down and Paul leaned across from the driver's side and signaled Cherry to pull over. He almost lost control and Cherry hit the brakes and dropped back while he swerved and slowed and fell in behind us again.

"I'm getting off," Cherry said, veering towards the first exit.

"No. We don't want to be on streets we don't know with him after us. Keep going. I can do something. When I say to speed up, hit the gas."

I opened the window and stuck my head out, watching the side of the road and making myself focus just a few yards ahead of the car. Paul kept making stupid moves and Cherry cursed and gasped for breath as she slowed and sped up, trying to get away from him.

We had gone almost a mile before I found something helpful. A piece of wood had fallen from a truck and splintered. I reached out with magic and grabbed it, dragging the wood along with the car, and then made a quick check of the surrounding area. There were few other cars on the road tonight. Good.

"Okay, on the count of three, hit the gas and get well ahead of him, Cherry."

"Okay. You won't hurt him, right?"

"Not intentionally. I can't stop him from doing anything stupid, though. He proved how good he is at that already."

"True. Okay."

I checked everything again and gave a nod. "One -- two -- three!"

She hit the gas, and I swept the piece of wood behind us and straight into Paul's right front tire. We heard the blowout. Sparks flew from the rim as he hit the brakes and swerved over onto the shoulder and stopped.

Cherry gave a laugh of relief and slowed back down to speed limit. I leaned back, trying not to show how much of a headache the little trick had given me.

"Thank you, Skye. At least we can head to the apartment and lock the door before he gets there. And if he shows up --"

"Darion said there are police watching your place. If we're lucky, they'll be around."

"Yeah, he told me about the police. This is such a damn mess, Skye. I'm sorry I called you."

"I've helped since I'm the first person who has found anything. That counts for a lot in my life, Cherry. This trouble may even be what I need to sway the fae in my favor, so I can live without fearing I'll overstep a line they never pointed out to me."

"You don't like them much do you?"

"If you had asked me that a couple of days ago, I would have said I don't like the fae at all. But I've met quite a few now who seem genuinely friendly and good people. I'm glad. I don't want to be a bigot."

"What do you know about Darion?"

"You've known him longer than I have," I pointed out. I looked back just to make sure, but there was no sign of Paul. "He was the best man at Lacey's wedding. He is Ambassador for Sapphire House. He's nice."

"What are they like in the clan houses?"

We talked about fae for the rest of the way home. We got back to the apartment in good time, and no one appeared to be sitting in the parking lot. If the cops were still there, I didn't look for them.

I walked up the stairs. I had a catch in my right knee still which was the last of the worst pains. Darion had been right because the food had helped. Dawn was less than an hour away. I wondered if I could sleep for a couple of hours again.

Cherry let us in, turned on the light, closed the door --

Someone was sitting on the sofa. I thought he might be Darion at first and stilled my hand. But the figure stood, and I saw someone stockier, darker hair. He held up his hands.

"It is safe, friends," he said.

"Fae," I said, watching him. I sensed nothing hostile, but I didn't trust him. Glancing at his hands didn't help. No rings.

No rings at all. Well-dressed. Not old, at least not the way I had sensed from a lot of fae.

No rings at all.

Oh, Gods.

"Sir," I said and bowed my head. "Sire."

"Oh, then you know who I am," he said and gave a little laugh. "I had expected Darion Sapphire Wilding to be here and introduce me."

I moved up to put myself between Cherry and the King of the Fae. Cherry didn't even argue this time. She must have realized there was something odd about this man.

This fae. Power hung around him like a wreath of light, and he moved with a scent of orange. I saw the magic circling him in waves and could sense the depths of chaos just below the surface. I would not have crossed this one for anything.

"Your cousin is safe from me, Skye Emerald McFaelyn," he said. He even gave her a very proper bow that I suspect the King of Fae didn't make often. "Forgive me for not introducing myself since I have no name I can offer -- not for a few more days, at least. I am the Fae King, and I severed my allegiance to any clan and family when I took the position."

"I understand," I said and wondered if I should do more than bow my head. My leg started to cramp. I braced myself and stood my ground. "May I ask, sire, what you are doing here?"

"I came to speak with you," he said. Something buzzed and buzzed -- ah, contact with others. It must have been nearly constant. "I came to deal with you since I worried that my compatriots might not be polite. Where is Darion?"

"He received word you learned something about the castle," I said. "He went to Sapphire House."

"Ah. Ah. Of course. There are drawbacks to secrecy.

Skye, I cannot stay long. I wanted only to tell you that the edict I passed to keep you safe may not have full effect in some quarters because my days as king are quite literally numbered. I suspect -- without any real proof, mind you -- that there may be a serious attempt to pervert The Choosing."

"Damn." I hadn't meant to say anything. I didn't know how to deal with the Fae King. I fervently wished Darion here right now.

"Damn them, at the very least," the king said with a nod. He sighed. "Please, both of you sit. I have a few matters to impart."

I nodded and limped over to the sofa. He noticed the movement and seemed worried, which sent a new chill through me. I didn't want to look weak in front of him.

Cherry and I sat on the sofa, side-by-side. I calmed. The Fae King didn't seem a frightening person. He might be what he presented himself to be, which I caught from the mirroring ability. I also reminded myself that this man had saved my life by pronouncing I had a right to live, and he had done so long before any of the current troubles. I would politely listen while he gave me information.

He didn't waste time after we had settled. "The castle you found is ancient, even by our standards," he said and made a slight shake of his head. "Whitestone is so old and filled with enough magic that it has become a living thing. But eons ago, Whitestone moved away from the fae to places where none of us could go. I can't say why it came back."

"Was Whitestone involved in anything wrong before this?"

"No," he said. He frowned, but that might have been at something he heard from elsewhere since the buzzing got louder for a moment. "But the place may have changed, or someone might have warped it to his own use. There have been other unusual happenings in this last age."

"Like the Unnatural that killed Lacey's parents," I said.

His eyes focused on me. "Yes. And you knew about this because?"

"Brand Lapis Landfair came here a few hours ago," I said. My heart pounded too hard as I watched the calculation in his eyes. "He told me about fighting the Unnatural."

"Brand came to you. Yes. Lacey. I see. That makes sense of things. I should have come to you earlier. You are far more ready with the answers than many others."

"Is it safe for me to be so open?" I asked. "Or am I making even more enemies?"

"I don't think you could make more enemies," he said.

He had not meant the words as a joke, but I laughed, and for a moment a smile played at his lips.

"But as you said, yes this brings to mind the Unnatural. And other, smaller problems which have shown themselves, ever since the last quarter of The Choosing began. This incident has been a far more exciting time than I cared to be saddled with at this time. And now that you are involved, the situation makes your position rather dire, Skye."

"More so than any fae killing me if they decide I might step out of line?" I asked.

Oh, and he heard the bitterness in those words. He sat stone still for a moment, and then nodded, but I wondered if the reaction wasn't to something else he heard. I would never want to live as he did.

"Prior to this, your clan considered you an embarrassment," he said. "A deviation which a few believed should not be allowed to live, but something relatively harmless. Now some see you are working in the sphere of fae politics, and they consider this a threat. Skye, if you wish to step away, I can give you help to hide, at least until the fae have settled this matter. You have been of invaluable help already. I would hate to see such aid paid back in full the way Topaz hoped to."

I hadn't expected him to offer me sanctuary. I considered the quiet peace of my apartment, and how I longed to sit there amid my plants again. But I still couldn't walk away.

"No, thank you, sire. I gave my word to Mrs. Weaver to look for Lacey. I might still be of aid. And, to be honest, I think if something is interfering with the rule of Fae, I want to have my hand in keeping things in line."

"Because we have been so very kind to you, of course," he said looking straight at me once more.

"Because I'm still alive, and from what I've seen of those who disagree with you, I can't much trust them, can I?"

"Ah. Yes." Pause, frown, and nod. "And you would want Ruby House's ascension to the rule to go without a problem. They are already more inclined to behave well towards humans, even without Lacey." Pause again. His eyes became unfocused, and then he shook his head and stood.

"Is there a problem?" I asked, standing as well.

"No more than before," he answered. "Sit down. You are not my subject. You owe me no fealty and have taken no oath."

"That doesn't mean I can't honor what you do," I said. But I sat down before I fell.

"Thank you." He paused a moment to look at Cherry

and gave her a slight smile. "I'm honored to have met you. I haven't been to this side in well over one hundred years. One forgets that humans are so fae-like, sometimes. Both of you take care. I will send Darion back --"

A portal started to appear behind the king. I thought Darion had returned but in the next heartbeat, I realized this wasn't him. The scent seemed wrong, like wood burning. The portal appeared behind the King who had turned --

I shoved Cherry down to the floor and launched myself at the King of the Fae, knocking him to the floor. Things went flying.

Light filled everything, or maybe it filled me. I tried to breathe, and I feared I had done something stupid. Voices shouted everywhere. The king moved out from under me, and he seemed fine --

Darion caught me by the shoulders and put a hand on my chest. He said words, but they seemed distant, blurred. I saw colors in them and heard the endless echo of a sound I tried to grasp. No air, no air --

I closed my eyes and welcomed the darkness and the growing silence . . . and the peace.

"No," Darion said, panic in his voice. "No, you will not die now!"

I gasped and opened my eyes to a world filled with colors so bright they hurt. Air filled my lungs and didn't seem to want to leave again. I wanted to grab the air around me and shove it inside and never let go.

"There. Better. There," Darion said. Did I hear Cherry crying? Others had gathered around us.

"K-King --" I whispered.

"You saved his life since his guards didn't react quickly enough. He has gone back over the Veil, Skye. It wasn't safe for him to stay."

I nodded, gasped and coughed. I looked up at Darion. Star and Blue stood over us, and Cherry sat on the sofa, her cat in her hands. Her eyes still streamed with tears, but she made no sound.

"All - right?" I asked, looking at her.

"They said -- you had stopped breathing."

"Better now," I admitted. But I didn't move, fearing that would be too much work, and I might stop breathing again, just from the exertion. "You must -- be tired of this drama by now."

"I want this trouble over," she said. But then she looked at Darion. She didn't want everything to end.

"Can I sleep now?" I asked.

Blue and Star helped me stand. They took me, despite my protests, into Cherry's bedroom. I was in no physical shape to argue about being nestled into the bed.

But I panicked when they started to leave, even though I hadn't strength left to make a sound. I wanted back out of the bed and out of the dark. Blue must have seen or sensed my reaction. He stopped by the door.

"Can I have a chair? I should sit here, just to make sure no one wakes Skye again."

Darion glanced back at me and then patted Blue on the shoulder. I felt like a child afraid to sleep alone in a strange room because there might be monsters under the bed. Or in the closet or --

Well, hell. There might be monsters waiting to take me.

They brought Blue a chair. He sat down and leaned back looking at me.

"Go to sleep, Skye. Who knows when you'll get another chance."

I didn't want to sleep. I had come within a heartbeat of dying, and now I found myself afraid to close my eyes. Whatever magic had hit me, I was certain it would have killed the King of the Fae if I hadn't moved so quickly. I had done what was right.

They spoke out in the other room. I listened to Cherry and Darion, two calm voices and sometimes a little laughter. Better. Calm.

I slept, and even the nightmares didn't wake me again this time.

Day Three

Chapter Thirteen

"**S**kye?"

I moaned and turned my head, letting the blanket fall away from my face. Cherry stood by the bed, frowning. I wondered what the hell had gone wrong this time.

"Wha?" I asked. My mouth wouldn't work yet.

"The police want the two of us down at the station to talk to them. If we don't get there within the next hour, they may send someone out to pick us up. I have enough of a bad reputation with my neighbors already from trouble over the last few days."

"I want to kill someone. Is there someone I can kill, and sacrifice to the Gods of Night so I can sleep for a few hours?" I asked.

She gave me a little smile. I must have slept for a long

time since bright light came through the windows and I heard a bird singing by the window. Voices came from the other rooms. Darion stood across in the kitchen, and I saw Blue and then Sand pass by the door. Scents of food cooking filled the air.

I had slept in my clothes again. I was getting used to it, which saved all kinds of time and embarrassment with the middle of the night emergency visits from everyone and their dog. Hell, I looked forward to a visit from a dog about now -- something sane and not dangerous to walk up and knock on the door.

I grimaced when I stood and tried to brush wrinkles out of my clothing without using magic.

Cherry crossed to the closet and pulled out a few things. I ran a hand through my hair and grimaced again. "I want my life back. My calm and somewhat unique life where I only had to wonder if a fae would walk in and kill me."

"Here," she said, handing me a silky black shirt and blue pants. "Those should fit you. Take a quick shower and then we need to leave."

I nodded. Darion came to the door as I hobbled out, but I waved him away.

I would like to say I felt better after the shower, but I didn't spend enough time in there to recover. Knowing the police wanted to see us didn't help at all. I tried to do my best to stay clear of anyone in authority who might question who I am. What I am.

"We'll see you later," Blue said as we headed to the door. "A few of us are going back over the Veil to learn what the news is on the other side."

"Be careful," I said. I doubt they needed my warning, but I feared for them and their association with me.

"You be careful, too," Blue said. He patted my arm.

Darion drove us to the police station and even came inside with us. He looked the same to me, but I sensed a spell, like a thin cloak thrown over him.

The emotions in this place where dark and ugly, but there hadn't been much evil through today, so it wasn't too hard to ignore the feelings that touched me. Darion grimaced as well. Barber met us in the hall and didn't realize the stranger had been the best man at the wedding. He suggested Darion sit in the lobby and wait, and told him we wouldn't be long, which sounded promising.

He and Cherry had been holding hands. They let go with reluctance that they didn't feign. It was like walking around with a couple of kids having their first high school crush.

Barber led us to a private room; a table, no windows at all, but I sensed someone watching us. I did my best to look like a normal human. Right. That would work so well, a blond oriental of indeterminate gender. I almost felt sorry for Barber having to deal with us.

"Cherry Shen -- is your first name Chun?" he asked, looking down at a piece of paper.

"Oh yes," she said and gave a little laugh. "Everyone calls me Cherry. I don't get called Chun more than once a year, usually on Chinese New Year when I visit the Venerables."

"Venerables?" he said, looking back at her with a little curiosity.

"Grandparents. They were born in China -- mainland China -- escaped to Taiwan, and then to America." She leaned back in the chair. "Cherry suits me better. I'm not Old World."

He nodded and then looked at me "Skye, I'd like to ask

you a few more questions about your background."

I wondered what I would say if he asked about magic, but Detective Barber kept his feet firmly on the ground, and I suspected I could have conjured a unicorn in his office, and he'd have found a logical explanation for it. That made talking with him far less fraught with worries.

He rifled through a few papers. "Your records show you left home when you were sixteen, but we show no new address for you anywhere."

"I left the country with my father," I said. I'd gone through this story enough times to sound sincere. "We traveled in the far east."

"Why?"

"Because he liked to travel," I said and shrugged. "I came back after I came of age. I didn't like travel as much as he did."

"Were you ever formally schooled?"

Cherry looked at him, a little shocked by the words, and then she looked at me with equal surprise.

"No. I didn't go to public school. I was home-schooled by both parents."

"Your father is wealthy."

"I suppose so. But I haven't dealt with him since I came back."

"Not a pleasant parting?"

I shrugged. He wrote more down a note.

"Why did you become a detective?"

"Because I'm good at finding things. It's a puzzle. I like puzzles."

He frowned, jotting yet more notes. He looked up again, and this time didn't look away from my face as he spoke. "Lacey Weaver's disappearance is a puzzle."

"Oh yes. Very much one," I agreed. "I've found a

couple of runaway kids for their parents, but that's as far as I go into people hunting. I'm not stupid. I'm not going to get in the way. Have I so far?"

"No, but you did show up at the house right afterward."

"Only because I'm Cherry's cousin."

He looked at Cherry and then back at me. I saw calculation in his face.

"Do you have any reason to believe Cherry might be involved?" I asked.

Cherry yelped and shook her head, but Barber settled back in his chair and put down the pen before he shook his head. "No, we don't. We thought we did, right until the three of you showed up here. Someone reported that they saw Darion Wilding at Cherry's apartment and with her occasionally since the disappearance." I frowned. He mistook the look, though, for incomprehension -- but I wondered who had reported the sighting. It didn't sound like the police. Paul? He could have gotten all the information he needed from news reports. "Darion was the best man at the wedding."

"Ah. And you suspect him?"

"No. The guy you showed up with is not Darion --"

"Oh," Cherry said with a perfect look of surprise. "I guess they do look alike, don't they?"

Barber nodded, embarrassed. Cherry didn't like playing this game much, either. We went through with the rest and answered a few more questions, and Barber apologized for calling us to the station. I felt another twinge of remorse since technically he had been right.

He escorted us out into the hall, and we went out into the hall and back towards the lobby.

"We lied to the police," Cherry said in a soft whisper

but with a growing look of panic.

"It's all right," I reassured her. I didn't use magic to calm her. "There's no reason Barber will ever think twice about it."

"Except you are working on the case," she said, looking at me. I feared, for a moment, she would ask me to walk away from finding Lacey.

"Don't worry," I said again. I even smiled. "The police and I are not going to cross paths, Cherry. We're not working in the same circles. And I am operating in a way the police cannot."

"Oh. Oh." She grinned at me which helped since I didn't think that looking panicked as we left the detective's presence would be a good idea.

Darion met us in the lobby and took Cherry's hand. They walked out ahead of me, and I followed like a younger sibling dragged along on a date.

For a moment, I wondered if my parents had looked like the two of them; the short, oriental woman with her hand held tightly by the taller blond man. Had they been happy in those first days? I sure as hell hoped this didn't turn unpleasant for Cherry and Darion.

My mother often told me how Cedric had lied to her, or at least never told her the truth about his background and what he was until far too late. Cherry already knew.

We were in the parking ramp, heading for the car when blackness swept over me so quickly that I thought I'd passed out. . . .

CHAPTER FOURTEEN

I feared I might be dead. Blackness encased me, so complete that I no longer sensed where I was. Magic swept through me, and I passed out.

Time had passed, and now something jabbed me right in the middle of the back. I shouldn't feel anything if I were dead, especially something so annoying.

I tried to move. The thing became the toe of a boot which kicked this time. I grunted.

"It's awake already. The spell didn't hold long enough. Get this boat moving, idiot!"

"I hate this fucking magic crap. Why didn't she come over and grab it?"

"Get used working this way. We'll live with magic forever after this."

The sounds seemed to come from a great distance, muffled by the surrounding blackness, but at least the words sounded like more of an answer to the entire situation than I'd had found so far. I stayed still and listened.   They grumbled moaned and complained about the boat, the magic, and the work, but nothing made sense.

And they complained about her, but they did so in hushed tones. They never spoke her name and after about fifteen minutes I had the strangest feeling they couldn't say it, which would be magically enforced. I had to strain to hear their words, which kept me occupied and I worried less about where they were taking me.

The boat moved across water. I wondered how long I had been unconscious, and where my friends were this time. Why hadn't Darion found me? Were he and Cherry all right?

I sensed no magic through the blackness around me though the darkness wasn't natural. No one would find me in this fold of darkness. I felt somewhat like being at the Clan houses as though I was just a little removed from the world.

Hell. I had to escape and get back to my friends. I would not like where they took me.

Did they intend to drop me overboard into the lake? Could I get free of this thing and I push the black off before we got too far from the shore?

I shoved at it, my fingers something almost solid --

"Little animal is trying to get free. Give me the rod."

Something struck me across the right shoulder and the side of my head. The black didn't swallow pain along with magic, and I slipped into unconsciousness again.

The boat dipped and bounced, dipped and bounced. A frigid, damp wind blew over us, and rain fell in torrents, passing through the enshrouding blackness which had seemed substantial until now. They might not plan to throw me overboard, but since I found myself in a growing puddle of water, I'd drown anyway.

Water got into my nose and mouth. I coughed, trying to pull my head out of the water. Someone reached down and flipped me over on my back. That helped although the water still brushed up over my neck and fell across my face. I still saw nothing but black.

"Where the hell is the wall!"

"We're close. We'll be in soon."

Both voices sounded panicked. The boat lifted and hit the water with a bounce that would leave plank-sized bruises across my back, though I wouldn't notice with all my other bruises at this point. Darion, I hope to hell you have an idea of where I am because I don't have a clue!

I hit my head. Rainwater ran into my mouth. I choked.

And then we hit . . . calm.

"Shit. I feared we'd lost our way, or She had closed the way to us."

"She wouldn't. She wants this little creature."

"Huh." A boot jabbed at my thigh. I coughed again but got more air than water. The percentage wasn't much better, though, despite how the rain had suddenly stopped.

The boat hit something and stopped. I bumped my head on more wood and would have cursed, but my companions grabbed me by the arms and hauled me out of the boat. We had reached our destination.

I had trouble keeping my feet under me since the black still engulfed me. I couldn't quite figure out where to step as we started climbing the slippery stairs.

"We can't carry it up. We need the black off."

"She might not like it."

A pause. A touch of magic.

"She doesn't mind. Get it inside. She's waiting and

we're already late."

The idea of making her wait bothered them a great deal. The black disappeared, blinding me with light, even though I faced a gray, diffused day. I blinked and looked down since the two men started upward, and I didn't want to bang my shins against the stairs.

Carved stone stairs, I realized, and we climbed a cliff side. I lifted my head to look at the building before me. Huge, with white parapets and walls covered in ivy and moss. Ancient.

I should have asked someone how you work with a magical castle so old that it had become alive. Given my run of luck in this case, we all should have realized I'd be dealing with the place before too long.

Welcome to Whitestone. Damn, damn, damn. I looked around and found that the two burly men who had grabbed me were both human. I wouldn't have looked at them twice on a city street though I wouldn't have wanted to meet up with them in an alley. Human, without a hint of magic; the realization shocked me at first and then gave me my first real hope.

Whatever waited in that castle, I didn't want to face the trouble alone. And that meant now would be the time to get away. I tested my ability to move by pulling my arm away from the guy urging me up the stairs.

And the one behind me shoved a fist into my back. I fell forward, slid down a few stairs, and they grabbed my arms and dragged me upward again. My shins hurt. I got to my feet and walked on my own.

Probably not a wise idea, trying to fight on the stairs. Wait until I was inside the building. Yeah. They wouldn't expect trouble there.

As I came closer to the building, I felt a strange,

peaceful magic, as though Whitestone, though alive, slept and watched through dream eyes all that passed within view. Should I try to awaken the place like I had the plate?

That didn't sound wise at all. No. Better to get away. We went through an archway and into a courtyard. I remembered Darion telling me about the tournaments, and I imagined one here, with crowds along the walls, horses in the paddock, pennants . . . and for a moment I almost thought they were real as I heard the shouts and cries of the people.

"Damn, I wish it wouldn't do that. Like walking through ghosts. I hate this fucking place. Should have stayed in the city rather than come back."

"Yeah, right. Stayed and become one of the sheep."

"Or come here and be one of her slaves."

"Shut up!"

I heard the panic in his voice. Apparently it was unwise to talk about her that way. Their hands tightened around my arms, and they glanced about as though expecting trouble to leap from the walls.

I did my best to map out the features in those few minutes as we went up a flight of stairs and into the building proper. I found something surprising once we went through the immense wood door. The interior looked like a layout for Architectural Digest; sedate and in no way ancient. Glass covered the windows -- not the ripple of old glass, but clear, perfect modern glass. A loveseat, somewhat incongruous, sat where the person had a lovely view out over the water to the city skyline which stood clear despite the storm and rain. Magic, of course -- but I suspected the distance might be right.

Everyone had been looking all over hell -- or at least all over fae -- for this place. Maybe I should be amused. We never considered looking close to our shore.

We passed a latte machine with lovely bone white china cups lined up symmetrically around it. My. Someone liked their comforts and their show. I stumbled as we passed another window and managed to get them to go closer. The window did not look out over the courtyard. The walls dropped straight down to a thin, sandy shore where waves pounded with the surf brought up high from the storm.

"Hey, I heard that this one's got no balls," the man holding me said. He started to grope -- disgusting perverted bastards -- and I shied away.

"Ah, come on, animal," he jerked me back.

"Not even an animal," the other one said. "They got balls."

I straightened a little and met the second man's look. "I may not have any balls, but I know what they're good for."

He smirked.

And I kicked him right in the groin.

He howled and crumpled. The man holding me spun me around, his fist raised, his dark face almost purple with rage. I lifted my arm, made a fist and timed my blow as I mirrored his blow back to him.

Hurt like hell, both ways -- the hit and hitting. I feared I broke my hand, but the ploy worked. He slumped backward, his eyes rolling up, and almost pulled me down with him before his brain made his hand let go.

The other had struggled back to his feet and tried to grab me, but I managed a quick spell and the surge of magic to knock him down and hold him there. I knew damned few fae spells, but this one helped.

Voices grew louder as people came closer. I could see

only one way out that would be fast enough to get clear. I charged straight at the window, spreading a spear of power ahead of me as I leapt, glass shattering around me. In the next moment, I flew.

Too bad about that lack of wings.

I was heading either for a spectacular head landing or a body flop that would smash my chest against my spine. I used magic to break the fall and came down on my legs.

Pain shot up through my right ankle and knee. Broken bones beyond a doubt, somewhere in there.

Lightning rent the sky above me. The storm seemed to grow right over the castle, reflecting someone's anger.

"Kill it!"

A rifle fired. I wrapped magic around my leg and did my best to deaden the pain which proved difficult since magic creates pain for me. No matter. I had to get out of here. To the small row boat on the little dock just around the curve of the island --

I stumbled in that direction until a bullet slammed into the back of my right shoulder and sent me flying into the ground again. I didn't even feel the pain yet.

"Get it! Get it!"

I rolled over and saw a few figures leaned out the broken window. One had a rifle, and another waved arms and yelled. That would be her. I wished I could see the woman clearly.

I couldn't reach the boat, but I could reach the water. The lake stood only a few steps away. Better to go there, out of her immediate sight, and hope for something helpful to come along.

As I rolled, a bullet burrowed into the sand where my head had been and gave me more impetuous to move. I dropped the magic around my leg and threw up a shield which would not hold up for long. A couple of bullets bounced off it as I leapt straight into the water.

I lost the shield as I leapt -- fell -- into the lake. More bullets swept by and I watched the churning of the water where they passed me.

Damned cold water.

But I had survived to make it this far. I dropped under the surface and swam. Hell, at least I didn't have to worry about sharks attracted to the blood. I would have to stop the bleeding in my shoulder before I became any more light-headed.

Surfaced, breathed, and kept going. I had turned towards the boat, believing the craft was my only hope of escape. I needed something --

By the time I had gotten around to that side of the island, people stood everywhere on the dock. I had swum right up under the dock before I noticed.

"Blood!" someone shouted, the words muffled by the water as I came up beside the boat. "It's close by!"

Damn. Idiot. Of course she sent people here to watch.

I pushed myself back down under the water and mentally reached up to the bullet hole in my shoulder where I created a small, tiny spell to cover the wound and stop the bleeding. The magic still swept more fire though my battered body.

I should have walked away from this case when I could walk at all. The icy waters of the lake had numbed the problem, but it wasn't possible to forget since the broken leg dragged through the water. My arm didn't want to move now.

And I didn't want to die here.

Everyone moved above me, searching, searching. I

had slipped under the boat and watched the shadows of shapes moving nearby. Someone jumped into the boat. It rocked and hit me on the head.

I needed to breathe. I needed air.

People were looking, though, not with magic. She might be the only one with magic here. A fish swam close by, curious about me. I grabbed hold, wrapping my hands around the body while the startled creature squirmed. I mirrored the fish. Air. Air. I could breathe in this water. But the tiny fish didn't have enough air. Panicked fish. Calmed fish. Breathe. Remembered that fish breathe through movement. Swept the creature back and forth, frantic.

Air, air.

I grabbed a larger fish. Helped a little, but I saw stars in front of my eyes. Did I want to die here or at their hands? Here. Drown rather than go to her.

The boat moved, dipping and bouncing again. People left the dock. I watched the movement, shadows becoming less distinct. People walked out towards the shore, still looking -- but not here.

I came up on the far side of the boat. The raging storm, which reflected her anger, covered me as I gasped for breath. I let the startled fish go.

"Must 'a got swept out," someone said. "She is not happy."

"Hell. I never expected something like that from the thing. Small, easy to take. Just goes to show you. I didn't even realize it had magic since it used none until then."

"You think she'll accept that answer? I don't want to be in your shoes. You ought to just throw yourself into the water and swim, Larry."

"I can't swim."

"All the better, 'cause you don't want to survive to face her anyway."

"Shit. I want it!"

"She's calling us back. Too late."

A spell dragged them back to the castle, the powerful magic sweeping everyone up into her will. Hell, I would have followed right to my death if I hadn't been so weak. Larry headed to his execution or maybe something even worse. I didn't exactly care right then.

Waiting in the water, holding on to the patch on my shoulder, was my only hope of survival since I'd already lost too much blood. I used the numbness of the cold water to help with my leg and did a quick, single surge of magic that snapped bones back into place and sealed them together. Not the best healing job either, and the doubled pain made everything go red for a moment, but I got the job done.

I did not intend to die here. All I had to do was get back to the city. The storm raged on around me, but I wanted to go there.

I pushed away from the boat, swam two strokes, and then shook my head in dismay. No, not swim, idiot.

I dipped back to the boat and grabbed hold of the side. The glorified rowboat, laden with magic, was the only craft on the dock. If I took it, would I trap those bastard humans here? Maybe. But the humans -- despite my battered body to the contrary -- were not the ones that caused me the most worry.

I pulled myself up to the side of the boat and looked inside and remembering all the bruises those planks had given me.

Should never have gotten involved with anything fae-related. Damn, Darion. Where the hell are you? I need help!

I had almost pulled myself up into the boat when I realized the magic surrounding the boat and tying it to the dock would make it impossible for me to take. What magic I had left couldn't wrest the craft out of the Lady of the Castle's hold and get me back to the distant city.

Swim after all.

But I wouldn't get there before I bled to death. And besides, the storm grew worse while I held to the boat's side. Was that intentional? She suspected I still lived.

I had no choice but to try to swim back to the city.

But I didn't want to die.

Nowhere else to go.

Unless. . . .

Unless I was very daring.

I looked back at the castle. No one stood between me and the tall building. Going up the stairs might be suicidal, though. And if I wanted a suicidal end, I might as well swim away.

Could I reach the broken window? I didn't think she had fixed it yet. The old castle had a covering of ivy and with a little magic of my own, I could climb.

I swam back the way I had come, all the time telling myself I was a fool to consider this idea. But she loved her comforts, and a full, modern bathroom would be a necessity.

My leg sent sharp pains up through my hip as I pulled myself up out of the icy lake since the broken bones were far from healed. As I moved, I feared bone shards might have torn into the muscles, and I had to keep myself from cursing at every step. I had heard no one since she called them inside, but it didn't make me safer, especially since I had headed right into the lair of the enemy again.

I stumbled over to the castle and grabbed hold of a

strand of ivy, but I feared if I climbed, tear part of the plant out of the wall. The ivy had been here for a damned long time, and that seemed an unfair treatment of something which had survived far more than this little storm of my life.

I like plants, and I feared my magic wouldn't keep it safe from being torn out. I started to look back toward the stairs again . . . and the plant changed. It grew sturdy enough to take my weight without help from my weakening magic. I brushed my fingers against the leaves, wondering why it had chosen to help me.

Old plant; magical island and castle. The ivy understood what it did and why. A long time had passed since anyone even noticed the plant. The ivy didn't care about good or evil in human terms. The world revolved around sunlight, rain on the leaves, and basking in life.

And because I took notice and cared if I damaged a strand or two, the ivy liked me. I thanked it with a whisper of words and climbed upwards. Strands reshaped where my foot needed to go and a tendril wrapped around my arm when I slipped.

I found the broken window and climbed in over the jagged edges of the glass, cutting my hand. There I stopped, insane as it was, and leaned back out to pat the plant and wish him well and a long, long life.

And the ivy gave me a gift. A piece of vine wrapped up around my wrist and released from the castle. I felt like a kitten had just latched on to me.

Where to go? I didn't want to use any questing magic here and risk awakening Whitestone as I had the dish. She would be attuned to the building.

I headed down the corridor for no particular reason until I realized I had touched on the emotions of others.

Weaker, frantic, and trapped.

I had found our missing fae.

And I was not stupid. I didn't even consider rescuing them, single-handed, with a bullet in my shoulder and the grinding of bone-against-bone in my leg. Hell. Where should I head?

A door stood on the right just ahead of me. I peeked in and sighed with relief to find a bathroom. Sometimes you get lucky. I stepped inside, looked at the too small mirror over the sink and cursed as I turned to leave the room. A full-length mirror covered the door.

The Gods were on my side.

I had a brief glimpse of myself as I touched the surface. I looked like hell again. Not a surprise. Blond hair, dripping wet, fell across my face and my green eyes and tan skin both looking bruised. I saw blood on the front of my shirt and realized the magical patch in my shoulder had come loose.

Time to go.

The surface of the mirror rippled with a hint of green along the edges and revealing the path I wanted. As I reached forward, the plant on my arm reached as well as though sensing something it wanted to touch far more than it wanted to be with me.

Shouts. I reached over and locked the door, as though that would help, and tried not to lose my hold on the link. The little vine helped, anchoring itself to the path.

I heard the sounds of running feet in the corridor and shouting voices. "I can sense the magic!"

She was close. I needed to get away. Concentrate.

The path steadied. I reached into the glass and pulled the green closer. I needed the link to stay calm and steady.

Go where?

Hell, hell.

The path faded. Panicked, I pulled the link back again. And this time, it came powerful and steady just as someone tried the door.

"Here!"

I stepped forward as the person on the other side of the door shoved it open, propelling me through the mirror and into the path.

I shut the gate behind me.

CHAPTER FIFTEEN

I stood alone in the familiar world of swirling green, but this time with no clear path to anywhere else. At least I had gotten away from her. I needed to go . . . go home to my apartment and. . . .

Why would I head there as though I believed myself somehow safe if I reached home base? This was no child's game. Think clearly, damn it. Think clearly. The others would look in my home first!

Mirrors. I knew mirrors in rooms outside my home. What ones had I seen recently?

The one in Lacey's room was the last I had last seen. I reached for that location and then stopped. What if Mrs. Weaver didn't happen upon me? Did I want to fall into the house of the man people said would be the next president -- the one with the missing daughter? Drop in there, battered and shot?

No.

My mind swarmed with pain and the path hazed

around me, like swirling green storm clouds. I wanted to sit down and make everything be still. I needed rest.

Ah. Yes. I needed a place of rest.

I visualized Cherry's bathroom and the mirror on the wall. People would look at her apartment, but Darion would have protection around her. I wouldn't be alone if I went there. Blue and the others might even still be there.

I could get to Cherry's place, partly because of the mirror, but also because my cousin was there, which helped, the extra draw of blood-to-blood. I might have lost focus for a little while, but that didn't matter if I kept moving.

I wanted to rest.

I sat down amid the green light. My shoulder bled, and I thought I should let go. No one would find me here before I died. No doctors in white coats and masks. No chubs. She wouldn't hunt me down to drag me away from here.

Green movement, swirling, bright: a hand reached for me. No face and yet the Guardian watched me. I smiled. I didn't hurt as much since I had stopped moving. Or maybe I didn't ache so much because I had stopped caring. If I let go, I didn't have to use the fire of magic to hold myself together. My body had relaxed; the pains of broken bones or even bullets didn't compare to the agony of using magic to get this far.

The hand still reached. I gently disengaged the vine from my wrist and held the plant up to her as a parting gift. The ivy was happy here, as though the plant had come back to a primal source of all plants, and perhaps all life. The vine released me and curled around the Guardian. She held the gift to her heart -- if she had such a thing. She made me smile, reminding me of a child with a kitten.

I closed my eyes.

And she gathered me into her embrace and stood. I almost protested, but I hadn't the strength. Besides, I remembered that if I survived, I could help Darion by telling him where to find the others. That would count for something.

"Cherry's home," I whispered, hoping she heard and understood. I tried to open my eyes, but I hadn't the strength.

We just moved and moved and . . . stopped.

She put me down on my feet. I felt stronger and braced my weak leg before I fell. We stood before Cherry's bathroom. The Guardian nudged me forward. I put one foot down on the bathroom floor, and it went out from under me, and I crashed down to my knees with a gasp of pain as I hit my head on the vanity. I knelt there, bleeding all over Cherry's tile floor. That bothered me.

And then I heard Cherry talking to someone. I struggled to my feet, holding tight to the doorknob, and pulled it open so I could lean against the doorframe and listen. Please let it be Darion.

"No, mama. I don't watch the news at all. I don't want to know what they're saying about Lacey." A pause. The clank of metal against metal, a splash of water. "Mrs. Weaver will call if they find her. Yes, really. Yes, I know her that well."

Splash, clank, splash.

"Uh huh."

Clank, clank.

She stood at the sink, washing dishes and talking on the phone which she held in place with a raised shoulder. The sight made me giddy with relief, which didn't help since I was already lightheaded from the injuries. I could step out there, draw her attention, and not have to worry about how we explained my presence and condition to anyone else. No fae here either.

"I don't like reporters," Cherry said with a hint of anger in her voice. "But I got lucky, and they've left me alone."

Splash.

If I stood leaning against the bathroom door long enough, I would bleed to death, which seemed stupid, considering all the work to get here. So I pushed away, and with a hand to my aching shoulder, I forced myself to keep heading towards the kitchen.

"I don't care about free publicity since I have more work than I can handle. I -- Holy shit!"

The phone dropped into a sink full of soap and water.

"I don't think you're supposed to wash them that way," I said.

"God in heaven, Skye! Shit. You're hurt! Sit down!"

She reached into the water and pulled the phone back out, shaking it. "Mama? You there? Barely. I dropped the phone in the sink water. I better go. I'm tired. Talk to you tomorrow. Yeah. Be good!"

She hung the phone up and threw it down on the counter and grabbed dish towels from the rack by the sink.

"I'm bleeding," I said, trying to wave her away as I caught hold of a kitchen chair. She maneuvered me down into the seat. "You don't want to use good towels --"

"Shush. Don't worry about the damn towels. Where are you bleeding? I can't tell. There's blood all over your back. What the hell --"

"Shot," I said, and caught my breath as she probed at the shoulder.

She stopped. I heard her breath catch. "Shot? Like

with a gun?"

"Rifle, I think. Marksman. What happened? I don't know how I got there."

"Someone grabbed you in the parking lot. Remember that?"

"Kind of." I leaned forward on my left arm, the right hanging down, blood dripping to the floor. My head pounded. Cold, shock -- fear. I couldn't speak for a moment, trying to decide what to do.

"Darion said humans took you," she said and sounded frantic. She tried to dab at the wound, and I tried not to shudder at her touch. "That's why he never sensed them coming. They used magic, but it was like a bag. You disappeared into it. We need to get you help. I'll call -"

I sat up and grabbed her arm before she moved away. "I cannot go to a human hospital, Cherry. You don't want me to go there."

She shivered, her eyes got wide, and her mouth clamped shut. She took a few breaths, her nose flaring before she spoke again.

"I don't want you to die here, Skye. Can't you do something?"

"I -- I might now that I'm no longer worried about someone else . . . killing me." I had started to drift there for a moment, just talking to her. Closing my eyes, I searched out the bullet with my magic, but as I touched the area the pain tripled, and my overwhelming weakness came close to killing me right then. I fell forward, and she caught me. Her eyes filled with tears. Fear came in the trembling touch of her hand, and I had trouble not mirroring since her emotions blended so well with mine. I feared if I didn't keep control over myself, I might do something really stupid.

"I can't go to the hospital," I repeated though I had trouble tracking the words now. "Darion. Where is Darion?"

"I don't know, but I thought he had the place under watch so he would know --"

"Ward the door." The few steps looked like a hell of a long hike across the room. "He can probably feel portals, too, but I came through the mirror."

"How can we reach him?" she asked, still trembling.

"Help me up. Let's go out the door and back in. If I can set off an alarm --"

"Yeah. Put your arm over my shoulder. Can you stand at all?"

"Barely. They took me to the castle, Cherry. I know where to find it. I think the others are there, the ones who had gone missing. We need Darion."

"We'll get him here. Come on."

I would never have walked to the front door on my own. The room melted and moved around me in a haze of blood and pain, and Cherry carried me by the time we reached the front door.

I could feel each labored beat of my heart. The air from the open door -- night outside -- damn long day -- blew across me with the chill of ice. Cherry got me out. She even closed the door. Did the police still watch? Not after having decided Darion wasn't the person who had turned up here.

Cherry somehow kept me to my feet, and I fought to stay conscious and hold the pain at bay. I wanted to slide down into the puddle of water on the steps. I wanted just to go away, but Cherry would not let go of me.

"You better open the door, Skye. Use a little magic when you do it. Can you do that?"

"I want to rest now," I said. I wanted to sit down here in the rain and wind despite the cold.

"Open the door, Skye. Open it now."

I sighed and reached out, sensing the touch of magic in the knob, and the power of the ward around the apartment. Darion's work. Darion liked her. He would keep Cherry safe --

"Skye, please."

I turned the knob and pushed the door open. Cherry pushed it the rest of the way with her foot, nearly losing her balance. I heard the pounding of footsteps up the stairs.

Only it wasn't Darion.

Paul had returned.

"What the hell is going on here!" he demanded. "What are you into, Cherry? You keep shoving me away for this -- is he shot? Are you dealing drugs, freak?"

Paul made the mistake of reaching for me. I'd had enough of rude, cruel people for one day, and while my mind tried to temper my instincts when he caught hold of my wounded shoulder and tried to spin me around, I reacted.

Magically.

He landed against the door frame. If he had been standing in the other direction, he would have gone flying over the banister to land in the parking lot. I might have killed him, but the realization didn't temper my feelings.

"Don't touch me," I said. Anger welled up, and magic played around my hand, green light like tame fireflies. "Don't come near Cherry or me again."

He struggled back to his feet, and I could smell his fear now. "Devils. Devils and drug dealers and --"

I nearly pulled away from Cherry to go after him. I wanted something to fight, even in those last moments when my body and soul might tear apart. The last magic had almost killed me, and yet I kept the power flickering in my hand. Mirror -- he wanted to fight. He wanted to hurt and kill and even in the depths of abject terror, those other emotions still came stronger.

But when I brushed the magic towards him, he fled.

"Well, hell," Cherry said. "I suspect he won't be coming back this time, but you know . . . I think I'm going to move."

"Sorry," I said, as she got me inside again. She kicked the door closed. We reached the kitchen chair, and the cat came and climbed into my lap. "Sorry. Shouldn't have. Magic. Shouldn't --"

"You did fine. He was out of control, Skye and we didn't need him here tonight. God, I need to try to stop the bleeding. I don't know how long Darion will take --"

But Blue arrived in a swirl of color and the scent of apples and roses -- good, pure magic. Cherry yelped and leapt backward.

"Damn!" Blue pulled me down onto the floor, stretched out on my stomach, which hurt like hell. I wanted to curl up into a ball and . . . sleep.

"Stay with me, Skye." Blue's magic played across my back, and down the wound. "We need Darion here, fast. I can't do this one alone!"

"Where is he?"

"Off at Williams' house." He paused. "There. I sent him word. He had to make an appearance if just for the sake of show since having him disappear now would cause problems. And he wondered if there might be more answers at the Weavers."

"I should have gone there," I mumbled. "I would have been closer to him."

Or maybe I didn't say the words aloud. I had no strength left.

"I've slowed the bleeding," Blue whispered.   "The bullet has to come out.   It's torn the hell out of his shoulder. Did Skye say anything?"

"She said she'd been to the castle."

"Did he? Damn. Darion!" And more magic went out -- a frantic message. "If not Darion, who else can I get? Ambassador Peren. Maybe --"

"Is there anything I can do?" Cherry asked the fear growing in her voice.

"Hold on to his hand," Blue said. He brushed his fingers over the back of my head, a gentle touch as though he wanted me to know he cared. And then he sent out a message again. "Darion -- Darion, get here now!"

Cherry sat on the floor and took hold of my hand. Blue's magic surged up over me again, but I sensed he had spent every bit of strength he had. "Sand," he whispered. "I need help."

I heard a sound of worry and new magic added to the flickering power Blue still used.

"What the hell happened," Sand asked. "That bullet -- it has magic."

"I know. It's why I can't get it. Darion will have better -- ah. Here he comes. Praise the Goddess. I don't think we can keep him alive much longer."

Like listening to a radio program or a television show in another room: I was not part of the scene. My body had gone numb which might have been Blue's work. I wanted to thank him.

Darion arrived. Good. "I'm sorry. The alarm went off, but I didn't realize -- I felt Paul and thought Blue must have -- oh hell!"

Magic swept in over me. Warmth. Life. I gasped for breath and wished I'd stayed numb for a while longer. It hurt to breathe, to move, even to think.

"Take little breaths, Skye. Easy. I'll get the bullet out. Blue, call in Star and as many of the others as you can. Right now. I don't care what they're doing or who they are with."

"Yes, sir," Blue said, his voice shaky.

I had not heard Darion sound like someone of power until now. How odd. Darion touched the back of my head, and magic moved in as he placed a shield between my head and my body. I could barely breathe, but I could think.

"I was at the castle, Darion," I said. My voice sounded soft and hoarse.

"Quiet. Not yet. Be still."

"No. Listen. It's just off the shore in the lake. Probably no more than ten miles. It's not in Fae at all."

"Ah. Yes. Thank you. Now be still."

"The others were there. I couldn't get to them. I'm sorry."

"You did well, Skye." For a moment, he brushed his hand over the back of my head with the same gentle calming touch Blue had used, and I relaxed again.

I had told him something important, in case I didn't survive. I had the very distinct impression that I might not.

People arrived and went right to work though Cherry never let go of my hand. Magic whispered through my body. Star said something about a broken leg.

"If he were full fae this wouldn't be a problem," Blue explained to Cherry. "But this is harder because the magic doesn't work with same."

Good he told her because I didn't know. Something

moved like an uncomfortable pressure inside my shoulder, probing around in there for the bullet. Even with all the other deadening I suffered a new jolt of pain when Darion located it.

"Sorry, Skye. But I have the bullet now. I'll do this quickly."

He pulled the bullet back on the track it had taken in, tearing along the same flesh and muscle. I felt other magic follow behind, healing the bloody path. The bullet must have impacted the shoulder bone because I felt a deep, bone ache of something broken. I wanted the numbness back.

"Okay. Let me seal this wound. We got it, Cherry. With the bullet out, we can repair the damage. The damned thing had a spell to do worse damage to anyone with magic."

"She wanted me dead," I whispered.

"She? She who?" Darion said, suddenly interested in what I had to say.

"Don't know her name, anything about her. Only saw her at the window when I jumped out."

"That how you broke your leg?" Star asked. Her hands were on the leg, repairing the damage there.

"Yes."

"And you swam back like this?" Darion asked. He must have finished his part of the work. The others carried me to the sofa. My place. My pillow and blankets.

"No. Didn't swim. Wouldn't have survived. I climbed back into the castle and found a mirror."

"You leapt out a window and then climbed back in," Cherry said.

I nodded. I wanted to explain more, but no one else asked. Maybe what I said had made sense. I feared, though, that this was just something they expected from me.

"We need to get people working on what Skye found," Darion said as he stepped back from the sofa. He looked pale, shaken, and furious. "I will put more protection on the apartment, Cherry and a key specifically to Skye. Skye will sleep for several hours, and I'll be back as soon as I can. I need . . . Damn, I need my people, Cherry."

"Go. Take them. We'll be fine as long as you've left us some protection and can get back soon if we need you. Is there a way I can reach you if Skye needs help?"

"Yes. Call my name three times," he said. I saw him put his hand on her forehead and set a spell there. Then Darion reached down and touched the side of my face, his fingers cool. I blinked up at him.

"Be careful. Be still. I'm sorry I can't stay with you right now and protect you, but I'll be back in a heartbeat if anything goes wrong again. I promise you. We just to go now."

"The island will move," I said, understanding. "She has it shielded, or people would have noticed. I should have asked how to deal with the castle."

He blinked and then shook his head. "I suspect no one knows the answer. Whitestone is unique. Like you."

"Huh."

But he looked down at me again as though what he had said meant something important. Then he lifted a hand and signaled his people, and the group of them stepped away -- and disappeared.

Being here with no immediate protection, no matter how fast they got back, worried me. I didn't want to sleep, fearing what would happen to me, to Cherry, even to the cat who climbed up to nestle under my blanket.

"Hey," Cherry said and reached for her.

"No, please. She's alive. She's warm."

"Ah." Cherry looked at me with her head tilted much the same way Darion had watched me. I wondered what they suddenly saw in me. "Do you want anything to eat?"

"No. Just sleep."

She nodded and slipped away. I closed my eyes, my hand still resting on the warm fur of the cat. She purred, moved to get more comfortable and then gave up, much as I did.

I didn't sleep, at least not right away. I considered the problems which might follow me. Even though I knew it unwise, I still reached out with a tendril of magic despite the pain. I looked for trouble. Trouble would come for me --

I found it and far too close.

This wasn't magic trouble. I found Paul, still lingering out by the parking lot, huddled in the bushes like an animal. I wouldn't even have noticed, except a little of my magic still clung to him, drawing my attention.

His rage far outweighed his fear, even after what he had experienced with me. His emotions were extremely . . . bad. He wanted Cherry. Wanted to possess her as he did everything else in his life. Not just to share moments with her, but to control everything in her life. The idea she spent time with people he didn't even know enraged him.

He had learned to dull those kinds of feelings with liquor.

And we had taken the ability to get drunk away from him.

The sexual overtones in his aura made me half sick. I had brushed up against those feelings before when I had first learned to use my magic, back on the streets. What people like him experienced never came close to love though Paul didn't realize the difference.

"Skye, are you all right?" Cherry asked. Her hand brushed against the side of my face, and I blinked at her, trying to hold my focus on Paul. I didn't want to lose him. I didn't trust him. "Skye?"

"Better," I said, but she still stared at me. "I checked and found Paul is still outside, hiding in the bushes. He's not going away."

"Hell." She shook her head in dismay and then looked towards the door. Her stare changed to one of determination. "Rest, Skye. I can handle this trouble all on my own."

She crossed the room, though not toward the door, so she didn't intend to confront him. Good. Instead, I heard her on the phone though I didn't listen. I lingered with Paul instead. Paul had started back towards the apartment building. Paul had a weapon.

I started to sit up, but the pain knocked me back to the pillows. I laid there on the sofa, gasping and hoping I hadn't done any damage, and tracking Paul as he headed our way. What could I do -

I heard the sudden spurt of a siren and saw the flash of red light at the window as a police car arrived. Cherry went to the door and watched. A police officer came that far, but lucky for me, he didn't come inside the apartment. There might still have been blood on the floor, and with me shot -- using magic to fix that mess might have killed me tonight.

"We got him, Miss," the cop said. "And he's put up a fight. We found a gun on him. It's a good thing you called."

She spoke with the police officer, and while they

talked, I planted trouble for Paul, though just the whisper of Paul as a dangerous stalker whom they needed to watch.

Paul wouldn't be coming back here. I had done something that would help, and Paul wouldn't even be hurt in the process, except what he brought on himself.

When the door closed, I drifted off to a troubled sleep.

Cherry went to work cleaning up the path of blood I'd left from the bathroom through her house. I existed in a state of half-sleep while my body, imbued with what magic the others had left in me, continued to heal at a rate that took away almost as much as it gave. The spells would still help, in the end, and I didn't fight the magic despite the needles of pain. I would survive this night, and the realization gave me hope again.

I might yet help in the battle and find Lacey. We had lost nothing, yet.

CHAPTER SIXTEEN

I am destined never to sleep for long at Cherry's apartment. I realized this when I awoke to the sound of someone jangling keys outside the door. The person turned the lock and walked into the room. It hurt to move, but I had my hand raised, and I would have used whatever power I had left on the intruder --

An oriental woman stood inside the door. She looked younger than Cherry, with the same shape and build. I hadn't seen Mei in years, but I still recognized Cherry's sister. I eased myself back down on the sofa, taking short breaths and trying to make certain my head didn't explode.

Mei had never been my favorite of the three daughters. Even the few times I had met her when we were younger, she had seemed pretentious and annoying. I didn't want to face that kind of interaction now.

"So, I find you scrubbing floors on a Saturday night? You have less of a life than I do."

"Not tonight, Mei, please," Cherry whispered. "I need

time alone."

"Hey, what's wrong?"

Mei came into the room, swung her purse around the sofa and just about dropped the thing straight on my chest. Cherry leapt to her feet and caught the bag in mid-air.

Mei looked down, frowning. "Hell. I didn't -- Damn! Skye!"

The smell of stale beer and the haze of a drunken glow in her glare didn't make her any more likable.

"You know I've had contact with Skye," Cherry replied and reached over to put a hand on my arm, looking protective. Mei might not be my friend, and I couldn't guess why.

Her dark eyes narrowed, and a little color came to her cheeks. "I didn't realize she lived with you."

"She doesn't. Skye is ill, and I didn't want her staying alone at her place. So we opted on here. Now, you want to leave so she can sleep?"

Mei looked down at me and frowned a little. "What is it? The flu? Or withdrawal?"

I heard more than a slight hint of maliciousness in the words. I couldn't guess what she wanted or what she wanted or what she expected me to do, not even with a touch of mirroring. Mei didn't know what she wanted, either, and that her anger was habitual and not aimed at me.

She wasn't like Li, the youngest of the three sisters. Li had been wild and stupid until the night she almost died. I'd saved her life, and though she accepted what I did, she had avoided me afterward. Cherry seemed to enjoy the idea of magic and things in the world that she didn't understand.

But Mei? I sensed nothing but an odd dislike of everything from Mei. She felt constant irritation because others had things she didn't. She knew Cherry cheated, somehow.

I found the word I needed when I looked into her face again: envy. The emotion ruled in every cell of her body. She hated that Cherry did so well, lived here in a pleasant apartment, had a good business and nice rich boyfriends.

All those feelings came to me in a couple of eye blinks. I understood her far better than she would ever understand herself. Mei didn't have a blind spot but rather a purposeful attempt to be as bad-tempered as she liked and never had to take the blame.

I wondered how Cherry kept her temper with Mei's obvious bad manners.

"Skye needs rest, Mei." Cherry took her sister by the arm and pulled her towards the door. "Is there a reason you came by?"

"I didn't think you would be here, Saturday night and all. Doug and the kids are having a screaming match at home. I needed a little quiet time. But obviously, you need to help Skye more."

"Mei, I don't mind if you stay," she said, but she lied. "It's just been a long couple of days. Paul turned psycho, and I had to call the cops. I want quiet."

"Paul, psycho? Huh. Wonder how you pushed him into that one. He's such a great guy."

"Yeah, right." Her voice went hard, and even Mei knew she'd stepped over the line. "Visit a friend. Or go driving. I'll tell you when Skye goes back home."

Out the door and closed.

I sat up, trying not to gasp. "I'm sorry."

"You have absolutely no reason to be sorry, Skye. Mei is a bitch. She made an unhappy marriage, and she wants the rest of us to be just as unhappy along with her. Well, there are nights when I won't sit here while she drinks my beer, gets weepy and accuses me of creating all her problems."

"You?" I asked, trying to understand the dynamics. I grabbed at the sofa back.

"Rest while you can, Skye." She came around and sat on the chair. I settled against the pillow and turned my head, more awake and alive, if not better.

"Tell me about your family," I said. "My mother made certain I wasn't around any of my relatives often and never alone."

"She used to come over to the house all the time, but she always left you elsewhere. I wanted her to bring you too. I wanted to talk to someone who was not my little sister, especially when we were in our teens. You were exotic, and I imagined you knew a lot more about life than I did."

"Life, as in sex," I said.

"Yeah. Funny how that turned out," she replied with a laugh.

And I grinned, too.

"Li is the youngest, and she grew up wild. I think mama and papa were both tired by the time she came along. They expected her to be a typical kid, and I believe she was, in a truly American way. They didn't expect the sudden change with the tattoos, drinking, and smoking."

"Why did she do it?"

"Because she was the youngest and because she has the type of personality that has to outdo everyone else. She never believed anything could hurt her. It's dangerous to be that kind of kid, you know." She stopped and shook her head, and I imagined she remembered the night Li nearly died, and I saved her. "Mei, though . . . Mei never did anything outlandish. She never took a chance at life at all,

Skye. And now she's tied down with a loser husband and three small children, and she wants to fly. Only it's way too late, so she's looking for people to blame."

"Like you."

"Yeah. She told me I should have stopped her from marrying Doug. She says it was my responsibility since I had dated Doug --"

"But that's the reason she wanted him. Because you had dated him and she wanted to one up you -- and couldn't do it without 'stealing' something of yours."

"Oh, you hit that one right on the head," Cherry agreed. "You must be a good detective. Are you always good at seeing human motivations?"

"I've spent my whole life trying to figure out humans." I almost shrugged and stopped just in time. My shoulder hurt even when I breathed. "I wanted to understand. I still do. There is so much people do that I can't begin to comprehend, and little of it has to do with sex."

"Have you ever been in love?" she asked, her head tilted.

"That's not something I can experience --"

"Bullshit. Love has nothing to do with sex." She looked into my face and nodded at whatever she saw there. "You have been in love."

"I have loved someone, but I kept the feelings to myself. We would meet for coffee and gossiped about our neighbors. She moved away to California and married, but she still writes me sometimes."

"That's sad," Cherry said. "I understand, but it's still sad. This discussion doesn't help me with my decision about Darion though. I like him, but I'm not sure where we're going."

"I can tell you this: If you want someone who will

stand by you for the rest of your life, and be there for you when you need him -- yes, Darion is the one. If you want someone to grow old with . . . no. He can't do that."

She nodded. "I hadn't considered the aging part. Sometimes he seems older than he looks, but I thought that came from his position with the clan."

"I suspect time and age don't equate much to the fae."

She sat back in her chair. Outside a siren wailed by the apartment and I wished everyone involved well. We didn't need more trouble in the city from any source.

"I like Darion," she said, as though she only now realized. "So I'll see where this takes us for a while. Besides, I don't think either of us wants anything permanent."

"Always wise to know what you both want going into a relationship," I said. Then I shrugged, regretted it, and grimaced. "But then, what do I know?"

So we talked about family for a while instead. The discussion helped her get a few things out of her system. Cherry had no one to turn to about her problems with Mei and Li. And as the oldest sister, she seemed to take their problems far too personally.

"Dad's oblivious, but then he always has been. He has the grocery business, and the store is still his whole world. He's so proud of that place. I'd still be envious of the store if I didn't have my own business and understand now."

"You envied the store when you were younger?"

"Yeah." She looked embarrassed. "I felt towards it the way others feel about an older sibling. Dad always talked about the store doing this, the store doing that. You wanted to be The Store, just to get some of that praise."

"And that's why you went into a food-related business? To get his attention?"

"That is what first drew me, but it's not why I've done so well."

"You have to truly love what you do to be this good at the work."

She smiled as though I had just given her a shiny new present. "Yes, you're right. I love my job. And now dad and I have more to talk about than we ever did before."

"And your mother?"

"She's tired of listening to Mei's problems and Li just scares the hell out of her. She and I can have calm, sedate conversations about housekeeping and cooking that aren't fraught with end-of-the-world or my-life-is-ruined overtones. My sisters' lives are one drama after another. I'm the calm, quiet, proper one."

"With a fae boyfriend and caught up in a drama which may change the world."

She looked startled and then laughed again. "You're right. Hell. Do you want something to eat? To drink?"

"Some tea would be nice," I said.

She went off to make tea. Cherry liked helping people; so much so, she hadn't looked at the larger picture of what had been happening around her.

While she made the tea, I tested my body's limitations by trying to sit up once more. I felt a dull ache of anxiousness -- the kind I always got before something important happens. Given the circumstances of my disappearance and return, I knew a lot of magic filled the air tonight. I didn't want to wait, helpless on the sofa, for something to find me. I still wasn't certain who to count as my friends or my enemies.

It hurt like hell to move, but I had expected the pain. I had even gotten used to it, which annoyed me. I sat with my bruised back against the couch cushions and my arm resting in my lap.

Then I had the clarity of thought to wonder why she had sent her little human minions to grab me. Why hadn't I considered that part until now? If she wanted me --

"You look worried," Cherry said. She put the cup on the table beside me. "What's wrong?"

"I shouldn't be here, Cherry. I have someone very dangerous after me, and I don't even know why --"

"If you try to leave, I'll knock you down and sit on you. Or have Yo-Yo do it. You aren't strong enough to outfight the cat."

"Cherry --"

"There is nowhere else you'll be safer, Skye. Darion made certain no one can easily get in here. He already said you faced danger and offered to take you back to Sapphire House, but we both agreed you might not be safe so close to those who already tried to kill you once, especially since most of the people of Sapphire House are out looking into the trouble."

I couldn't argue with the logic. And abandoning Cherry would not make her safer. So I nodded and picked up the cup of tea, which made her happier.

"Do you see my mother often?" I asked mentioning the one family member we had skirted around for the entire conversation.

"Sometimes, at family gatherings when she brings your sisters and brother --"

"Brother?" I said, my head coming up with a start.

"Oh. I hadn't realized -- sorry. Kelly, Mary, Veronica and Ian the Third. Veronica was born after you left. She's nearly nine. Ian is seven. Not bad kids. But I realized there was something perversely wrong when the moment you left, she brought the others around."

I had never considered there would be other children and had a hard time getting my mind around that concept of more siblings. Human siblings. I had gotten along well with Kelly, who was nine when I left. Mary had been two. Cherry, seeing my discomfort, changed the subject back to the family store and her home life. I didn't ask about my mother again.

Sirens swept past the building and faded away into the distance once again. The night had turned cold, late and quiet. The prickling worry and anxiety which had gotten me to sit up remained, gnawing at me. I wanted to pace now and refrained. Something was not right.

"I wish I knew what's going on out there," I said with a wave of my hand, which was almost steady. "I hope they found the island and are settling everything, but there is something in the air I don't like."

Cherry watched me and then gave a decisive nod. " I want to make cookies. Want to sit out in the kitchen with me?"

"Yes, thank you. I'm better than I was now that the magic has worked for a while. Darion made certain I'll heal well."

"He said not to be surprised. I'm relieved."

"Me, too."

She still had to help me out into the kitchen and to the chair. My leg hurt when I put any weight on it. I didn't get dizzy; I might be up to a tussle with the cat by now. Cherry brought me a different shirt and helped me get dressed. I apologized for having ruined her clothing. She shook her head and patted my arm.

I watched Cherry go to work. She had an amazing ability to open cabinets and pull out exactly what she needed. I stared in utter amazement as the ingredients for oatmeal spice cookies filled the counter before her.

"I wouldn't have even found the cookbook yet," I said.

She laughed. "I cook to help me through any worries since I calm down."

"I play my harp," I said and grinned at her look. "Yes, I know. Fae, harp, cliche. But the music helps."

She laughed. "Are you any good?"

I started to say no, but ended up giving a little shrug instead, and then put my hand on my shoulder as a twinge of pain shot through it.

"I'd think you would remember not to do that," she said, dropping flour into a bowl.

I watched entranced as she worked not only without a cookbook or measuring devices. She dropped things into the bowl in rapid succession, stirred, added more, tasted and nodded.

She had just put the first batch of cookies in the oven and pulled out apple cider

I heard keys in the door again.

"I'm tired of this crap," Cherry said and headed straight for the door, her face set in anger. I stayed at the table, unwilling to come between them.

Mei pushed open the door and stepped in, but she didn't come alone this time. The woman who followed stood half a head taller than Mei, but the height came from the heels of her perfectly shined black boots. She dressed as if she were twenty rather than over forty.

My mother.

"What the hell are you doing here?" Cherry demanded. She signaled me back into the chair, but there was no way I would sit there with my mother at my back. I hadn't consciously considered her an enemy until then, even though I had always known the truth.

"Mei called and said you had slithered your way into Cherry's home," she said, looking at me.

"Out," Cherry said, moving towards her aunt. The woman stared back at Cherry with comically shocked surprise. I wished I could appreciate the humor. "Get the hell out of my apartment. I will not put up with any of this crap."

"You don't understand about Skye," she said. Her voice shook with hatred and fear. I had followed Cherry into the room and stood beside her, barely able to keep standing, but I dared not show weakness, which my mother would exploit, if not now, then later. She had to believe I had power and strength. I needed her to fear me and to leave me alone.

"I know everything about Skye," Cherry said. My mother's dark-rimmed eyes went wide. "Out. Both of you out of my apartment, right now."

"You shouldn't have come back," my mother said, looking at me as though she had thrown me in the gutter and never expected me to drag myself back up again, which was the truth in many ways.

"A thousand dollars just doesn't buy what it used to, does it?" I said.

"You want more money to go away? I'll get you more money --"

"I never wanted your money, and I'll send you back the thousand, in fact. You can't buy me out of here."

"Give me the keys, Mei," Cherry said, walking over to her sister and holding out her hand.

"You can't!" Mei looked panicked for the first time. She snatched her hand back.

"Give me the keys to my apartment. Then you and Aunt Tay leave and never come back again."

"Skye is trying to ruin the family. Can't you see?" my mother said, glaring once at me before she turned back to Cherry. "She'll tear us apart. She's evil!"

"Cherry --" Mei began.

Mei still had the keys in her hand, and Cherry yanked them from her fingers and pushed Mei back to the door. My mother didn't like standing alone facing me. She backed up several steps and got to the door before Mei did. Mei looked dismayed and angry when she turned as though she hadn't created this little drama all on her own.

"Cedric said they killed your kind," my mother said, stopping in the doorway. Mei looked at her, a little shocked as though she only just now realized what the woman had been saying. "I'm going to your parents, Cherry. I'll tell them everything Skye is doing to drive you away from them and your sisters."

"Go. Have a nice visit." Cherry shoved Mei into Tay's arms and herded both of them out the door. She closed and locked it, waiting until she heard them heading down the stairs. Then she walked back into the kitchen, snagging my arm and steering me into the chair again.

The oven chimed. She grabbed the pot holders and pulled out the first batch of cookies and sat them on the counter. My hands trembled with reaction. Cherry looked at me and nodded.

"You should have these." She tossed the key chain, and I caught it out of surprise. "That's my apartment, my car, and my business."

"I shouldn't --"

"Take them, Skye. You'll be a lot more responsible than Mei ever was. She wrecked my last car. Had a hell of a hard time with the insurance, too. I am still paying for her mistakes."

"You shouldn't have made them mad," I said, waving my arm towards the door. Fear almost took hold of me; I could have been standing outside the bus terminal again. "Damn, Cherry. I should go. If I stay, you might find yourself cut off from everyone in your family."

"No I won't," she said. She slipped a warm cookie onto a plate and sat it before me. "I'll still have you."

"I'm not --"

"You are family. But don't worry. Mei and Tay won't drive me away from my parents. Or away from Li. Cider or milk?"

"Cider," I said, accepting that I belonged here, at least for tonight. Mei may never have learned when not to argue with her sister, but I saw the look in Cherry's eyes and stopped before I made her mad. I didn't need to be lectured tonight.

She got the cider and the phone from the counter and then took the chair across from me. "You know, this thing works better since I dropped it in the water," she said and punched in a quick series of numbers. "Hi, Mom. I wanted to give you a head's up. I have Skye staying with me for a few days -- she's been ill --" A pause. "No, much better now. We even have cookies. But Mei came by and then took it upon herself to get Aunt Tay. No, it wasn't pretty. I took Mei's keys away and kicked them both out. I suspect they're heading your way. Oh, yes. A run out for pie and ice cream would be a good idea right now. Yes, I'll tell her. Have fun!"

She hung up the phone. I had the glass of cider half way to my mouth, frozen in mid-movement.

"Mama says she hopes you're feeling better."

I put the glass back down without tasting the cider. I don't know what I felt, but I suspected it came close to stepping into an alternate reality. I had spent all my life cut off from family. It only now realized I had let my mother stand between me and the others.   Chance alone had brought me to Cherry and Li.

Or maybe the Gods had smiled on me for a moment.

We ate cookies, talked about anything but the end of the world and my mother, and around midnight, we both crawled into her huge bed. I had never slept with someone warm nearby. She fussed with my pillows to make certain I didn't strain my shoulder, and then wrapped an arm around me and gave a gentle, wordless, hug.

I had never slept so well.

DAY FOUR:

CHAPTER SEVENTEEN

Sometime after dawn a wave of magic invaded my sleep like fire ants running over -- and through -- my body. Something monumental and bad had happened in the fae world. I realized we faced horrible trouble long before I opened my eyes to a new, gray rainy day.

Sounds came from the other part of the apartment: Cherry's voice, soft and urgent, and Darion reassuring her. I drifted back to sleep because I did not want to know what had gone wrong.

I didn't rest well this time. Something else invaded my sleep with a black emptiness far worse than when the men took me to the castle. If I slipped away I would never find my way back home. Fear gave me strength, and I almost awoke.

And the dark dream started again. And again, and. . . .

"Wake up Skye," Darion ordered. He had fingers placed on my forehead and magic spiked down through my head. I opened my eyes, going from deep sleep to instantly awake in that single heartbeat. Everything pounded with pain, but Darion pushed the discomfort aside with another brush of magic that hinted at lilacs. "Good, that's better. I'm sorry. I should have checked on you sooner."

"What?" I asked as I moved, but my arm shot pain up into my shoulder and I collapsed again.

"We're trying to find out what happened. However, you better get up if you can and join us in the kitchen while we wait. The sleep isn't helping you."

"What happened?"

"There's a current running through fae. Something has gone wrong and I can't say what, but you locked on to an aspect of the trouble."

"I got the feeling there are many people involved," I said as I slid towards the edge of the bed.

Darion stood and frowned. "Did you? I didn't even get that much. You might have been more receptive, being asleep. We'll have the news soon, I'm sure."

Darion left the room. Cherry had laid more clothing out on the chair by the bed which had to be for me. I needed to take her shopping after all of this madness ended.

Providing the world survived. I had an odd feeling that last night we had gone far closer to the edge than any of us wanted to know.

When I came out of the room, I found Darion and Cherry at the kitchen table, their hands wrapped around them cups of tea. They looked like a couple used to being together in the mornings. Companionable. I hated to intrude.

"Sit down before you fall down," Cherry said, waving to another chair. She already had the tea on the table, and the cookies, too.

I sat and looked at Darion. He shook his head. "I'm still waiting. This is bad though. I can sense something horrible has happened."

I sipped at the tea. Outside the wind blew hard against the window, the sound of ice in the mix. An early winter, I feared.

I looked at Cherry. "Any word on our little family encounter last night?"

Cherry shook her head, but Darion grimaced. "She told me about the show," he said. "They're both lucky I wasn't here."

"Oh yeah. I can just imagine my mother's reaction to another tall, blond fae in the family."

"She'll have to get used to it," Cherry said, and in a tone that stopped both Darion and me from saying anything else on the matter. "Mom called to tell me she had a phone call from Tay at seven this morning and it ended when mom hung up on her. I think that's something my mother has wanted to do for a long, long time."

"I hate to cause trouble in your family," I said, shaking my head.

"You aren't. Tay and Mei are. And it's about time those two face the problems they've created for themselves. Do you want breakfast?"

"No," I said with a more vehement shake of my head than I should have given. I moaned and sipped the tea. They both took pity and didn't ask me again.

I began to wonder how long we would have to wait for information when I felt a tingle along my spine. Darion looked up from his tea and stood, and I stood beside him, ready to do whatever I had to --

I didn't expect Ambassador Peren from Ruby House to appear right in the living room. Neither had Darion who looked as though he still considered using magic to send the man right back to his Clan House.

"Peace," Peren said, somewhat breathlessly. He looked pale and haggard. I saw a spot of blood on his shirt. "Please. We need to talk."

Darion signaled him to the last chair at the table. Peren looked unsteady and ill and I didn't want to hear whatever tale he came to give us. Blue and Sand had not returned yet, which made me even more worried. I wondered if Darion had heard from them.

"I am Ambassador Peren Ruby Day," Peren said, giving one glance to Cherry who looked as though she considered leaving.

Darion settled in a chair beside her, waiting for the other man to speak.

"Sit down, Skye," Peren said. He put a steadying hand on my arm, for all the good it did. *He* trembled. "The news is not good, though mostly bad for Ruby Clan. Last night someone used magical creatures to kill all possibilities for The Choosing."

"Hell," Darion said before the reality of what Peren said even filter through my head. "How did this happen?"

"We don't know." Peren shook his head, looking sick. "We're working on finding the answer. Some of your people have already volunteered to help. Other clans are stepping in. If we'd had any idea last night, we might have gathered a few of the younger ones --"

He stopped and took a deeper breath. An entire generation of his clan had fallen. The numbers might not have sounded like many deaths to humans, but those forty represented almost every Ruby child born in the last hundred years or more.

"Lacey is the last hope we have for The Choosing." Peren looked at me. "However, I have to tell you that if I believe she has been compromised, or she is a willing part of this monstrous act, I will kill her myself, and Ruby will pass The Choosing on to the next clan."

"She isn't involved," Cherry replied emphatically. "She would never be part of something so horrible. Not the killing of others."

Peren looked at her, surprised by the words, no doubt because they came from the only true human at the table. Cherry had been her friend though. She had known Lacey long before Darion became the woman's secret guard.

"Let's believe Lacey isn't involved, and she is still alive, for whatever reasons those who took her might have. This woman Skye found hasn't killed the others outright," Darion said. He looked worried and pensive. "I knew her pretty well, too. She wouldn't have even wanted to worry her friends, let alone take part in the rest of this horror."

"I wish I had met her," Peren said. "I wish Brand had at least brought her to someone in the clan -- but never mind. It's done. And I still stand by what I have said. I must consider what is best for all the fae. We dare not take the chance with her."

"Don't talk as though this is already settled," Darion said. "Nothing is yet. And what does your clan leader say about it?"

"He died last night while trying to protect his son, who is also dead."

"Dear gods," I whispered.

"We are doing the best we can," Peren told us,

desperation in his voice. "I have some authority, but as you can guess, we're divided on which of us should lead at a time like this. I did not have leave to come and talk to any of you, but Skye . . . Skye is the closest we've come to finding an answer in this trouble, and by all the gods of every realm, we need answers and quickly. Until last night we had several possibilities for The Choosing. How could we know she would be the only choice left, providing she even survived?"

"You intended to let her marry a human," Darion said, taking up the conversation.

"Yes. The marriage didn't offend us. We have never hated humans. However, as long as her human husband lived, there would be no children. Time enough for her to find a fae mate, later." He stopped and looked at me again. "Would that have been cruel?"

"No," I said. "It was a practical answer."

He stared at me, silent. I had something to ask, and now seemed as good a time as any, under the circumstances.

"Why was I allowed to be born, let alone live?" I asked.

Cherry winced. Darion looked at me and then away. Peren did not turn away from the question.

"We didn't know about Cedric's relationship with your mother, even for a long time after Emerald Clan knew. Your father is -- well, he's a devious bastard who didn't want to ruin his good name with the rest of the Emerald Clan by letting it be known he spent time with a human woman. And that, Cherry, was his version of the world, not mine."

Cherry gave Darion a look of worry.

"I'm ruined already," he said with a barely concealed grin. "Obviously everyone knows where to find me."

"Not to mention the fact you're an egotistical bastard," Peren added with a snort. "I didn't come here looking for *you*, after all. Skye, the choices Cedric made concerning you didn't make him popular anywhere. That, however, is not a reflection on your existence, but rather because he thought more of himself than anyone else. If others from Emerald had known before your birth, they might have taken action. Afterwards . . . I understand that no one sensed your fae blood until you reached your teens."

I nodded. There had come a time when odd stuff happened around me: lights flared, things moved, and even wild animals came to my hand. This change had made me ill, so I never pursued the power. My mother kicked me out and expected the fae would kill me for her.

No one had done so yet. The fae were honest with me. I wanted to ask more about my own life, but what more could I learn? I was neither human nor fae and I was alive because of lies, chance, and deception. It didn't matter. I had reached a time and place where I might help.

"What do we do now?" I asked.

Peren leaned over, his hand brushing my chest and easing injury and pain with a sweep of more magic. I must have looked startled. I never expected kindness.

"You have abilities, Skye, and we have damned little time left before the Choosing which happens tonight. We need you to find the island again. It moved, and we can't track where to, though Whitestone hasn't gone back over the Veil because we had a watch set. You can find it again, can't you?" Peren asked. I saw desperation in his eyes. "None of the rest of us have been able to do the work, or at least haven't admitted they could."

"There are people you don't trust."

"Right now, there are far too few people whom I do

trust." Peren replied, dismay and worry growing again.
"This is a dark time for the fae, Skye. There hasn't been a
massacre like this in thousands of years and several of the
fae believe we're slipping back into chaos. I don't want to
live in chaos and have to fight my way back to civilization
again."

"I can't point the island out to you, but I can go back
and lead you there," I said. "I can't take you through the
path I take, though. I'm not sure the Guardian would allow
it."

"I'll go that way with you," Darion offered. "I'll take
my chance with your guardian, since she was kind with the
other members of Sapphire House. Peren, you can use a
magic link to find us. When?"

"We're still organizing across the Veil," he said. He
reached over and put a hand on my forehead, his fingers
warm. Magic surged through with a sharp pain although
gone again in a heartbeat. "You'll know when we're ready.
And when you arrive at the island say these words: *Come to
me in the dark of the night.* Those words will be a beacon for
us to follow you."

I sensed the link back to fae lands, one far stronger
than I ever felt in the past. I can't say this gave me
confidence but at least I might still help in this trouble. I
would be ready.

CHAPTER EIGHTEEN

P eren left a few minutes later. I didn't like the look of hope he had turned my way before he hurried back across the Veil to ready his people. Darion left as well, saying he'd return soon. He looked worried, glum, and troubled, but he still managed a smile and even a kiss for Cherry before he left.

They would do well together.

"I hate waiting around," I said. I helped Cherry clean up, doing no more than limp thanks to Peren's magic. "No, don't tell me to go sit down. I can't sit and wait for something to happen like I can turn my brain off."

"How do you feel about all this?"

"Like I wish I wasn't a focal point in a lot of the trouble," I said. Then I shook my head. "But that's not true. I want to help. I want to prove myself --"

"You don't have to prove yourself to anyone, Skye. The longer this goes, the more I regret I called you. If I hadn't --"

"I would have awoken this morning, all alone, knowing something terrible had happened, and I would have no idea what trouble waited out there -- at least if those people hadn't already grabbed me. Instead, I have a slim hope of helping fix this."

"Can you get back to the castle?"

"Yes."

"God, I hate all of this, Skye." She took hold of my arm, her fingers tight. "I want nothing to happen to you. I've seen you close to death too many times in the last few days. They shouldn't ask you to do this --"

"I have to do something, Cherry, and I want this group to win because I don't trust the other side at all."

Her eyes went wide with fear and shock as she realized I fought for my life.

Someone pounded on the door. We both looked that way with the same angry, confrontational glare. Ready for trouble.

"Paul or Mei?" I asked.

"I don't care which one." Cherry stalked toward the door like a jaguar about to attack, and I followed in her wake, a limping jaguar. "I told them both to get the hell out of my life, and I meant it."

When she opened the door, Mei stood there, her shoulders straight, her eyes behind sunglasses. I should have realized. Paul didn't have the guts to show up in the morning, sober and in the full light of day. Besides, he might still be in jail.

Mei had returned because she didn't know better and because she lived for drama.

"What is she still doing here?"

"Are you that stupid?" Cherry asked. She did not move out of the way and let Mei into the room.

"We need to talk. Privately. Aunt Tay told me some relevant things you need to know about Skye."

"I'm sure she did. All about the devil and magic, right? Did she say the word fae at all or did she stick to the biblical version to make this all palatable for you?"

Mei's head jerked back as though Cherry had slapped her. "You can't -- you don't realize how evil that thing is. How it's destroying us! Look at how you are treating me -- "

"Mei, for once take responsibility for your own stupidity," Cherry said. I leaned against the wall and let Cherry handle this trouble. Despite what Mei thought, I didn't want to become involved in any family problems. "Mei, you are a self-centered woman who looks to everyone else to take the blame for the stupid mistakes you have made. Not this time. Not ever, if you continue to stand by Tay. Now go away."

Cherry started to close the door. As Mei tried to push her way in, Darion arrived behind us, stepped up to the door, and looked Mei right in the face.

"Who the hell are you?" Mei demanded.

"This is Darion Sapphire Wilding, Mei. He's my new boyfriend. He's a fae Ambassador."

"No! God have mercy, Cherry! They're devils! They're evil!"

"So this is your sister, Cherry?" Darion said, ignoring the hysterics.

"Yes, she is. Goodbye, Mei. Or would you like to come in and have breakfast with us --"

Mei fled and tripped on the stairs. Both Darion and I reached out with a little magic and steadied her. Cherry didn't close the door until she had driven away.

"Are most humans so dense?" Darion asked. "Or are

you blessed with more than your share of people who don't understand terms like go away?"

"It must be my curse in life," she admitted.

"I can take care of that you know," Darion smiled. "I'm kind of good with the curse sort of stuff."

We laughed, which took me by surprise. I didn't laugh often enough. Muscles hurt where they seldom moved.

I left Cherry and Darion to work in the kitchen because they deserved to have at least a little privacy. I sat down and willed myself to relax.

Yo-Yo came over to keep me company. I noticed she still limped, and this time, she had trouble getting up on the couch, so I reached down and pulled her up into my lap. She settled in, purring, though I realized I sensed something wrong.

I used a little tendril of magic to search out the trouble. Yo-Yo had a growth on her bladder. Poor baby. With soft, small strokes I took the trouble away. The magic hardly hurt me as I did the work. Others might consider this a stupid waste my power by helping the cat when so much else stood at risk, but doing this little kindness felt right.

She purred when I finished, and I swore she knew what I had done as she rubbed against my face. I had never experienced anything so happy and friendly. In the next moment, she leapt down and pranced out to the kitchen, her tail up in a moving question mark as she yelled at Cherry.

"Yo-Yo," Cherry said. She sounded surprised. "Feeling better, sweetie? That's her food cabinet, Darion. She hasn't eaten much for days. I wanted to take her to the vet, but all this started -- yes, food. I understand, silly cat."

Darion came into the room. He stared at me, a little

surprised. "What did you do?"

"She had a growth on her bladder," I said. "I took care of it."

Cherry looked shocked and touched. Yo-Yo was munching away on something. She still purred.

"How did you know?" Darion asked, sitting down on the chair across from me.

"Just because I can't sense something wrong the way fae can doesn't mean I can't see. She'd gotten worse just in the couple days I've been here. You would have noticed, too, if you had been around for long."

He leaned forward in the chair. "I've petted Yo-Yo. I should have known."

"You have a lot of other things on your mind," I reminded him.

"And you don't?" He picked up Yo-Yo, who had come charging back in, so full of energy she seemed years younger. Or perhaps she only acted her age. Darion petted her and nodded again. "You did a good job."

"Thank you, Skye. She means a lot to me," Cherry said, taking the cat from Darion.

"Do you want to experience the way fae see the world?" Darion asked. "Can you mirror me if I open to the full feel?"

"I don't know." I looked at him, surprised that he'd offered.

"We can try if you like."

The possibility intrigued me, but would I regret afterward when I went back to being myself?

I'd never been afraid to try something. I nodded to Darion.

Cherry looked both intrigued and worried. She stood beside Darion's chair and waited. I saw Darion close his eyes for a moment, his hands moving a little as though he brushed something aside. And then he looked back at me and nodded.

I usually only mirror out of panic, but I knew how to draw the power. Painful to use the magic but I let my mirror reach out to Darion and. . . .

I got lost in sensations I couldn't even describe, except this felt like being born: Painful and wondrously aware of an entire world you had not known existed. I didn't want to let go as I tried to touch everything -- Darion, Cherry, Yo-Yo, bugs in the carpet, trees outside, the wind, and the birds. The world burned through me with the magic that hurt to use, but this time, the pain came with ecstasy.

For the first time, I felt whole.

"Damn, Skye, let go," Darion said. He sounded worried, and the worry worked into the mirroring, so I let go. I tried to grab the link again, but Darion blocked my magic this time.

"Sit back," he said, standing over me. When had he moved? "Take deep breaths. You shouldn't have held when everything hurt so much."

"Hurt but so much I wanted," I said which sounded lame. I had captured a little of Darion in that mirror, which happened sometimes and I understood him a little better for it. Good. "I can't explain. It's like -- like seeing and hearing, both for the first time."

Darion looked intrigued. "You don't realize, but when you mirror, you project a little of yourself back with the image. So not only did you see my vision of the world -- which I'm obviously far too used to -- but I caught a glance at yours."

"Huh." The revelation made me uncomfortable. I often mirror instinctively to hide who and what I am, not to show myself to others. I tried to push the worry aside, gave up with a shrug, and turned to another subject. "Is there any hope we can go past my place before all hell breaks loose? I have a couple of knives I'd like to pick up so that I have weapons."

"That sounds like an excellent idea," Darion agreed. "I can get weapons from Sapphire House if you like. Something with a little more bite."

"I want my own weapons. Unless you can make me instantly comfortable with yours, I need something I am used to using."

He nodded and smiled at Cherry, who didn't look happy about the weapons. "Do you want to drive?"

"How come I don't get to drive?" I asked.

"Well, if you want, you can play chauffer with the two of us in the back seat," Cherry said, smiling wickedly. "That would be all kinds of fun."

I rolled my eyes. They laughed and smiled at one another, and if I had felt better, I would have driven for them and let the two have those moments in the back seat.

Darion drove, and I sat in the front beside him. The rain still poured, so we didn't put down the top. I frowned as we pulled out into the street by Cherry's apartment building. Everything looked drowned, and there was a hint of ice in the air along with something more troubling.

"Does this storm have magic in it?" I asked, waving my hand towards the stream of water washing down the side of the street.

"The weather picked energy from beyond the Veil," Darion explained. "There's considerable sorrow on that side today, and the emotions have transferred to nature. Sometimes the emotional backlash washes over everything, which is one of the real problems with being aligned with nature. And in the places like this one, where the two worlds brush up against each other, one can inadvertently affect the other."

"There are other worlds?" Cherry asked, leaning forward. She sounded intrigued.

"Many. Countless," he said, maneuvering around a UPS truck stopped in the middle of the block and in the middle of the street. "But the farther away from here you go, the less the places are akin to your home world, which means the places a few steps away are relatively safe, and you won't stand out. However, if you go too far, you risk ending up in a world where you can't even breathe the air. The fae go exploring sometimes. A long life and boredom will get you to do many stupid things. Some go too far and never come back. Rumor is there are places without magic just like there are places without air. The fae can get stuck there, which would be hell." The car in front of us belched out a white smoke as the driver hit the gas, spun tires on wet pavement, and tore across the street in front of an oncoming bus. "Although the air part is getting iffy even here these days," Darion said.

I made a muffled sound of amusement and looked away as we passed a building. A dozen homeless had taken refuge on the stairs under the portico. Someone would be along to roust them out into the cold and wet again, but for a moment, a couple of kids in their teens passed around the butt of a cigarette and glared out at the cars that passed. I hadn't meant to look, but I always do.

"Skye." Cherry touched my shoulder, and I winced. She looked contrite as I glanced back at her. "Sorry. But I have a couple questions for you. Personal ones."

I frowned. "I might not want to answer."

"That's fine. The first one is something which only

now occurred to me. You weren't born in a hospital, right?"

"No," I said. "My mother said I was born at home with a human midwife who had her memory erased or altered afterward by my father. My mother said he wanted to kill me. She said no and regretted the decision ever since. He left that night and never came back. Later, when I decided to become a Detective License, I magicked some information into the proper places, so I had a birth certificate and a few other records."

Cherry seemed to take a moment as though considering the next question. "After you had left, your mother said you went to live with your father, but you couldn't have gone to him. Where did you go?"

"I never left the city," I said.

"But where did you go?" she asked again and must have figured everything out. Darion glanced my way but then went back to driving with a single-minded attention which meant he had no intention of stepping into anything family-related. Wise man.

Cherry didn't speak again, but I relented. Besides, Darion had already picked up a good amount of the story from the link in the Weaver's kitchen, and it hardly seemed fair for him to know when she didn't.

"The day before my sixteenth birthday, my mother herded me out to the car and drove me across town to the bus station." I tried to keep the anger from my voice. "She handed me a thousand dollars and told me never to come back."

"That bitch," Cherry said the anger in her voice strong enough to sting. "If I had known what she did, I would have thrown her down those stairs instead of just kicking her out the door. How could she do that to you?"

"I scared her," I said and admitted that much of the truth to myself. "Some of my talents by then and I accidentally mirrored her when she went into one of her rages. She didn't like what she saw in herself."

"Accidentally?" Darion said.

"If I'm panicked, mirroring just happens sometimes," I answered and gave a little shrug. "Kind of an instinctive hiding maneuver."

"That is an interesting concept," Darion replied. He stopped at a light and glanced at me. "Sorry. That sounded way too damned clinical, didn't it?"

"Better than other reactions I've gotten. I scared her," I continued, determined to get the tale done. "And she didn't want to explain anything to Ian. Ian's a wonderful guy. If I had gone back home and told him what happened, my mother would have been the one sitting at the bus station wondering what to do with her life."

"Why didn't you?" Cherry asked.

"Because of Kelly and Mary. I knew if I left then my mother would turn normal. Fear can do odd things to people."

"You shouldn't make excuses for her, Skye," Cherry said. "There are none. You didn't leave the city, though. Why not? I would have run."

"Fear all my own. I had never been away from the house for more than a few hours at a time, and never alone I knew nothing about living in the real world except what I read and saw on TV, and none of that was good. I was scared, but I did a few wise things right away, like getting rid of the damned frilly dress and covering my blond hair, so I looked less odd. By the way, I have never been able to get any dye to take. I found a cheap place to live and brought in a young girl who was out on the street too. She helped me figure out normal though she never realized. Still, that first winter was damned hard."

"Why didn't you come to us?" Cherry asked.

I glanced back at her. She had the look of someone who felt herself betrayed. "Cherry, I didn't know you. I had only met your family a few times in my entire life. You were as much strangers as everyone else. Besides, you had a link to my mother, which I feared. That wasn't your fault since it was my mother's doing. I had no concept of family to whom I could turn."

"So you were sixteen and lived on your own," she said. She shook her head. "I'm twenty-seven, and I still don't have the knack of it down. How did you manage?"

"I had to get a job. A thousand dollars got me through the first winter, but it wasn't easy. I found jobs, made a little cash and lived cheaply. I sent the girl on to relatives who would take her, in and take care of her and I made certain she was all right. One day I started making money by finding stuff for people. I fell into the work. And I could help others."

"You did well, Skye. Better than a lot of kids would have."

"A lot of kids would have had their bodies to sell," I said. "I couldn't do that."

"So you had to use your brains instead."

"How did you two get back together then?" Darion asked. "I caught a little of it in the link, but not how you got there."

"Total accident," I answered. "I was looking for some punk gang-bangers I intended to beat the hell out of and take back the little necklace one of them had stolen from his grandmother. Afterward, I was heading back when I saw two women attacked and stepped in. Turned out to be

Cherry and Li."

"You make the meeting sound so straightforward," Cherry said. "It wasn't."

"I suspected as much," Darion said. I pointed him down another street and wished we had gotten closer to my home. All this talk made me uneasy. I had always been a private person.

"Li had gotten into trouble," Cherry explained with a shake of her head. "She'd seen a murder and the guy she was dating was trying to kill her. She called me to come and get her. I arrived, and the guy came out of nowhere and stabbed her."

"Hell," Darion whispered.

"Then he grabbed me and intended to do about the same. That's when Skye arrived."

"I mirrored him back to himself with all the horrible, maggot-infested thoughts, all the slime in his mind, and the memory of killing others. He didn't stick around, and the police caught him without any trouble. He turned evidence against the others."

"He had killed Li, though," Cherry whispered.

"No," I said, glancing back at her again. "She wasn't dead. Nothing I do would have helped her if she had been dead, but it was close."

"That kind of magic is hard on all of us. For you --"

"I spent a couple of days recovering," I said. I remembered that part in a haze. "Cherry stayed with me."

"And you learned about family," Darion said.

I suppose he was right.

"We have dinner now and then, and I've called Skye to help me some problems. I knew about the magic after the encounter, so when Lacey disappeared, I called Skye immediately. I wish I hadn't."

"You did the right thing," I said yet again. "I would hate not knowing what's going on right now. I can feel the trouble in the storm, Cherry, and this would have driven me mad. And besides, they also came after me. If you hadn't called me, I would have been all alone in the trouble and without a clue what was going on."

Lucky for me we arrived at my building only a couple minutes later. I didn't want to discuss life on the streets. Darion had seemed distant, and I caught several of those annoying bug-like buzzes which meant communications with another fae. I suspected important events happened elsewhere.

The two followed me up the back stairs, braving the rain-slick steps. It looked as though fall had taken a toll on my outdoor plants. In a few weeks, the little balcony would be covered in snow, and the plants would sleep until spring. I almost wanted to join them this year. Just the walk up to the door had nearly worn me out.

A squirrel dropped onto the railing, startling Cherry as he chattered incessantly at me.

"Yeah, yeah, I know. I'll get the damned food."

Darion grinned. I pushed the door open and let the two go ahead of me. The squirrel food sat in a huge bin just inside the door, and I popped the lid and got out a big scoop, stepping back out into the rain to fill the feeder. At least I couldn't get much wetter.

"He has you well trained," Cherry said, amused.

"Better than having him pound on the door. And yes, he has done that in the past."

"Nice place," Darion said and seemed to mean those words. "Green."

Plants hung at every spot of sunlight, and a few more lined the long set of windows across the front of the apartment. Cherry had been here before, but she still looked around with a whisper of shock, as though she had forgotten I lived in a jungle. Though maybe I had added a few more plants since the last time she came to visit.

"Plants help me relax," I said with a shrug. "I'll get the knives."

"The others know about this, right?" he said.

"Others?" Cherry said.

"This?" I asked.

"The others who have come from over the Veil to check on Skye. They know about the plants, right?"

"Oh, sure." I shrugged and let my fingers trail over the leaves of the plants I passed. "A few of them have shown up here. Is this supposed to mean something?"

"Lots of healing plants here," he said, letting his fingers brush against the leaves of a gorgeous Diane Marie chirita with a few bell-like purple flowers. The plant sat on my desk. "It means you connected with the very things that would help you recover each time you were ill from magic. I keep finding you are far more fae-inclined than anyone has admitted."

"I wish I want to more," I admitted.

"Good. I can teach you," he answered. Then I heard a little buzz of sound, and he frowned. "Later."

"That was it, was it?" I said. I caught a little touch of warning as well, the hint that others had prepared.

"Yes. They're ready to go."

"I'll get the knives," I said and headed towards the bedroom.

"My people are waiting at Sapphire House." Darion looked distant for a moment and then nodded. "Blue says they have several others waiting at different houses. All we need is for you to get there and say the words to open the beacon."

"Good." I gave Cherry a smile because she watched with fear plain on her face. "It's okay, Cherry. I'll make this as safe and quick as I can."

She nodded but wasn't any more reassured. As I went into the bedroom, she crossed to Darion. I turned and saw them embrace. They deserved time together. It seemed unfair they had found each other in such a dark time that would send him into danger. I could fix that . . . at least for a little while.

CHAPTER NINETEEN

I shut the door and quietly turned the lock. It wouldn't keep Darion out for long, but I wouldn't need much time. The knives sat in a case just inside the closet. I pulled two out and placed one in a sheath and hooked it to my belt. The other was small, thin and far less conspicuous; I strapped it and a sheath around my left leg and pulled my pants down over the weapon.

No time. No time at all.

An odd strand of ivy grew around the mirror by the window. The plant hadn't been there the last time I was home. The leaves spread out from the glass and curled upwards, reaching for the light at the window. I hadn't expected to find the gift I had given to the path guardian. The plant gave me hope.

I placed my fingers on the glass and called back the image of the bathroom in the castle from which I had made my precipitous escape.

"What the hell --" I heard Darion shout. The

doorknob jangled. "Skye!"

I stepped through into the corridor of green, closing the magical door behind me, though almost not fast enough. The bedroom door burst open, and Darion charged into the room looking crazed and angry with Cherry behind him, frantic.

I turned away and started down the long path to Whitestone. I still hadn't learned how to deal with an intelligent building. Ah well. It was the people inside who would be the problem.

The Guardian stepped out of the darkness. Trails of ivy hung across her body. This time, she moved in front of me. I realized she didn't want me to go the rest of the way.

"You've always helped me and this time I have to help others. You understand what's happening, don't you?"

Did she understand or care? She didn't move and blocked the way. I feared I wouldn't be able to help the others who had all helped me and had done something stupid, wasted time. Should I go back and help figure out another way that would get to the castle? Too much depended on us getting to Whitestone and rescuing the others. The fate of the fae and the humans --

A hand reached out with long green fingers, ivy trailing from her hand. The fingers brushed across the side of my face.

Be safe.

She stepped aside.

The mirror to the castle bathroom stood on the other side of her. With a single deep breath, I walked forward and out --

And someone hit me across the back of the head. I fell, turning as I tried to grab at the person. Boots. Kicked.

"She was right," someone said with the sound of glee

in his voice. "It came back through the mirror."

I gasped for breath and tried to speak. "Come to... me..."

"Oh, no magic this time!" Someone grabbed me by the hair and shoved a cloth into my mouth and tied it around the back of my head. They grabbed my hands and tied them as well.

I tried not to panic.

The two men dragged me out of the room and into the hall. She had replaced the glass. They kept tight a hold of me as we went past.

People shouted and rushed up around us. Humans, all of them, and so happy they acted like a gibbering band of monkeys.

I had made a major, probably fatal, mistake. I was the only one who could draw the others to this place and in my stupid wish to protect Darion and Cherry, I had ruined the only chance everyone else had to stop this evil. If they killed me now, what would happen?

At least I wouldn't know how badly I had screwed up if she killed me. That might be my only hope though I feared she intended to leave me alive and I would see everything fall because of my stupidity.

I wanted to howl. I didn't care what the humans did; how they grabbed at me, smirked, and kicked. They dragged me down the hall and then down a set of old stone stairs. How plebeian. We headed to a dungeon. I would have laughed, even now, at the cliche.

The stairs curved downward in an odd, uneven spiral. The farther we went, the more it seemed chilly, though not the cold of the world, rather something touched with magic, brushing against me like a darkness waiting to devour my soul. Or was that a cliche as well? My head hurt.

I wished I had done better.

At the bottom of the stairs, we entered a well-lit spacious room and with none of the conveyances of a fantasy dungeon. Several people stood secured in a magical circle near the center of the chamber, and a few had severely treated. The room stank of magic -- a lot of vanilla and cinnamon, but it seemed to have mutated into something foul. I would have gagged at the stench, except for the cloth in my mouth.

Aria, my less than beloved half-sister, stood trapped in a magic circle, ropes made of spells and power holding her and the others in place. I knew the faces of some of the others from the mirrors. And I recognized Lacey, who stood in the center of the circle. Lacey? Lacey doing this --

No. The chains of light held her in place, and the desperate look she gave me said she wasn't here anymore willingly than the others.

"Ah, just in time," a woman's voice all but purred. The figure stepped out of an alcove where she had been sitting, sipping tea. Not very pretentious looking, even for a fae: straight dark yellow hair, gray eyes, average height and slim. When she came closer, I sensed powerful, chaotic magic, and when I looked into her eyes, I saw something else: madness, hunger. These two emotions were a troubling combination in a fae.

She had a familiar face, but I'd never met her. I glanced at her hand. Ruby Clan. How odd. And young enough, I guessed, to be one of the groups born to The Choosing.

She saw where I had glanced and gave an imperious nod.

"I am Earis Ruby Day." Ah, the Ambassador's

daughter. I felt sorry for Peren, who must not know what was happening here. "And you are the infamous Skye Emerald McFaelyn. I am so glad you walked in here when you did. You are just what I needed to finish this little passion play."

I tried to work the cloth out of my mouth. Earis had taken hold of my arm and dragged me towards the circle of others.

"You did well, my humans," Earis said, and I almost gagged at the patronizing bullshit tone, though the humans still danced around like --

Hell. Spellbound to her, without a doubt. The woman had power and the potential to use magic in dark ways. I liked this less and less.

Lacey looked at me, frantic and frightened, and I knew I had just made things far worse. Earis wanted me here for a reason, right? Had I walked in and given her everything she needed to complete her plans? I didn't like the feeling much at all.

"Where shall we place you? Oh, next to Emerald and before my poor Ruby cousin. Yes, there."

She waved her hand, and people moved like figures on a game screen, sliding aside, and forming a slightly larger circle to make a spot for me behind Aria.

I wanted the damned cloth out of my mouth. Did she know what would happen if I spoke those words? I didn't think so. Earis seemed someone who would gloat over anything she had learned. So she might still make a mistake. The magic of the circle snapped around me like a vise, so I could hardly breathe. But I didn't need magic. I only needed a moment to speak one line which would trigger magic made by others.

"Oh, look. It brought a little weapon." She drew the

knife from my belt and held the blade in front of my face. I took a breath, trying not to gag at the look of pleasure in her eyes. "And what did you intend to do with this, animal?"

She reached towards my chest, sliced down through shirt and skin.

I had panicked, of course. I shouldn't have -- I knew at the moment I mirrored that she would make me pay for the reaction. She gave a cry of shock and put a hand to her chest where blood welled from a wound that mirrored mine. She slapped me and then leapt backward in comic shock when the blow rocked her head back. This woman didn't think straight when angry. I could use that, maybe --

"Oh, what a cunning little animal you are," she said, her voice a hiss of rage. Her finger traced the wound on her chest, and it disappeared. Mine did not, alas. I would have liked to have mirrored that moment, but I'd lost the hold as she calmed. She brushed a hand over her face, and the bright red spot disappeared. No bruise for her.

But I had annoyed her. She wanted to hurt me. A nod to one of her little human puppets and that one slammed a fist into the small of my back, but he collapsed from the pain, and I almost got free.

"Oh, this just will not do," she said as though I was a troublesome little puppy who had just peed all over the good furniture.

Earis moved through the circle of power, and a ripple of light flowed where she had passed. I watched, trying to get an idea of how to fight, and ignoring how the rest of these fae in this circle would have figured this out without me if there had been an easy answer.

"We have time, still," Earis said. She sighed, as though time with nothing to do bored her. "I hate to waste the moment. Shall we have some entertainment again, my fae friends?"

Distaste, discomfort, dislike: The emotions rose all around me. But the others didn't fear her. I realized they would not give her the emotion -- fear -- that she wanted. So I didn't either.

She still had my knife in her hand. I wished I had not brought the weapon or the other one she hadn't found yet, which sat heavy and cold against my ankle.

She came forward and laid the knife against the side of my face, looking into my eyes. "No, I am not stupid. Aria, you despise your sibling. So you are going to have the joy of making it a little more tractable for my work."

Earis turned Aria who stared, hatred in her eyes. I didn't deserve her anger. And when Earis pushed the knife into my older sister's hand, she didn't fight, even knowing the pain and the wound would mirror back to her.

"Ah much more entertaining," Earis decided. She brushed a hand along the side of my face, cold spider-like fingers against my skin. "Cut here, Aria."

Aria brought up the knife. I saw her face harden, preparing to deal with her own pain, though not a moment of compassion showed in her green eyes.

The knife caught at my skin just below my right eye and pulled downward with a fire that spread through my entire face.

I would not mirror. I fought against the instinct to turn the pain and wound back on the person who caused it. I didn't care if Aria hated me: I would not be an animal and perform in a show for the perverted woman who had captured us.

Earis caught hold of my hair, jerked my head around and slapped me. I mirrored that right back at her again.

"Damn."

Blood ran down the side of my face and spread, a warm brush of liquid against my neck. Earis turned me back around and waved her hand. Aria jabbed the knife into my side. If the magical field hadn't held us up, I would have fallen as pain shot through my body, and when she twisted the blade –

I would not mirror.

"Well, isn't this fascinating, children?" Earis said, in a pretentious tone of voice someone should have slapped out of her years ago. "It seems the little animal will not hurt one of his – no, pardon me, its – own blood. How about another? Shall we try? Or shall we let Aria play some more? Don't fight me, Aria. Jab a little more."

I looked at Aria and found her face bathed in sweat, and she must have bitten through her tongue or her cheek because blood ran down her chin now. She fought Earis this time, and when she looked into my eyes, I didn't see her usual hatred.

"I said jab harder."

The knife came out and then pushed back in so quickly I gagged on the cloth and would have passed out if Earis hadn't brushed a hand over the back of my head and kept me conscious with magic.

"You are the animal, Earis Ruby Day."

The words, spoken with apparent disdain, drew Earis's surprised attention to Lacey Weaver.

I hadn't been able to look much at Lacey before this. I should have been here to save her, but instead, I feared I had made everything worse. Could I get the gag out of my mouth before I became too weak to speak?

Lacey Weaver wore the rags of her wedding dress, the lace soiled and torn. Her long golden hair hung in limp strands down the side of her face, and her perfect makeup had long since smudged. She looked like a little girl's bride doll, left out in the yard in the rain weather.

There was nothing to be toyed with in the stare she gave Earis.

Earis turned her attention from us, and Aria gave a muffled sound of relief as she dragged the knife back out again. I almost wish she hadn't withdrawn the blade because the pain tripled and the blood flowed far harder and faster now. Perhaps she did so in hopes I would die before Earis used me in her plans. That might be the best answer.

"I'm sorry," she whispered.

I'd never expected those words from her, even now.

Earis cast one glance at us, frowned and waved a hand; the bleeding slowed, but didn't stop, and the pain didn't ease at all. She turned to Lacey once more. I must not have been as entertaining as she hoped.

"You aren't any better than this little animal my boys dragged in," she said, pretentiousness melding with disdain. "Fae-raised human. I am disgusted to see one of our own reduced to this --"

"Oh shut up, you pompous, stupid bitch," someone else said.

Earis spun at the words, her face bright red. Oh my. She didn't like to be insulted. And now -- now she was the show. I would have enjoyed this far more if I thought I would survive for much longer.

"Oh, does that upset your sensitive little fae ears?" Lacey said and drew her attention back once more. Earis spun like a puppet on a string.

Someone else laughed.

"She hasn't the ability to see beyond her illusion. Blind

and stupid," Aria said. The more they talked, the harder it became for Earis to stop them. I wanted to join, but the gag -- damn the gag!

"Shut up," Earis ordered with magic in those words. They stung.

"Oh you can take your stupid orders and shove them up your tight little fae ass," Lacey said.

Earis choked, rage growing with each breath. I saw power ripple in the circle, turn dark red and swirl, as attuned to her as the storm had been when I escaped.

She spun and ran up the stairs, her humans galloping after her like a pack of mad dogs after a bitch in heat.

CHAPTER TWENTY

"**D**amn!" Lacey cursed after Earis had disappeared.

"We came closer," Aria replied. I heard the agreement mumbled elsewhere.

"Wha?" I muttered into the gag.

"When she gets mad, she loses control," Lacey explained. "We've almost gotten free once that way, but it got one of us killed."

"Ah." I coughed into the cloth and shook my head trying to get it loose. I tried to say the words, even with the gag in my mouth, but it came to jumbled. Damn, damn! I shook my head again.

"Careful," Aria said. "Be still."

"Na. Gag."

"Who is he?" Lacey asked with a lift of her head towards me. "Another Emerald? She doesn't need three of any other clan. And she fears him and wants whatever power he has to add to the mixture."

Aria's green eyes narrowed. "This is Skye. He's my father's half-human child."

"Half-human? But from what you told me -- oh. Oh." She blushed, which annoyed me, but then she looked me in the face and nodded. "You are unique, aren't you? That counts for a lot for what Earis is trying to do."

I looked at Aria, far more panicked. "Ki' me."

She still had the knife in her hand. I wasn't sure if she could bring the blade up against the force that held her, but she understood what I had said.

"Not yet," Aria replied. "And not by my hand."

"Ou hate me."

Her eyes flashed, and she looked at Lacey and away. Had she wanted to appear noble before the woman who might, even still, be her next queen? I didn't care. I wanted to provoke her into anger and for her to hold to that anger and use it if she got the chance.

"No one dies," Lacey said. She fought against the power that held her, which blurred and brightened, coalesced and braided. "No one else, not yet. And Skye, your death wouldn't change a damn thing at this point. Oh, you might give the bitch a little more power, but right now she has all she needs with us in her hands."

"Wha?" I asked again. I should have passed out by now, but whatever Earis's magic held me here. I suspected her magic couldn't keep me from death, not if we tried hard enough. "Wha she wan?"

"She wants to rule," Aria answered. She gave a little shrug, and that sent eddies of light through the circle. "Not just be the chosen Queen, but to rule everything forever. Earis knew she didn't stand a chance at The Choosing. So she killed off her rivals."

"Na chance?" I said and tried to spit out more of the

damned gag. I could barely breathe for the pain. My mind wanted to wander, and I had to fight my attention back again.

"Easy, Skye. The more you fight, the harder you will bleed. You can't last long like this," Aria said and for a moment sounded as though she cared.

But I looked into her face and kept fighting, trying to tear my hands free or to spit out the gag -- to do anything but wait.

Aria frowned, as though I was a somewhat stupid younger sibling. "Earis grew up believing she would be the chosen one, no question," the man from Ruby, now standing at my back, said. "But then, we were all treated that way. Only she found out the others were better than her. Wiser, better with magic --"

"She hunted for other ways to win," Aria said. They must have talked about Earis a great deal. "She studied books and even old manuscripts on magic. Earis decided that if she would not be chosen, then she would make sure she took the throne another way."

"Ah. This?" I lifted my head, trying to indicate the circle and Lacey. Lights flashed before my eyes. I wanted to understand before I died.

"She found an old spell," Aria said. "One which allows her to siphon the magic from others. She gathered us into a single spell and then implanted part of the magic in Lacey. Then she linked herself to Lacey's power, so she can draw on all the magic at once, without having to deal with several threads of magic which would have made her too vulnerable. When The Choosing begins, the spell will drag all the power and life from each of us, siphon it into Lacey and on to Earis in one thread. She will be invulnerable at The Choosing, where she will then be able to drag in more power and destroy every clan leader, Councilor, and Ambassador there."

"Why La?" I said with a nod of my head toward Lacey.

"Lacey is the one the spell will draw to The Choosing. Earis has done her best to make certain of it by killing off every other person who had been in the running," the man from Ruby said behind me.

"She'll be able to use the power -- more power than any single fae has held -- and she'll be unstoppable at that point," another added.

"And quite mad," Aria said.

"Right. Like she's sane now," Lacey replied. Others laughed.

For all their joking, I sensed the undercurrent of desperation in their voices. We had too little time before The Choosing and too few options.

"I wish Skye could tell us if we had any hope of getting out of here," Lacey said.

I nodded so emphatically I spattered blood on Aria. She frowned.

"There is hope?" she said.

I nodded again. I shook my head, trying to get the damned gag loose. It was just cloth! I should have been able to will it away. I should --

"He needs to talk," Lacey said. "Hell, we should have considered that seeing how desperate he is to get the gag off."

"Oh." Aria sounded embarrassed. I wondered if she had just been glad to see me silenced when I arrived. "Yes. Get the gag off. I'll try."

It wouldn't be any easier for her, but at least she understood. I stopped long enough to take another deep breath. Gods of all peoples, I would not last much longer.

Aria worked to move her arms, her muscles straining, the sweat pouring from her face. I wanted to help, but I remained still instead, for fear I would lose the ability to speak if I worked harder. I blood flowed from wounds and down the front of my shirt and pants. More of Cherry's clothing ruined.

Earis came back down the stairs only a few moments later and far too soon for Aria to have done anything. Earis held her anger in check though I could still see it in her eyes. She understood her own weakness, and yet couldn't stay away. Was that another weakness we could exploit, somehow?

She stopped in front of me, her hand brushing against my hair. I didn't understand the touch at first, but then fire spread down through my body. More of the wounds healed, but not completely, and the healing hurt worse than the knife blade. I gasped.

"Oh, you felt that, did you? Well, I do not want you to die, Skye. You are the prize jewel in my crown, so to speak. I'm sure the others have explained, haven't they? I will use them to take the throne, and I will rule forever. Only I faced one problem. I could draw all the powers from this group and even from the others at The Choosing, but those powers would only make me a more powerful version of them. They might still join and overcome me, using magic I took from these others. But you are unique, my little pet. You have powers no one else has. And once I take those powers, no one will ever be able to counter me."

I felt the truth of what she said and knew I would be the one who made her invincible. No, I would not allow such a thing to happen. If I could have wished myself dead right then, I would have. She grabbed my head when I closed my eyes and slapped me hard. I didn't have time to mirror. With all the magic coursing through me, I could hardly think at all. I did not want -- I didn't want to have done something so incredibly stupid. I didn't want --

Something tickled against my skin. I shivered.

"Oh, even you can feel it, can you? Yes, that's The Choosing, my children." She stepped back from me, almost dancing with joy. Then she whispered something, and I felt a tendril of magic slip from me to Lacey; it showed green among the other colors. "We begin! That was the first call to The Choosing. Soon! Oh soon! I will be where I was born to be -- and that doesn't mean kneeling at the feet of a human-raised creature who doesn't know what it means to be Fae!"

"Gods protect the Fae," Aria whispered.

"Oh, they are, child," she said. "That's why they have given all of you to me. Don't you see? I am only doing my duty."

She looked my way, and I purposely mirrored her insanity back at her. Her face grew red. I should have looked away -- but I didn't. I dragged her anger up until she snarled, grabbed the knife from Aria, and jabbed again, but this time, she got a lung. I gasped and gasped and couldn't get enough air --

"Damn. Breathe you stupid little animal," she ordered. Tendrils of magic circled back towards Lacey, who sobbed, everything beyond her control. The summons tried to pull her away, but Earis wouldn't let her go until she had the power from all the others.

I stopped breathing. I closed my eyes.

"Breathe, I said!"

She slapped me. It didn't help.

But then she yanked the gag from my mouth.

I looked into her face and took a single small breath --

"Come to me in the dark of the night."

Maelstrom, chaos. The scents of spices and flowers grew so strong they obliterated the stronger foul scent of her magic. The surge of power won a profoundly shocked reaction from Whitestone itself. I hoped we had not awakened the castle and wouldn't have to deal with him.

"Portals, lady! Portals are opening everywhere outside the building!" someone shouted from the stairs.

She spun and raced for the stairs, panicked. The control on the circle weakened, and Aria dragged herself out of the circle and collapsed, nearly senseless, only a few steps away. She had broken the circle of magic, and a few of the others fell as the power holding us lessened.

Earis stopped half way up the stairs. I saw her turn slowly, steadily.

"You are the only ones who know who I am and what I plan. But if you are all gone, then I still have another chance, don't I? What is another one hundred years, after all?"

"Stop her," Heron Sapphire Wilding said. He reached my side and went to his knees. "Stop her."

"Oh, but you can't, can you?"

I heard fighting above us. Darion would be here now. I wanted to redeem myself for the stupidity I had already done. I would not fail a second time.

The bleeding had gotten worse as the field lessened. I realized that if I tried to use magic on myself, the pain would kill me this time.

Nothing I could do. The bitch looked at me and smiled.

"A shame about losing you, but in one hundred years -- yes, in that time I can make a few like you, can't I? Grab a few fae and humans and breed my own. Ah, such a good idea."

And that enraged me beyond anything I had ever known.

She lifted her hands, casting in a way you rarely see in fae, who use their inner powers with no outward show. She knew old powers from ancient books, and she knew how to wield them.

Power formed in her hands and expanded, taking the shape of a human -- fae -- monster, all stone and faceless. Lightning played along the creature's arms. It took a step down the stairs, but she shook her head and grabbed its shoulder.

"Multiply and destroy my enemies," Earis said, laughter in her voice. And it multiplied. The stone monster reached out a hand and grew another of itself, and another, and another --

They each took magic from her to create, and she stopped them at five. She lost all hold on the circle by then, and the captured fae had all broken free -- except for Lacey, who fought against the other spell that held her while another power tried to drag her away to somewhere else.

The others came to stand at my side, and we fought against both the stone creatures and the humans she sent against us. I would have spared the humans if they hadn't been so firmly in her control. Even Aria tried to wound and incapacitate rather than kill, but sometimes we had no choice.

I had drawn the second knife from my boot -- surprised Aria when I used it to stab a man who had wrapped an arm around her neck and almost killed her. And then I saved Heron. He took the human's weapon as his own. Despite the mistreatment, he still looked like a model which amused me. We fought, and even her monsters succumbed to us.

The castle did not like this conflict and trembled. I knelt, there in the midst of the battle, and hoped the others kept me safe.

"Peace, Whitestone," I said aloud. "We mean you no harm. She wants to kill us, and we dare not die and let her live, to do this again. Peace. Help us."

"Have you gone mad?" Aria demanded. She grabbed my arm and jerked me back to my feet. "Get the hell up and fight with --"

But the building stopped trembling, and the stairs moved, dipped and dropped Earis down to the floor before us.

I smiled at Aria. Whitestone had chosen his side. Earis, startled, scrambled back to her feet and scurried to the side of her last monster. The battle in the castle drew closer. We only had to hold a little longer. We would not fail.

And damn if I didn't stand the line with the fae that day and destroy the creatures that would have kept Earis hidden and doomed everyone to play this perverted game out again at another time. We fought and one after another the enemy fell.

I feared she might yet escape. I tried to get closer when I saw her raise her hands once more and saw power come to her fingers -- darker, this time. Wilder. She barely held on to the spell.

"Go take the male and female, human and fae, and scatter the flesh and bones of my enemies to the wind!"

I felt the brush of a sinister breeze, the prelude to destruction. The others sounded dismayed, but I took a step forward as a small storm of black and wind came down at us. I swept a line of magic out and entangled the spell with my own magic. The power burnt and I feared the spell would get past me and to the others --

I took a deep breath -- as much as I could -- and mirrored the spell back at her so now it sought my enemies. She should have chosen a different spell; one that didn't include male and female, and the magic would have killed me. But I was neither. I was only a mirror, reflecting back. . . .

"No!"

Earis tried to run, pulling the few humans in around her like a shield. I prayed to hell Aria stayed behind me and out of the way of the spell though I hoped she was no longer my enemy. This cloud of death would not turn on her.

I watched as the storm caught Earis by the stairs. Whitestone would not let her climb to safety. The unholy howl of the wind covered her screams as lightning wrapped around her and the humans who stood close by their leader. The lightning dragged her up, pulled her into the light.

And in a moment, the wind blew and scattered ashes. Nothing but ashes.

But the storm still moved.

"Oh hell," I whispered. I stumbled forward, trying to figure out a way to draw the power back and destroy it. I didn't want this loose. Gods knew who might be my enemy out there since I was not the most beloved in this group.

"Skye," Aria said. She had gotten to her feet and came to my side.

"Get back!" I ordered, holding to my bleeding side and not much power in my words at all.

"You can't order me," she replied, anger back in her voice.

And the storm turned and spun back towards us like a miniature tornado caught in the room.

"Oh hell," she whispered.

I shoved her down and reached up with bloody hands to grab the thing Earis had created. I got hold of the magic which felt alive and frantic to do the work. Not intelligent, but driven. I didn't know what to do now. Mirror? Mirror what? How? Destroy it? How?

Enemy. This spell was now my enemy. I reinforced the need for it to destroy my enemies and then forced the magic to see itself as my worst enemy.

The storm dissipated in my hands, and the world grew suddenly calm around me. I heard the distant shouts of others and the sounds of battle and wondered how many damned humans had she taken in here? What other magic monsters might protect her? The others -- they could handle --

"Lacey. We can't let her go. She's still --"

The other spell Earis had set with the others, but not yet for me.

"Damn!" I wanted this over and kept finding another piece of the problem. I spun back to find the others trying to hold Lacey here against the call for The Choosing. Three lay dead already. Another fell away as I watched. Lacey cried out, trying to do anything but what two different spells compelled her to do -- one dragging her to the fae lands and The Choosing, and the other drawing power from everyone in reach and pouring into her.

I grabbed her arm.

"No!" she cried out.

The spell swept down and tried to devour me.

And I mirrored one more time.

The pain from the magic alone would have killed me if others hadn't added their own powers. I mirrored the spell which had been made to siphon powers from others. I made the magic pull the power back out of Lacey and return it to the others. If Earis had still been alive, we would have had a very messy fight because she still would have still held the power. Instead, the magic gave way rather spectacularly in the end.

I flew across the room amid light sound, magic, fire, pain -- I don't know what I hit. The wall? The stairs? I would not survive. I took a last breath. Nothing else.

Just let me have peace now.

Voices. People rushed past with an array of footsteps within my sight. I feared someone would kick me. They usually did.

Darion knelt and laid a hand on my chest. He had a cut on his arm. I wasn't certain he noticed how he bled.

"Stopped her," I whispered. "Earis."

"Damn," he said. "Be still. You are an idiot."

"I . . . know."

"No, no. Stay with me, Skye. Hold on. I need help!" he shouted to someone else.

"Others," I said. "Others hurt. I tried to save them, Darion. I'm sorry."

"You did well. We knew what was going on down here. For a moment, we had lost everything when she cast the spells that created her creatures, but you destroyed them and that second spell. She was a fool, Skye. She sent the storm to destroy her enemies, and she would have destroyed both worlds because no one was her friend."

"Oh hell." The shock of what he said brought a surge of trembling and almost the power to move -- but the false strength passed in the next ragged breath. I had done all right. And I had saved them, not only from Earis but also from Earis's own stupidity.

Darion poured magic into me. Someone else knelt to help, but my vision was still dimming. I saw someone nearby --

"Aria!"

My father rushed past to grab up his beloved daughter as I closed my eyes.

DAY FIVE:

CHAPTER TWENTY-ONE

They took me back to Cherry's apartment. I awoke in the night with another storm raging outside and the lighting so bright and constant I clearly saw the room.

I hurt with every breath and every atom of my body and my soul. I felt bruised and battered, and I couldn't say I cared one way or another why the storm raged or even why I still lived.

Cherry sat on a chair beside the bed, staring into the darkness and not even flinching at the sudden flashes of light.

"Cherry?" I whispered.

She leaned forward and her lips brushed against my forehead. I had seen such acts of kindness in movies and television, the touch of someone who loved another. I shivered.

"Be still, Skye. Everything is fine."

"Darion?" I asked, panicked because I had expected him to be here.

"He left for The Choosing. He suspected the magic would awaken you. You need rest."

"The others?"

"Darion says you saved the world, and while they lost a few fae, far worse almost happened. He said to tell you to stop worrying."

I was glad we had stopped the trouble.

"I'm sorry," I whispered and recalled how I left her at my apartment. "But I had to do it."

"I understand.". Her hand brushed against the side of my face. I almost flinched. The last person to do that had been Earis, and the touch had been the prelude to agony. "Rest. You'll get better soon."

I closed my eyes wishing for oblivion again.

I got something else.

There a voice whispered in my mind.

An odd dream, like none I had known experienced. I stood with others, watching a large area of monolithic stone blocks and felt as though I shared companionship, made a part of the whole.

Lacey Weaver stood on one of the monolithic stone platforms, her tattered dress looking regal. People had gathered in clans on the lower ground. A pennant flew above each group, bright jewel colors rippling in the breeze. I realized we stood neither in day nor night, but rather a perpetual twilight that didn't change as I watched, expecting either sunset or sunrise.

The day felt warm, pleasant and very much unlike the weather back in Chicago. I stood with the Sapphire clan.

Cedric and Aria had gathered with others beneath the Emerald banner.

"She cannot be made the queen," someone from Amber said. "She knows none of the traditions, and she is tainted not only with humanity but with the power of the Ruby witch who tried to rule us all. Even if the Guardian chooses her, we must not follow!"

The words made me angry, and I wasn't the only one. The others had voices to shout their displeasure, even if I did not.

I realized I wasn't dreaming; I watched The Choosing through magic created by the Sapphire Clan people. I wondered why they had brought me here and if I should be among the fae at a time like this.

We wanted to bring you in body, Darion said -- quite clearly Darion this time, there in my thoughts. However, you wouldn't have survived. All the same, you have the right to be here, my friend -- more so than many of the others.

Voices rose in protest and counter-protest on all sides as they debated Lacey's right to rule. I watched, more enthralled with how well Lacey seemed to take the situation than anything else. Perhaps her time with Earis had given her a unique ability to deal with the fae.

"You have no idea what Lacey is," Heron said at last. He stepped forward, holding to Darion to keep to his feet. I sensed the power of his conviction, though, and his anger at the others who questioned Lacey's abilities. Everyone fell silent, looking towards him. "You weren't in Earis's hold. But I was there with Lacey. I learned about her strength of will, her fairness, and her power and yes, I'll follow her."

"You -- you and your clan are all suspect!" Lord Iron

was a skeletal man, his hair a dirty blond, and his face somehow aged, despite the eternal youth of the fae. I remembered his icy fingers on my skin. "We know what you've brought to watch us."

I tried to pull back. Darion would not let me go.

"Skye saved your miserable wormy life, Lord Iron," Darion said despite my silent protests. "I suggest you show at least a little respect. Yes, Skye watches through us. Are you going to tell me he didn't win the right to at least see what he helped to save?"

"He? He?" Iron said with a derisive snort.

"He, she -- does the term matter?" Peren demanded. And a few others agreed which shocked me even more. "Or would you prefer 'it' just so you can feel smug and superior? You aren't. Skye is here. Skye watches. I wish Skye were here in person, but he took the brunt of the battle that saved Fae from my daughter's insanity and stupidity. Let us get back to the matter at hand, shall we? Lacey is the last of the children born from the Ruby Clan to be Chosen. If the Guardian decides in her favor, then the rest of you can decide if you follow her . . . or follow the way of Earis instead, who had worked so hard to upset this The Choosing."

Oh, now those words brought shock, cries of dismay and new anger that anyone would be put in the same category as her. I was rather glad not to be there in person Better to watch, like a movie. A dream.

Lord Iron still tried to order that I be banished, but Ambassador Syna Diamond Sky and her Lady put an end to that discussion before even Darion said anything. Lord Iron looked stunned, but he backed down before the two women.

No one paid me any more attention. They continued

to debate The Choosing, to grumble and attack one another's morals, but from the way Darion just shrugged everything off, I wondered if this might be the way all such meetings went. How odd -- and likely why they didn't meet in such groups often. I wondered how often such gatherings came to blows. They seemed a contentious group. So much for the idea of fae as polite, pretty elves.

"There is one thing to consider," Darion said. Silence fell everywhere. They wanted to hear what he had to say. "If, no one from Ruby Clan is found suitable for the throne, then the choice passes to Sapphire -- and not to a Sapphire born to the age, either. Consider that information before you petition for Lacey's removal."

Voices rose again. Louder. Darion grinned this time and Blue shook his head.

"You love to stir them up," Blue accused softly.

Darion didn't disagree.

While I understood little the ranting, I enjoyed watching the people. I saw far too many who reminded me of Earis though. Those said 'human' with that same curl of the lip that couldn't have made their disdain any plainer. They looked to Lacey, Sapphire and even to Emerald clan with the same snarl.

I watched Aria and my father for a while. Aria stayed by his side, but I noticed there wasn't any warmth between them. The looks he gave her now and then showed just a whisper of disbelief as though she betrayed him. He looked once towards me, the hatred so obvious that Darion even stepped between us.

And then sudden silence fell over the group as though they had all taken a single breath and held it.

"Now it happens," Darion whispered.

The monolithic stone on which Lacey stood glowed

with pale dancing lights. Lacey lifted her head, ready for whatever judgment came to pass. She had never sought this place. I wondered how she felt just then, caught up in something she might not understand much better than I did. We had that in common; neither of us taught the ways of the fae.

All the colors of the clans rose through the stones. Green twisted and twined with the others, and I sensed the guardian from my path. I bowed my head to her; she knew of my ephemeral presence among the Sapphire clan.

And the colors kept rising, twisting and turning and gliding up over Lacey --

"Gods all," Darion whispered, unexpected awe in his voice. "Legend. There has never been a show of their power, not in as long as the fae can remember."

And the fae had very long memories. This show came from their own myths. A different magic filled the air, and the Old Ones arrived without show. Not just one, but a dozen, and another dozen and before long they outnumbered the new Fae.

"What does this mean?" Blue whispered.

The lights still swept up around Lacey. Rainbows and stars formed around her, and she lifted her hands, letting globes of light play along her fingers. She laughed and the light sang.

"This is your queen," one of the Old Ones spoke. She lifted her hand to Lacey and bowed her head at the same time. "This is our Queen. Never doubt her. You are blessed to live in the time of such a Choosing when magic shall live again, and the worlds will heal."

They bowed to their knees, the old fae and then the new, and I, who was not there except in spirit, watched over it all like a benevolent ghost.

CHAPTER TWENTY-TWO

I awoke. The day outside the window looked bright and sunny, and I wondered if I had dreamed the gathering of the fae.

No. I had been at The Choosing, if not in body, at least in spirit. I would have to thank Darion. I'm not sure even he realized how much this meant to me. My body protested as I tried to lift my arm. No matter. I wouldn't have to fight anything today. The world felt right.

I sensed a little breeze of magic from Fae as though something so special had happened and essence drifted over the Veil to share with the life here.

Magic shall live again, and the worlds will be healed.

I slept once more and when I next woke, I braved aching muscles, weak limbs and a pounding head to get out of bed. A robe sat on the chair by the bed, and I pulled it on over bruises, scratches, and healing bones. I didn't remember the magic that had saved my life again this time.

My heart labored with the first few steps, and I had to catch hold of the different pieces of furniture, but I reached the door. I might not make it back to the bed, though.

I saw Darion and Cherry in the kitchen cooking together. How cute. They looked at me. I grunted and headed into the bathroom.

I decided on a shower. It was a sit-down shower, but the water ran over me and muscles relaxed. I slept for a couple minutes, but the water turned cool.

"I have clothes for you, Skye," Cherry said at the door. "You have company."

"Ugh."

She pushed the door open, sat the clothes on the counter, and left again.

I pulled on the clothing and ran Cherry's brush through my dripping hair. I looked into the mirror. Not too horrible. Might as well face the fae who had come seeking me.

I had not expected Aria. I might have retreated if Darion hadn't crossed the room and helped me to the sofa. Aria sat on the chair across from us and looked me over as though she had never seen me before this meeting. I suppose, in some ways, she hadn't.

My hand almost went to my side where the pain of the knife wounds lingered. I forced myself not to move. She hadn't been the one to create those injuries, even if she had held the knife.

"You did a good job," Aria said at last. "You know what you did, right?"

"I did what I had to," I answered.

"No. You didn't have to do anything, and you had no reason to help the fae. And yet you risked your life to save a handful of us and in doing so saved everyone." She stopped and looked at me, her head tilted a little. I wondered what judgment she made this time and if I should care. "Father has returned over the Veil. I doubt he'll be back for a long, long time."

"That means nothing to me," I said. She frowned a little. "I've only met him once, Aria. I know you better than I know him."

She blushed, no doubt remembering our first meeting. Then she nodded. "You need rest, Skye. I'll come back to see you when we've both put a little distance between us and everything that's happened. I'd like to get to know you. I promise that if you don't kick, I won't."

I smiled despite myself. "Deal."

She stood and gave Darion and even Cherry a polite nod. "Good cookies. I'd like the recipe later."

All so normal and mundane a scene that I shivered. But she left, and I stared at the chair where she had been sitting. Her visit marked a change in my life. I had a relative from across the Veil who admitted to my existence and who must claim me if she intended to visit again. I wondered how I should handle those new feelings.

It would take time for both of us.

While we ate an early meal, Darion explained how they had dealt with Lacey Weaver's reappearance in this world.

"We created a servant who had worked at the house for a short time," Darion said. "We created all the background material, planted a few memories of her in the human's minds, and then had her leave a suicide note and leap into the lake. They won't find her body, but they located Lacey in an abandoned house, a little battered, but none the worse for the situation. Lacey told everyone that she didn't know what happened because she was drugged. Everyone will love the little mystery. I can't wait to read the ideas humans come up with to say how it was done."

"So the incident is covered, no one takes the blame,

and Lacey is back where she belongs . . . only she doesn't belong there," I said. "She is the Queen of the Fae."

"Yes, she is. That doesn't prevent her from being Lacey Weaver, daughter of the man who might be the next president. In fact, many of us like that link."

"Have the fae manipulated things so Ted Weaver is more attractive as a candidate than he should be?" I asked.

"No," Darion answered. "Ted is genuine. We do not mess with human politics. We have enough troubles with our own."

Darion would lie so I let that last little nagging worry go. I wanted to leave this mess with the fae behind and get back to my own life. Only I didn't want to escape and abandon Cherry just because she was dating Darion. Part of me looked forward to seeing Aria the next time, just to see if we managed another conversation that didn't end in blows.

I ate a little soup with them, but even eating half a bowl and grunted a few monosyllabic answers to their questions and I might even have fallen asleep with my hands wrapped around a cup of tea afterward.

Cherry and Darion took pity on me and said I should go back to bed. The thought of lying down and sleeping got me temporarily to my feet.

But this was Cherry's apartment, so I didn't make it as far as the bed. Even with Cherry's help I was only half way across the room when I stopped. Someone knocked at the door.

"Fae," I said with a resigned sigh.

Darion headed for the door. He seemed a little worried when he opened it. I recognized the man who stood on the other side. He was -- no, he had been the king of Fae. I bowed my head as he came in and checked the ring.

Emerald and chieftain, which shouldn't have taken me by surprise since the Emerald Clan stood before Ruby in the sequence. I hadn't had time to consider the implications before now.

"Sir," I said belatedly. I tried not to let my fear show but my heart beat harder, and Cherry's hold tightened around my waist as I trembled again.

"Please, can we sit down?" he asked, nodding towards the sofa. "This won't take long, but we have all had a few hard days."

I resigned myself to at least sitting if not sleeping. I sat between Cherry and Darion on the sofa which seemed symbolic this time -- caught between human and fae, between female and male.

"Now that I am no longer King, I can give you a name," he said with a slight smile. "I am Donal Emerald McFaelyn, chieftain of the clan. And I have come here to redeem our honor and do something years overdue. Give me your left hand, Skye."

Darion's breath caught. I held out my hand, which trembled with weakness. He took gentle hold of the fingers and then pulled something from his jacket and. . . .

He put a ring on my finger, with a single emerald in a band of gold.

"You are accepted as a member of Emerald Clan, Skye Emerald McFaelyn. Continue to live in honor, as you always have, and know you can call upon the clan in times of danger." He let go of my hand and then stood. "And go get some sleep."

I looked at my hand. Up at him. "Sir?"

"We'll talk again later," he said. He turned to Darion. "Thank you."

Even Darion looked a little startled, but he went with Donal out of the apartment and discussed something with him. I hoped I would reach the bedroom with no one else stopping me.

With Cherry's help, I nestled back among the pillows and blankets. Birds sang outside the window. Tired, but I couldn't sleep yet.

The ring felt heavy on my hand. Unnatural. I looked at the stone and considered all the changes that had happened since the call from Cherry. I had even met my father, though I had lost that brief, bitter moment under the weight of everything else. Even my mother's tirade didn't outweigh all Cherry had done for me.

I had found acceptance in many places where I had never expected it, both in family and in friends, and with the clan ring on my hand, I realized there would be changes in my future. This meant far more than Aria accepting me as kin.

And had I changed? Yes. A person cannot be a mirror without capturing part of the reflection. I still sensed far too much of Earis Ruby Day in my soul, and I shivered at the taste her anger and disdain. I had known no love, but she had felt no love . . . and I knew the differences between us.

Still, she lingered there and a long time would pass before I would completely drive her out. I would need time before I found peace with the world and could play my harp again.

But I still heard the music in my soul, and when I looked at the ring again, the memory of Earis already seemed to have dimmed.

THE END

###

PREVIEW: MIRRORS 2: REFLECTIONS

Something, somewhere, had gone wrong, and I felt the trouble coming my way.

I put aside my harp, packing the ancient instrument back into the case and placing it in the cupboard by my desk. This was not a day to play music. The late afternoon had already gone gray and dull. Snow brushed against the large window obscuring the view of the street from my second-story apartment. A chill took me as I watched the wall of white outside, even though the apartment felt -- and looked -- like a jungle. I like warm and green and often asked myself why I haven't left for somewhere warmer because I could go anywhere.

I should have left years ago when my mother took me to the bus station and told me never to come back home. She gave me a thousand dollars. I should have gone to California. Or Hawaii. The idea of tropical beaches appealed to me until I thought about the news stories that covered tropical storms. I at least understood snow storms.

Yes, fear has kept me here. I've learned to hide among these humans, who never look beneath my carefully chosen clothing to see that I am not one of them. Back then, when my mother abandoned me, I had never been out of the house alone and had never left the city. Even now I haven't traveled far.

Well, as long as you didn't count a quick, and exceedingly chilly, trip to the fae lands across the Veil when a few rather annoying members of the Topaz clan tried to kill me. I'm not popular with many of the fae. Darion Sapphire Wilding likes me, but that's because he met my cousin Cherry through me, and he really likes her, even though she is human.

I live in an odd world. I do my detective work -- small scale jobs -- and it pays well enough finding lost dogs and stolen trinkets. The rest of the time I can hide out in my jungle of an apartment. I'm happy, except I don't like snow and watching the growing wild white of the current blizzard made me want to curl up in bed and not come out until spring. I couldn't stay hidden here, though because. . . .

There was something in the air, besides the snowflakes, that made me suspect I would be out in the weather soon. I made a mental note of where my hat and scarf were, and to make certain, I left food for the tame mice and the persistent squirrel who often came to the door. I wanted to retrieve my harp and play so I could bury the sense of trouble, but instead, I pulled up the ledger for McFaelyn Investigations and did the math. Not my favorite job, but the work took my attention and kept me focused on anything but the storm and growing dread that kept seeping in around my attempt at concentration. I had made a profit for the first time in a few months. Not just a few dollars over my bills, but enough to bank some money. That was a pleasant thought

The last case had tipped the scale. I had found a dog for someone. Not just any dog; this was a very expensive Shih Tzu worth close to two thousand dollars. Someone had stolen the pooch from the owner while they walked in the park, a slick job of getting the human's attention just long enough to grab the animal. I knew from the start that this had been a professional job. I used a little magic and not only located him, but I also lead the police to a band of people who were stealing expensive dogs and selling them overseas. The case even made the news, with my name there, for all to see. I hoped it brought in a few more solid cases. This one had come by way of Ted Weaver -- yes, the man everyone says will be the next president. He didn't know what part I'd played in helping to find his missing daughter (who was now Queen of the Fae), but he seemed to like me.

I need little work. I want enough to keep the power company happy and the mice fed.

My life keeps changing, though. A few months ago, I was nothing more than a half-breed fae, mistrusted by my father's people -- the fae -- who had never let one of my kind live this long. Half-fae is a dangerous thing to be. Most have had powers but no ties to the land like the real fae, and that means they have nothing to counter them. The fae killed those of my kind in the past. Many of them still want to kill me, but so far I'd stay out of trouble.

Well, except for early fall when I helped to save the soon-to-be Queen of the Fae and hundreds of other fae from death. I won my place in my father's clan, and I wear the emerald ring of a member. Sometimes seeing it on my hand still surprises me.

I may be accepted by a few, but I am not one of them. I can't be. Being half-fae and half-human is something too odd. I am genderless. I'm not fae or human, I'm not male or female. I'm just me. It's always been enough.

So I stay clear of the fae and keep my secrets hidden from the humans. That seems the best answer for all of us. I do my work, and I have contact with Darion, who is the Sapphire House Ambassador besides being in love with my human cousin. He's also my guard since he made himself responsible for my life back in that mess last fall. At least he no longer feels obligated to follow my every move. I've seen my fae half-sister Aria twice since the Lacey Weaver trouble, and we have neither kicked nor drawn weapons, so the relationship is on an upturn. I have not gone to Emerald House, and everyone is happy to let it stay that way.

Except . . . I can still sense when something is wrong. Like today.

I leaned back and closed my eyes, hoping for a nap, right there in the chair. Nightmares had plagued me the night before, most of them about being held against my will. Those same nightmares had bothered me last fall. Earis Ruby Day was dead, and no one wanted to pick up where she left tried to go before she died.

I wanted to rest, but the moment I slipped away, an inexplicable terror took hold of me, like something clawing at my stomach, and far worse than what I had suffered during the night. I came back awake with a heart-pounding thump and almost shot out of my chair and had pulled up magic before I even realized what I was doing. I saw nothing to fight and let the power go again, gasping and shaking.

Gods of all people, I had never been afraid of shadows and nightmares. Why now? Why at this moment when everything was going so well? I had broken out in a cold sweat, and not all of it from that call of magic, which I find painful to use. It's another part of not being one thing or the other.

This wasn't good. This wasn't --

The phone rang.

If I hadn't already let go of the magic, I would have blasted the device. I keep an old-fashioned land-line at my place because it's far more reliable around magic than cell phones, at least as long as I don't attack it. I took a breath, and another and picked up before the phone went to voice mail.

"Hello?" My voice sounded a little shaky.

"Skye. This is Ian."

Not the person I would ever have expected to call me. Ian had married my mother long after my birth. We lived in the same house for several years while my mother did her best to make certain he guessed nothing about me, including that I wasn't a 'daughter.' Those had been tense years until my mother sent me away.

"What's wrong?" I asked because something had to have happened. Was this what had been plaguing me for the last couple days?

"Kelly is missing, Skye. She disappeared yesterday morning on the way to school. I wanted to call you earlier, but your mother --" He stopped and took a ragged breath. "We've only told the family. It's been almost thirty-six hours. The police have nowhere new to look. You -- you can help, can't you?"

Kelly was his oldest daughter, my half-sister on the human side. The thought of something having happened to her made me shiver for a new reason. Even so, I had to be truthful.

"Ian, my mother and I don't get along. I'm not sure what I can do. I'll try, but I don't dare come over there."

"Your mother is irrational." He spoke as though he was not talking about his wife and with no emotion in the words. "I don't know what happened between the two of you, and I don't care. I want help to find Kelly."

"Do you have any ideas at all?" I had not even seen Kelly since she was ten, almost eight years ago. She would graduate soon, I supposed. The realization gave me a chill: the child grown up who had always been a little girl in my mind.

"Your mother is at the police department, Skye. I heard. . . ." He stopped and took a deeper breath. "I heard that you're good at your work. We need help. Please."

"How long will she be with the police?"

"I'm not certain. She's filling out reports."

"I'll be over as quickly as I can get there and see if I can find anything. The police don't like private detectives working in their major cases, and my mother will be angry. I don't suppose we can keep it a secret from her."

"I don't think so. Does that really matter to you?" he asked, sounding lost just then.

"No it doesn't, but you don't need more trouble. If my mother shows up, this is bound to get ugly, and we don't need that right now."

"Skye, I don't know what happened between you and your mother --"

"None of that matters. I'll be there as soon as I can. Can you get me a picture of Kelly? I haven't seen her since she was ten."

"You haven't met Veronica and Little Ian."

"No, but Cherry told me about them, so they aren't a big shock." He was trying to hold on to the conversation so he didn't have to face other things. "I have to go, Ian. I'll see you in a few minutes."

"Thank you."

He hung up first. I held on for a moment longer, wondering what the hell I was getting into this time. I wanted to help find Kelly, and if anyone had hurt her, there would be hell to pay. She had been a sweet little girl, and I'd played dolls with her sometimes. That seemed like another lifetime though I remembered her face with laughing brown eyes and bright smile. She had reached the age where she wondered why our mother didn't treat me the same as her and Mary. She had gone to school while I was (supposedly) home schooled. I had learned everything on my own from their school books and television. My mother wanted nothing to do with me.

As I stood, I caught at the desk as a wave of nausea passed over me. Was that fear? Was it the worry of going to my mother's house and facing her again? We'd met at Cherry's apartment last fall in the midst of all that other madness. She hadn't changed, except to grow more angry and bitter.

What had happened to Kelly?

Blood calls to blood. I might track Kelly if I found a link to her. My abilities gave me opportunities that the police didn't have, and that realization gave me the strength to go over to the door, pull on my jacket, gloves, hat and scarf and head out --

I was on the steps leading down to the alley when Darion and Cherry arrived in his little sports car, even in this weather. I hadn't been expecting them and Cherry hurried out of the car, rushing toward me.

"Skye --"

"Kelly is missing. Ian just called me and asked me to help."

She looked worried and frantic. She hadn't even put on a hat and snow dusted her jet black hair. Darion stood and gave me a grave nod. Missing children bothered the fae. They have so few children of their own that they are instinctively drawn to protect any child, whether fae or human. Maybe that instinct had kicked up for me, too.

"You're going over there?" Cherry asked and looked worried for whole new reasons.

"My mother is at the police station. This might be the only chance I get to see Kelly's things."

"Ah. Okay. Darion --" she said, looking back at him.

"We'll take you, Skye. Come on. You look like hell, and I'd rather be driving than worrying about whether you'd make it that far before piling up your car somewhere."

"I'm fine," I protested even though I wasn't. Then I gave way to my macho pride -- or whatever it would be in my case -- and nodded. "You two might help, anyway. I want to look in a mirror, if I can find one, and to get a feel for her. I can't do that if Ian is there."

"True. Come on," Cherry said and took my arm. They offered me a wall of protection, and I felt safer with them at my back.

The two had the same looks of worry on their faces, which was odd in people who otherwise looked so opposite in all other ways. Darion stood tall, his long golden hair pulled back in a tie, his face ageless in the way of the fae. He might be the age he looked -- which was doubtful considering Darion was a fae Ambassador -- or he might be a couple thousand years old. I had never asked. I wondered if Cherry had breached the subject, or if she wanted to pretend that age didn't matter.

Cherry was very much human -- a petite Chinese-American woman with a bob of black hair, and an overpower presence that belayed her small size. She was a chef and ran a bustling catering service that sometimes served at very prestigious events.

Winter was her slow time, though. Most of the occasions where she worked were summer, spring, and even autumn parties. In winter, all the 'better' people retired to the warmer climes, and Cherry (who didn't like the snow any better than I did) took care of small events and stayed close to home. She made enough the rest of the year not to worry about the downturn, and she paid so well that she had little trouble hiring back her best people each spring.

She bundled me into the back seat. The snow was coming down harder. If it hadn't been for Darion's magic, I doubt we would have gotten out of the alley behind my apartment. A lot of city would soon be impassable, at least for most cars. I suppose people would think something odd when they saw Darion's sports car taking those streets where trucks bogged down in the snowdrifts.

Did I care? No. I wanted to get to Ian's house as fast as possible, check everything there, and then find Kelly. Darion would get me there faster than if I had driven. Then, if I could refine my link to Kelly, I should be able to track her, just as I could find Cherry. I even used Cherry as a tie on the other end of a magical path and go to her sometimes.

"You all right, Skye?" Cherry said, looking back over the seat at me.

"Worried," I admitted and pulled the cap back off my

head. Darion kept the car warm. "I haven't seen Kelly since she was about ten."

"It's funny," Cherry said with a tilt of her head. "She looks like you, only not as blond-haired fae exotic."

"That might not be good. Not with my mother."

"Do you suspect her of having a part in her disappearance?" Darion asked.

"I suspect her of being part of everything bad," I replied. "That doesn't mean it's so. Do you know where we're going?"

"Cherry took me by your mother's house a month ago."

"Why?" I asked, startled by the news. "Trying to torture her or Darion?"

"We didn't go in," Cherry said with a quick smile and then lost it again. "He wanted to see where you had lived."

I wondered what had drawn Darion there. His eyes in the rear-view mirror narrowed at an unpleasant thought. I didn't want to pry, but the house had been part of my world, not his --

"I saw so much of your life when I scanned you that I felt like what I had from you was only a dream, and I needed to get the facts grounded I reality so I could sort things out from some of my own thoughts and reactions."

"Ah. Sorry."

"You have no reason to be sorry." He took a turn and slowed. A truck spraying out sand made slow progress down the road ahead of us, another truck ahead of it, clearing the way with snow shoveled out to both sides, creating a narrow, white corridor. "Damn. We would have gotten there faster without their help."

I leaned back as my stomach cramped. I fought the pain back and took a deep breath. "If the roads are this bad, it might slow my mother too. I don't want to run into her."

"Good thing Darion and I are along, then. We can help out there."

"True. Though if she sees Darion she will react just as badly as she would at seeing me. She knows he's fae."

"True enough. We'll be careful. There's no reason to make this worse," Darion said and quieted Cherry's start of a protest. "This isn't the time to take her on, Cherry."

"No time is a good time," I said and saw Cherry give me a narrow-eyed glance. "What happened between my mother and me is far in the past, Cherry. Don't get into a war with her on my account. I would just as soon forget everything about my past."

"Can you forget?" Cherry asked.

"No. That doesn't mean I want to re-fight that battle. I've moved on."

She relented with a sigh of resignation. "Sorry. I shouldn't push you about her, especially not now. I'm worried about Kelly. She's a good kid and works hard, and I don't want to see anything bad happen to her."

"She was always nice to me. Mary was too young. But Kelly . . . Kelly had figured out things were not right, which may be another reason my mother panicked and got rid of me."

"There is no excuse for what she did," Darion said, a touch of anger in his voice. "Or for how she treats you now. But then, there's no excuse for your father's behavior either. They are both egotistical bastards."

I gave a little laugh and the tightness in my shoulders eased. "I don't need them, Darion, and I would rather not get caught up in something involving either of them, but I'll do what I can to help find Kelly."

Darion nodded and fell silent. So did Cherry. I wondered what they thought. I wouldn't have minded more conversation to keep my attention. Every time my mind turned to Kelly and the trouble -- and the fear of crossing paths with my mother -- I felt a twist in my guts that said something horrible was happening. I hoped it was my imagination.

"Darion, I kept sensing something odd in the air today and last night and thought I caught something fae-related. Anything going on?"

"Nothing I have heard," he said. "It might be your link to Kelly."

"I wish I had better control to sort this out faster."

He turned down a side street, where we made better time despite more than a foot of snow. "Sometimes being fae isn't the answer."

"Yeah, I know." I slouched back on the seat to hide a sudden bout of cold sweats. Maybe I had the flu. Great timing. "I would just like any kind of answer, to be honest."

He nodded and said nothing more again.

We were getting closer to home.

Oh, now that was odd. I hadn't considered this building as home in a long, long time. I had my home, and I loved my place, but there would always be a link to the place where I'd lived the first years of my life, spending almost every single day of sixteen years there. When the ranch-style building came into view, I felt a draw I had not expected. I had grown up here, dressed in pink and frills, and I had left to be. . . . something else. I sometimes wondered what I had changed into in the years since I left this street.

Most days it didn't matter.

Darion pulled up across the street. I stared at the unassuming white house with blue trim, surprised that they hadn't changed the color scheme in all these years. The window to my bedroom sat at the end of the long side. I looked away in haste. Snow piled up in the driveway and along the walk to the door, but there had been many people in and out, trampling out a path.

I took a deep breath and followed Cherry out of the car. When she started to cross the street with me, I stopped her there. "You don't have to go with me, Cherry."

"Yes, I do. And she's my cousin, you know."

"Oh. True. You know her better than I do," I said, depressed at the realization. I should have tried harder. Maybe I could have protected her if I had spent more time with Kelly.

Maybe doesn't get you anything in the end.

We crossed the street. Ian came to the door, looking frantic, his hair barely brushed, his shirt not even tucked into his pants. I had never seen him less than dapper in all the years I had known him. He hadn't aged much. It was odd to come up and see him watch me, judging things.

"You've changed, Skye," he said.

"I got rid of the damned dresses," I said and won a brief, almost bright smile. Then he stepped aside and let us both inside the door.

"Cherry. It's good to see you."

"I was already heading over to tell Skye, so we drove her over."

"Oh. Thank you." He looked past us into the street. "Is your friend there? He can come in --"

"He'd rather not intrude," Cherry said which was true. "I'm sorry this has happened, Ian. I pray she's all right."

Ian nodded and pushed the door closed behind us.

I felt peculiar being back in this house. I experienced a strange resonance with walls as though the house and I belonged together. We passed from the entry hall towards the kitchen. I glanced in the living room and saw three children watching TV -- quiet, frightened children, which made my stomach tighten again. They looked my way, and I thought they recognized Cherry, but even Mary wouldn't remember me. I hurried past, almost running into Cherry, who glanced my way and then at the children, and then gave me a nod of understanding.

The kitchen was better because they'd remodeled. The old white cabinets were gone, the sterile whiteness that I had scrubbed and re-scrubbed every day had given way to rich wood and marble counters. This didn't look like home. I felt safer here in this place I didn't recognize.

Several boxes of cereal sat on the counter, and dirty bowls and spoons littered the sink. Children's drawings covered the refrigerator almost hiding a grocery list. All common, family things. This was not my home.

Ian leaned his back against the counter and waved us toward the chairs by the table. He watched me. I met his look, worried --

"I had forgotten how different you are, Skye. Your mother has no pictures of you. She will not speak about you."

I gave a small shrug. "That doesn't matter. We need to talk about Kelly. I can't stay long and risk running into her. Have there been any problems, Ian? Anything in the last year you can remember that of that might have led to this?"

"You mean between her and your mother?"

"No, I mean any problems at all. School? Boyfriend?

Girls she hangs out with?"

"Nothing I know about," he said and glanced around the room as though looking for an answer. "Nothing at all. The police asked the same thing. We went over everything, Skye. She has good grades and is checking out colleges. Kelly and her friends had a sleepover a week ago here at the house, and everything was fine. She doesn't have a boyfriend right now, and the last one moved away. They didn't have a bad breakup and they keep in touch on the computer. The police took the computer to an expert to search, but I don't think they'll find anything." He ran a hand through his hair. "There is nothing that might give a hint. I wanted something, Skye. I don't want this to be random with no hope of finding her."

"What about Kelly and her mother?" Cherry said with a hand lifted to stop me from saying anything. "Skye doesn't want to ask, but I will. I don't trust her, Ian, especially after what she did --"

I grabbed her arm, frantically trying to stop her from going on, but Cherry looked at me and shook her head. "No, Skye, baby. He needs to know because if she did that to you, she could have done something like it to Kelly."

"She had her reasons --"

"What the hell did Tay do?" Ian demanded and stepped away from the counter. His face had reddened, and he looked both angry and dangerous. I had never seen him angry in all the years we'd shared the same house. I didn't want to change that memory now. He and Kelly had been my link to a whisper of a happy childhood.

Cherry touched my hand where I still held to her arm. I knew she was right, but this wasn't a conversation I wanted. Not now, not ever. "He needs to know for Kelly's sake because you can't know that she didn't do the same to her."

"She had no reason --" I said again, protesting.

Cherry shook her head and looked at Ian, who appeared to have lost the last of his patience. "When Skye was sixteen, Aunt Tay took her to the bus depot, gave her a thousand dollars, and told her never to come home again."

Well, there it was out. I saw Ian blink several times, shook his head and stopped again. "Son of a bitch," he whispered. It was the first time I had heard him come even close to cursing. He leaned closer, staring into my face. "This is no time to lie, Skye. Tell me the truth. Did she do this?"

"Yes."

He nodded. Why didn't he doubt? I was a stranger here and didn't even look like the step-daughter he had remembered. I watched him, curious why he would trust this story. He forced himself to lean back against the counter once more and held both his hands together before him, his head bowed. I waited and after a few breaths, he looked up and spoke.

"The marriage hasn't been good for years," he said, his voice neutral. He stared out towards where the other three children were still watching TV. "We sleep in the same bed, but that's as close as we get except for dinner with the kids. We kept together for the children. I never thought she would hurt the children --"

"We don't know that she has," I protested.

"Even after what she did to you?" he asked, confused now, his gray eyes meeting mine.

"She had reasons," I said.

"I believed you must have been into something bad. Drugs and that was why she sent you off to live with your father. But she didn't, did she? God, please tell me you went to him. That you didn't live on the street --"

I had not expected to see Ian appalled for my sake. I hated adding to his emotional turmoil. His voice had risen, and I signaled him to stay quieter before the other children heard. "I managed. I'm here. Let's move on to Kelly."

"Why? Why did she do it?" he asked.

I considered lying and saying he'd been right about the drugs, but I didn't want him to think badly of me, which seemed odd. I realized he was, perhaps, closer to real family than I had ever admitted, and I wanted one of my parents not to hate me. Since he had already admitted that he was not happy with my mother, I didn't need to cover for her now.

"It had more to do with my father than with me," I said, which was true. "I was too much like him. She had to be rid of me."

"Why didn't you tell me? Even though you aren't my daughter, I always treated you well."

"You were always kind, Ian, but I couldn't come back because things would have gotten worse. I didn't want trouble here for Kelly and Mary any more than you do for the children, which is why you've stayed. We did it for the same reason: because the kids didn't deserve to be caught up in our problems. I couldn't have come back to live here, Ian. All I could have done is caused problems for everyone."

He took a breath, his face paler as he nodded. "I don't know what to tell you, Skye. I don't even know why I called you. I'm just -- I'm panicked."

"What bedroom does she have?" I asked, glancing at the hall to the right.

"Your room," he said, and he saw me shiver at those words. "Skye --"

"I'm just going to take a look. I won't touch anything," I said.

He nodded and would have followed, but Cherry caught his arm and shook her head. "We need to talk, Uncle Ian."

I suspected she planned to talk about me, and I wondered what Cherry would tell him. It would not be about the magic at least. I wanted to stay and listen, but I left anyway. I had work to do.

The kids looked my way as I passed and watched with wide, frightened eyes. Had they known about an older half-sister? Kelly would have remembered me. Had she told the others? Should I want to be remembered in this place?

I wanted a family. This place reminded me what it was like to sit at a table with others. Sometimes everything had been normal when my mother didn't stare at me, fear and worry in her face.

The room that had been mine had changed, praise the gods of all peoples. My room had held dolls, a pink canopy bed, and pink lacey curtains. I still have an aversion to pink. Kelly's room looked more like a normal teen's room with a lot of yellow and blue, but no unifying theme. She had a desk in the corner by the window and a still an unmade bed. The closet, standing open, showed normal, teen clothing. She had good taste.

A teddy bear sat on the bottom of the bed. I brushed my fingers over the fur and got my first sense of Kelly and for her, and for her worries. Nothing seemed out of place. Teen things: grades, friends, summer job.

The mirror still stood on the back side of the closet door. I pushed the door open with my foot since I did not want my fingerprints anywhere in this room. How often had I looked into that mirror myself? If I stood here long enough, could I even pull back a memory of the child I had been?

This was not about me. I bowed my head for a moment before I lifted my hand and reached with magic to pull back the images buried in the mirror's memory.

I hadn't been able to work with mirrors when I had lived here. This was a power that came one day when I was helping someone locate her missing husband. I had looked into the bathroom mirror, wishing it could tell me something --

It hadn't, really. Oh, I had seen her husband shave with a dull blankness to his face like he did every morning before heading to his equally mind-numbing job. The realization gave me a hint of what had happened. Not long afterward I found him wandering through parks, watching the flowers bloom and free from all the things that had so weighed down on him. I found Ike a new job and last I heard, they'd moved out of their dull little apartment and into a house with a lakefront view.

I liked jobs that ended well and held tight to that memory while I reached forward and almost laid my hand upon the glass.

This was a bittersweet experience. I drew the image back to where Kelly had gotten up out of bed and then let the scene roll forward again. She resembled me, without my odd blond hair and green eyes. Kelly also had all the right bumps and curves I lacked. The sight made me self-conscious watching her come from the shower in a big fluffy robe and then dress for school, discarding one shirt after another until she had the right choice. I was right about her good fashion sense.

Mary came in and teased her as she sat, cross-legged, on the bed. I wished I had sound with the mirror and could hear what the two sisters said to each other. I wanted. . . .

I wanted to be Kelly with a sudden, unexpected longing. I wanted to be normal and have a family and --

And I couldn't. Kelly was missing, and my personal feelings would not help her. Nothing here gave me a clue. She wasn't distraught the morning before she disappeared. I needed to search elsewhere, but I was unwilling to step away.

Then I saw my mother come into the room and walk up behind Kelly. My breath caught in sudden fear, but she only put a hand on Kelly's shoulder and gave a quick smile, then brushed down the side of my sister's hair to get a strand in place.

The little kindness hit me like a knife -- that moment when mother and daughter stood together before me. That would have been me if I had been different. This was torture, but I watched anyway and noted my mother's face when Kelly turned away. An emptiness came to her eyes that seemed more like what I remembered from her --

Kelly came back, patted her on the shoulder, and walked away. I bowed my head. Nothing had helped.

I looked back up, surprised to find my mother still there --

Only not there. *Here.* I spun just as she leapt, screaming at me.

ABOUT THE AUTHOR:

Hello!

I am an eclectic and prolific author whose has published in a number of genres, including Young Adult Mystery, Contemporary Fantasy, Epic Fantasy, Science Fiction and numerous works on writing. While I started on the outer edges of traditional publication with sales to small press and magazines publishers, I have since moved most of my work to the Indie world and I am madly in love with the new world of publishing and the direct contact with readers.

I live in Nebraska with my husband, my cats and a small but entirely useless dog.

Connect with Zette:

Web Site: http://lazette.net

Twitter: http://twitter.com/lazetteg

Facebook: http://www.facebook.com/lazette.gifford

Joyously Prolific Blog: http://zette.blogspot.com/

Smashwords:
http://www.smashwords.com/profile/view/LazetteG

FIND WORKS BY

LAZETTE GIFFORD

ON

CREATESPACE

SMASHWORDS

A CONSPIRACY OF AUTHORS

NOOK

LAZETTE.NET